**A PSYCHIATRIC HOSPITAL IN QUEENS
A DOCTOR EAGER TO RETIRE
AND A PATIENT DESTINED TO
CHANGE HIS LIFE**

"There is nothing sweeter than first and passionate love," said Don Juan. "It stands alone like Adam's recollection of his fall.

"The very first woman I ever loved fully, with all my body's power and my heart's delight, revealed to me the smiling secrets of the universe. I learned from her the answers to the only four questions worth asking: What is sacred? Of what substance is the spirit made? What is worth living for? And what is worth dying for?"

Don Juan paused for dramatic effect.

"The answer to each is the same. Love. Only love."

Don Juan De Marco

a novel by
Jean Blake White

based on the screenplay by
Jeremy Leven

A SIGNET BOOK

SIGNET
Published by the Penguin Group
Penguin Books USA Inc., 375 Hudson Street,
New York, New York 10014, U.S.A.
Penguin Books Ltd, 27 Wrights Lane,
London W8 5TZ, England
Penguin Books Australia Ltd, Ringwood,
Victoria, Australia
Penguin Books Canada Ltd, 10 Alcorn Avenue,
Toronto, Ontario, Canada M4V 3B2
Penguin Books (N.Z.) Ltd, 182–190 Wairau Road,
Auckland 10, New Zealand

Penguin Books Ltd, Registered Offices:
Harmondsworth, Middlesex, England

First published by Signet, an imprint of Dutton Signet,
a division of Penguin Books USA Inc.

First Printing, April, 1995
10 9 8 7 6 5 4 3 2 1

 REGISTERED TRADEMARK—MARCA REGISTRADA

Printed in the United States of America

I would like to express grateful acknowledgements to my sister, Melissa Blake Rowny, my daughter and her husband, Catherine E. White and Stuart A. Malone for their tireless support and suggestions, and Jeremy Leven, who wrote the screenplay, directed the movie, and took the time to guide me through the strange process of producing a book.

—JEAN BLAKE WHITE

Don Juan De Marco

Prologue: The Legend

*T*he origin of the Don Juan legend is obscure, but its essentials have been cherished for centuries. Don Juan himself was supposed to be Spanish, Italian, or Portuguese. His legend, however, was elaborated by the English, a colder nationality but one passionately desirous of warmth. After all, Queen Victoria's Empire eventually included a great many palm trees, idyllic islands, and warm-water harbors.

England also produced the works of the warm-blooded romantic and charmingly susceptible George Gordon, Lord Byron, who was given to romantic adventures of various kinds, beginning at a very early age. He loved Greek islands—and a large number of women. He was the author of Don Juan, *a* long and skillful retelling of the legend in verse, satirical but sweet. Some Englishmen, even today, have memorized large swatches of the poem and will whisper it to an appreciative young woman if the setting is just right and the mood sufficiently intoxicating.

The other man who kept the Don Juan legend alive was Wolfgang Amadeus Mozart, the composer of the opera Don Giovanni, *in which the wicked but adorable Don Juan is* consumed by the flames of Hell, defiant to the last. Few men can hum the great themes of this opera, but no one who has ever seen it can forget Don Juan's final repudiation of responsibility and repentance.

In both tellings of the legend, women in great numbers find the don utterly irresistible. His charm is overpowering, his attractions without equal. He is extremely obliging. He never intends to harm anyone, and though he keeps track of his totals, is not so much interested in scores as in playing well. He never thinks of himself as aggressive but as agreeable.

Don Juan never grew old, having been consumed by infernal flames long before wrinkles and gray hair could set in. In the legend, he remains forever boyish. Neither Don Juan's composer nor his poet ever reached, or perhaps wished to reach, middle age. Mozart died at the age of thirty-five. Byron died in Greece at thirty-six. Both fortunately expired before the prudish reign of Queen Victoria ever got underway.

We all recognize the legend's devotee when we meet him at a party or in a conference room, or even in advertisements in the personals sections of newspapers, though these days he is seldom equipped with a mask or sword or cape; he may even be detected masquerading in a thoroughly unboyish but enthusiastic body. He is often charming but growing cagier every day as women become more prone to laughter. His yearnings are quaint and his intense attachment to the past is rather touching. We must treat him tenderly, knowing so well that he's an antique. Like baseball cards or the book of Kells, he is to be preserved and lovingly appreciated but never to be played with again. However, Don Juan and his heirs do not, necessarily, yield gracefully to life on the shelf.

And thereby hangs our tale.

1

Don Juan at Home

*

In which Don Juan prepares for death.

Slender, young, and languid, Don Juan De Marco reclined alone in a bedroom clearly designed for seduction. His pajamas were silk, and his mask was new. He lay on red satin sheets, reflected in many mirrors. A small fire blazed in the marble fireplace, in front of which a magnificent wolfskin covered the hand-knotted Turkish carpet.

A leather notebook, a slim journal without a title, rested on Don Juan's knees. He was writing his suicide note. Sad songs played on his stereo, which would normally have been pouring out mariachi music, tangos, sambas, or seductive arias from Italian operas.

He had started writing his suicide note more than a month ago. Although his life was short, it had been eventful. He wished to do it justice in his swan song, and justice meant the inclusion of many luscious women and exotic lands, discoveries and losses, and tales of narrow escapes.

He had finally reached the point where it became necessary to explain his reasons for wishing to die. He took up his richly engraved gold pen and began to write.

I wish to end my life because of a broken heart. The woman responsible for this wish is Donna Ana, my glorious but lost soulmate. A world in which I must live without my darling Donna Ana is one in which I no longer wish to linger, even though I am still the world's greatest lover. I have made love to over a thousand women, a remarkable record for a man of my admittedly tender years.

The thought of the thousand beautiful women made him pause briefly. A tender smile played over his handsome features. His mouth was soft, formed like a cupid's bow. His cheeks were smooth, but since he had achieved his majority, he wore a modest beard and a dashing mustache. His hair was long and curled charmingly over his shoulders. He tapped the pen against his curved lips, a smile of rueful nostalgia continuing to flicker as he considered how best to state his story.

He began to write again in a well-formed calligraphic hand. He made no corrections and the words seemed to flow from his pen without effort.

Like music, gymnastics, or figure skating, the game of love occasionally produces a prodigy, blooming early and fiercely. I am such a prodigy. Zeus himself might have surpassed me in variety of species sampled, but never in zeal. No woman has ever left my arms unsatisfied, but that is of no great consequence now that I have lost the only woman who has ever mattered to me.

He arose from the tumbled sheets and put on a quilted dressing gown with a velvet collar, feeling that his sentiments required more formal garb than pajamas. Then he resumed his writing, a solemn expression on his gentle face, as he contemplated the end of his delightful stay on earth.

Thus at the prime of my life, at the age of twenty-one, I have determined to end my life this very night.

He paused to consider the best way to proceed. He realized that the name and beauty of his beloved might not be known to the stranger who would read his note. Yet some understanding of his staggering loss was necessary if the situation were to be properly appreciated by that stranger.

The incomparable Donna Ana was once all my own, then was lost to me forever. I was shipwrecked, washed up on the shore like a bit of seaweed, found by a beautiful girl and cast again into the deep. Blighted affections, that's my problem. But as you read my story, stranger, think of a blazing beach, coffee and ouzo, and the burnished shoulders of a silk-draped, cherry-tipped virgin warbling innocently beside the amniotic waters of the Aegean.

You will say, of course, that after all, I had her. We grappled naked as the cruise boats sailed past. A hoopoe perched on the columns of the ruined temple, watching our acrobatic couplings with avian amazement. You will be puzzled by my determination to die, considering the net of lust we crocheted around our laboring bodies, the giving and taking and tasting and rolling over and over, shameless, and both as beautiful as sunfish. I surely had her, you will think, this boy enjoyed the fondest liberties, the most intimate secrets of his darling, and he possessed her completely.

Don Juan stopped to mop his brow. The room had grown much warmer. He shed his dressing gown and began to write the end of his note.

You would be wrong, you who judge me foolish, because for once and forever, she possessed me.

There on the magic island, in the cool sea air scented with honeysuckle and thyme, in the shade of the olives, on the picnic table, she took what once was my heart and she threw it away.

Lewdness is no substitute for love. My genius was that I never gave less than both to any woman. Round or thin, blond, brunette or blue-haired, I drew out the best in every one of them, until an accident of navigation cast me up on that infernal beach, where I wooed and lost my darling Donna Ana.

His mind was flooded by poignant memories of geraniums beside a white-washed beach house. He remembered the wonderful mornings, the delicious breakfasts—sausages and strawberries with Donna Ana—beside the bluest possible waters, lulled by the sunlight and the pounding surf. He remembered the honey-flavored nights, the delectable midnight rambles along the moonlit beach. Happy though those memories were, he determined to stick to his task and complete his last document.

Now my love belongs forever to that single adorable woman. I will never again give my whole heart to every sweet lollipop the way I once did. Donna Ana owns me and she has run away from me, for no good reason. She has destroyed our happiness and left me only questions. Why did she trample on our perfect bliss? Why were my pleadings of no avail? Why was my most sincere sacrifice to no avail? Why did she flee from our Paradise without a backward glance? Donna Ana has given me my excellently good reason to take the plunge to oblivion, the dive into eternity. Memory, like a veil, obscures my eyesight, worse than my black silk mask ever was. I can no longer see a way to go on in this cold, cruel world.

He reached for his white silk handkerchief. His own prose and pitiful predicament had moved him to tears. He thought, with difficulty, of the pain his beloved might well be suffering. The thought gave him the strength to go on.

I don't know what she is feeling. I think she may be sorry, plowed under by regret. I'd like to think she misses me and that she finds all picnics dry and tasteless after the delicacy of our shared repasts. It would be pretty to think so. But I may never know whether she suffers as I do. That simple maiden to whom I gave my unstinting love may never have appreciated what a rare love she abandoned when she cast me aside.

A tear fell from Don Juan's eye to the page, blurring his words, making a perfect heart-shaped blot on the elegant page. He paused to dry his over-flowing eyes and regain his composure.

Donna Ana left me only the ashes of love, left me alone to undergo the bitter pangs of rejection. Others may know this fearsome pain, the awful humiliation of being cast aside by a woman. I never had been turned down before that day. My life had been nothing but happiness and love, and the worship of women. All of them always adored me, and I them, until Donna Ana ran from me on that dreadful afternoon. After she left, I wandered the island for days. I was like an orphaned puppy, calling and calling her name. Looking under bushes and into caves, asking after her at the port, in every taverna, asking the tourists as they poured from the cruise ships, inquiring of sailors and old women in the village square, asking them had they seen my Donna Ana. Searching and searching, never finding her.

Don Juan's face reflected the agony of those days in which he wandered over the island, finding out too late that his darling had fled over the sea. The final discovery was too painful for him to write. He was almost done with his note. He wished the unknown reader to feel something of the delicate love that he had enjoyed, the tangible delights of the perfect woman.

Whoever finds this note, I beg you to keep the vision of that delicious and vanished woman hovering in your memory as she hovers forever in mine. Her image haunts my every waking moment, even more tantalizing to you, who have never seen her, perhaps, than to me, since I enjoyed the bliss as well as the blight. Picture to yourself the dimpled knees of the perfect nude, frolicsome in the sunlight of a tropical island, remember the scent of flowers and seaweed, taste the salt of a warm sea breeze, and then imagine that it all revolves around you, that you are at the very heart of this feast for every sense and for the sentiments, that your every movement only increases your delight, that you are never tired, never hungry, never sad, but always bathed in bliss. Did I remember to tell you that her white silk gown flowed over her round sweet behind or her dainty feet so that she looked like a mermaid as she ran away from me? Did I tell you that? Too late now. I am for oblivion.

Don Juan closed the journal and put it on the nightstand, in plain view. He wanted to be sure the proper authorities would find it. Some well-trained, obedient, foolish detective was certain to poke around looking for clues to the fatal act, and would find Don Juan's swan song, his epic of a great love lost for no reason, his final confession. Of course, the plain, ordinary man could never be the same again after reading Don Juan's life story.

The young man smiled, thinking of the pleasure the unknown detective had in store for him, and the secrets of love he would uncover just by reading this slender book.

The young man stood up and stretched, his silk pajamas rippling over his sinuous limbs, his resolve firm. He was prepared to die.

"But first," he declared, "one final conquest."

2

Victoria

*

***In which our hero embarks upon a night
of love and suicide.***

Don Juan, still alone in his bedroom, readied himself
for his final conquest. There was an old saying in
the village of his birth: "A young man anoints himself
with scent when he prepares to meet a woman. An old
man merely bathes." Some say it is the other way around,
but Don Juan was young and loved the elegance of cologne.
Slender, serious, he put on his regalia as if he were going
to be wed. What he selected was no ordinary tuxedo. Rich
stuffs, velvets and brocades, filled his capacious closet.
That night he chose black for mourning and red for
passion, for he was the great Don Juan, setting out on his
last adventure.

His slender, nearly feminine hand seemed too fine for
its burden of gold as he slid his massive, crested signet
ring onto his forefinger, then covered it with a butter-soft
kid glove, black and cuffed in the style of a knight's
gauntlet.

He put on his black silk mask, which he had removed
in order to bathe his face and wash his long, curly locks.
His deep brown eyes were filled with sadness and yet they
contained a certain mischievous light as well. He gazed at

his own image in the mirror, closely but without vanity. He wanted his dress, his grooming, everything to be completely appropriate for this momentous evening. Finally he nodded to his image, satisfied that every detail of his appearance was correct.

Then he reached for his cape and swept it over his shoulder. In any other young man, the gesture would have been ridiculous. The dignity of this youth was such that even the grandest gesture could not seem outlandish.

He was nearly ready for his last experience of love.

Whatever the station in life of the woman he would choose, whether virgin or wife, lawyer or secretary, milkmaid or duchess, that woman, he knew, would enjoy the benefit of all he had ever learned. She might never realize the full magnitude of the favor he was about to bestow upon her. On the other hand, she would never forget the handsome stranger, and she would never be the same again. Far into the future, that woman would seek to feel the exceptionally magnanimous pleasures Don Juan would provide for her.

He smiled at the mirror, speaking to his own image as he planned to speak to the woman, not merely reminding himself of his gallantry, charm, and noble ancestry, but taking inventory, ensuring that all his best traits were still readily accessible and well displayed.

"My name is Don Juan De Marco. I am the son of the great swordsman, Antonio Garibaldi De Marco, who was tragically killed defending the honor of my mother, the beautiful Doña Inez Santiago y San Martine."

His introductory speech never varied. But this night would be his last. He wanted his speech as well as his costume to be perfect in every detail. He continued to rehearse the words while he strode to the place of assignation, his bootheels clicking on the sidewalk.

"I have made love to over a thousand women." He spoke aloud as if he were singing to himself an old folksong in a minor key, almost a lullaby. There was nothing of the braggart or the coarse seducer in his tone; he was merely stating a fact. In his experience, women found the sheer audacity of the number to be intriguing.

Not a soul in the street bothered to glance at him. He was, of course, in New York, a place where an oddly dressed man mumbling to himself in the street was hardly a rarity. A few of his fellow pedestrians may have felt the influence of Don Juan himself. He exuded an air of manly confidence and trailed the heady, seductive fumes of a classic eau de cologne. He was a striking and attractive figure as he threaded his way politely through the crowded sidewalks.

He was almost pretty, in the way of certain paintings of Italian Renaissance commanders. Botticelli had painted such men as saints, as warriors, as gods, and simply as themselves, with long carefully dressed hair and rich clothing. Don Juan swaggered as those young men must have done, but there was a touch of the lost little boy in his manner.

Beneath his cape he carried a sword forged in Toledo, but there was nothing in the least threatening about him. Hooked to his hip, the sword looked like a plaything and he was not intent on murder. Don Juan wore his sword everywhere because his father had bequeathed it to him. His thoughts were wholly concentrated on anticipation of a night of triumphant love and glorious suicide.

When he entered the impressive hotel, he was greeted warmly. Doormen and headwaiters recognized his noble character at once. Not only did he tip generously, but his demeanor was always affable. He was soft-spoken, polite to everyone, servants and potentates, demonstrating in every encounter the inherent nobility of his character.

As he walked through the ornate doors of the lobby, he flourished his cape and handed his sword to the doorman for safekeeping. *No accidents tonight*, he thought. *No quarrels. Only peace and love. I'm ready.* He entered the Ritz as if a fanfare of golden trumpets had preceded him.

He stood for a moment on the top step of the marble stairs of the elegant foyer. Polished, baroque brass and marble surfaces caught the light from crystal chandeliers and diamond earrings. He watched women in evening dresses walk past in the lobby below.

Horse buyers stand the way he did, slightly above the sleek animals in the ring, judging, appreciating, savoring. A svelte woman, not too young, returned from the telephone booth. She was dressed in an expensive, but tasteful, black satin gown, cut expertly to show off her perfect figure. The satin flowed around her hips, catching the light as she walked. She was obviously anticipating an encounter with an important man. A necklace of heavy twisted gold and pearls hung from her swanlike neck almost to her ivory décolletage. A diamond bracelet sparkled on her slender wrist, and a sapphire gleamed from her ring finger. She was confident, poised, and beautiful. Yet her face reflected sorrow, inner tension, and some annoyance.

She walked alone to a table for two and sat down, gracefully, refusing to betray the awkwardness of her situation by the slightest diffidence. She sat alone with perfect aplomb, as though she were daring her fellow diners to notice her solitude.

The woman's name was Victoria, but Don Juan would never know that. He preferred at times the faint perfume of regret and mystery which clings to the memory of nameless women, the pure essence of pleasure without history or complications.

Victoria looked up as he arrived at her table, where an excellent white wine and a generous plate of oysters Rockefeller had been served to her. There was no hint of invitation in her glance, and no hint of aggression in his.

Polite and personable, Don Juan gazed intently into the woman's eyes. He pointed at the empty chair across from her. "May I?" he asked, very courteously, but warmly, as if they had known each other for many years.

She said, slightly annoyed but unconsciously responding to his gentle manner, "Well, actually, I have a friend who'll be joining me. He's been delayed, but he should be here soon."

Don Juan sat down and introduced himself.

"I won't linger. I am Don Juan."

She laughed. "That's very funny. Is there a costume party in the hotel?"

He took no offense at her mirth. He corrected her politely. "No, no, I am really the great Don Juan, directly descended from the noble family of the original Don Juan of whom you have surely heard. *Don Giovanni*, Byron . . ."

This line was new to her, and though she had heard many, not a single one alluded to poets or operas or mythical lovers. The young man seemed harmless enough so she decided to string him along while she consumed an oyster.

"And you seduce women?" she asked, sharply. It was not so much a question as a reprimand. A lesser man might have considered it a rejection. Her reaction was not unanticipated. A reputation for predatory behavior was wrongly attributed to the young man's ancestral name. He gently set her straight, with engaging sincerity.

He said, "I never take advantage of a woman. I give women pleasure, if they desire it." The intensity of his concentration on her increased. He looked deeply into her eyes.

"It is, of course, the greatest pleasure they will ever experience." His manner was dignified and sober, as if he were a master craftsman about to embark on a technical lecture.

Victoria dropped her fork onto the plate with what seemed to her a deafening clang. She was embarrassed. Other people may have heard him. Her normally cool persona had been disrupted by a callow youth.

Victoria lowered her voice and fixed her gaze on Don Juan's wistful, velvety eyes, outlined by the silken mask.

For the first time, she became aware of his extraordinary allure. She could not quite make out what kind of man he was, but she began to realize just how susceptible she might become to his charms.

"You don't really expect me to just, to stop eating and go off . . . ?" she said, her voice beginning to lose its certainty, to waver toward a softer tone.

Don Juan, utterly composed, the soul of sophistication, answered casually. "It depends on how soon you expect your companion to arrive. I'm in no rush. Order dessert."

Victoria's eyelids half closed as she looked demurely down at the ring on her finger. Don Juan De Marco turned up the heat and took her hand in his own.

"There are some women," he said with a sigh, "dark, and with a certain texture to their hair, a curve to their ears that sweeps like the turn of a shell . . . These women have fingers with the same sensitivities as their legs. . . ."

Don Juan began to run his forefinger in circles around the end of the woman's finger. The world narrowed for both of them. In their imaginations they stepped onto an island big enough for only two. The woman was no longer smiling. Her face was serious as she paid extremely close attention to Don Juan.

He spoke, quietly and reverently.

"Their fingertips have the same feelings as their feet, and when you touch their knuckles, it is like passing your hands along their knees. This tender fleshy part is the same as brushing your hand along their thighs and finally . . ."

He lifted the woman's hand to his lips. He ran his tongue gently along the crevice between her fingers, worshiping at this small shrine.

There was action in the cathedral, too. Waves of heat washed over her, seeming to radiate from Don Juan's lips. The woman's other hand clenched convulsively, tearing at the tablecloth. Victoria and Don Juan raced to the elevator of the hotel, tumbling through nondescript hallways to

Victoria's room. In seconds, they were transported out of time to Paradise. They were as playful as otters.

Don Juan whispered his secrets to this anonymous woman, Victoria, who was far too distracted to appreciate them. She became an enraptured body, while he became an amorous oracle.

"Every woman is a mystery to be solved."

Don Juan De Marco mapped the woman's perfect neck, and memorized the dimensions of her collarbone with his fingertips. His face was masked by a silken device; hers by passion. He continued to whisper into her pearly ear.

"But a woman hides nothing from a true lover."

Her shoulders were perfectly shaped, but then, so were his. Their bodies were entwined, perfect harmony building between them. His mouth was buried in her hair, but he continued to talk.

"Her skin color can tell us how to proceed. A hue like the blush of a rose, pink and pale, and she must be coaxed to open her petals with a warmth like the sun, touched by the moisture of a summer morning's dew."

His accent was foreign, pleasant, formal, suggesting a Southern land filled with lemon trees and oranges, hot dusty villages, and red flowers. He nibbled her pale skin where she was most tender.

"If her skin is dark and ripe, like a fruit daring us to devour it, then her limbs should be more firmly pulled to us in order to yield the succulent flesh inside."

Victoria's navel moved up and down with excitement. Her breathing was quick and hoarse. She paid no attention to his sweet babble as Don Juan explained it all.

"The pale and dappled skin of the redhead calls for the lust of a wave crashing to the shore so we may stir up what lies beneath and bring the foamy delight of love to the surface."

The woman was definitely nearing foamy delight. The agony of pleasure she experienced made her toss her head, a restless mare under his eager thighs. Don Juan's breathing was peaceful, contented. He had still more to say.

"Although there is no metaphor that truly describes making love to a woman"—he spoke thoughtfully, tranquil in the storm, responding to the urgent rhythm of the woman, more than equal to the occasion—"the closest analogy is to playing a rare musical instrument."

Victoria gripped Don Juan's back with an almost painful force. They toiled happily, coiling together, glittering in the rented bed.

"I have often wondered," Don Juan continued to muse, "does a Stradivarius violin feel the same rapture as the violinist when he coaxes a single perfect note from its heart?"

With that, the woman sang her joy, a single perfect note to express a tormenting need at last satisfied. Victoria was at last freed from all restraint, transported. All the music in the world proceeds from that cry, the glad hymn of the female to her god. Or to herself.

Don Juan De Marco escorted his lady back to the dining room. She was far more cheerful than when he had first selected her. She danced back to her table, a rowdy, enchanting bounce in her step. Steam seemed to rise from the nape of her neck. Her hair was charmingly tousled, her face moist and rosy. She was unsteady on her feet, and to the initiated, obvious in her air of sensual satisfaction. She slowly regained her composure, but never again the same melancholy. Don Juan politely kissed her hand.

"*Muchas gracias, señorita*, for permitting me to partake of your extraordinary sensuality."

"No, no, thank *you* . . . really, thank you so much." Her speech may have been girlish, but her voice was full of a womanly warmth he loved to hear. It was his cue for departure, an exit as perfectly part of the performance as the entrance. He twirled his cape, turned on his heel, and slowly began to withdraw.

As he left, a nondescript man in a suit brushed past him, heading for Victoria's table.

"Sorry I'm late, honey," said the man, his mind elsewhere. "It was unavoidable. I hope you went ahead without me."

The woman nodded, a smile of ineffable appreciation on her swollen lips. She looked across the room at Don Juan De Marco, who bowed his head once more, a perfect knight of love. For just an instant, they were together again in the tropical isolation of their feverish paradise. And then Don Juan De Marco walked out the ornate doors to the dark, cool midnight air . . . . and to death.

3

Dr. Jack

*

In which Don Juan is plucked from the jaws of death only to fall prey to the powerful Don Octavio del Flores.

Although Love had almost always obliged the great Don Juan, Death would not be so easily won. Somebody called the cops after seeing a man in a mask and a cape perched on top of a very large billboard, apparently intending to kill himself. The distance to the ground was great and the masked man had a sword strapped to his hip.

Police and firefighters arrived in force, with siren music and flashing, gallant lights. They were part of the brigades ranged against the dashing suicide, knights of life as he was the knight of love. They, too, wore regalia. Their badges of rank were pinned to uniforms connoting bravery. They wore polished boots and carried weapons far deadlier than Don Juan's sword.

Don Juan had traveled over many miles of subway track to arrive at the perfect spot for his death. He paced gracefully, surefooted on the narrow catwalk above the billboard. The picture above which he prowled was that of a beautiful woman wearing only a bikini, lolling on the sand of an obviously tropical beach. From the ground a shadow fell across her eyes, almost like a mask.

The billboard was actually a gargantuan travel poster, advertising Spain and the Canary Islands, but only the woman's curves resonated with meaning for Don Juan De Marco. Only a woman's image could have drawn him all the way across town in the dead of night. Only that particular billboard could express his problems so graphically.

The tiny figure above the crowd seemed to be guarding the woman on the billboard as he measured the lofty path, patrolling back and forth above her glorious body.

Firefighters and police milled around in the street, drinking coffee, and talking in low tones. They wanted to prevent a catastrophe. The ambulance attendants waited, too, without much hope of salvaging the wreckage of his body if he decided to launch himself into space or fall upon his sword.

Passersby, drawn by curiosity, stared up at the lonely figure pacing above the billboard. Individuals in the throng were struck by the nobility of the small, fragile human being in such peril as he occupied his narrow strip of territory so far above them.

Don Juan's thoughts were of the sweet faces of Donna Ana and some other women, all as beautiful and precious as ivory, as gold, as rubies, as the Earth itself. The searchlight of the rescuers blinded him to all but the glowing images that soothed and warmed his final hours. It naturally took some time for him adequately to review such a rich, full life and so many wonderful women.

He waited, like the police, for someone special to arrive. He needed a partner for this last act. He needed a collaborator to help him express the glorious, immortal perfection of his sorrow and his love. He had absolutely no intention of making an undignified exit. He intended to die as stylishly as he had lived. No regrets, no remorse. Only beauty, respect, and happiness.

Far below Don Juan's exalted perch, the grownups conducted a conference. The last crucial player had arrived, Dr. Jack Mickler, a psychiatrist and suicide specialist. Like the police and the fire fighters, he had his own kind of uniform. A great bear of a man, his clothes were nondescript, but he wore the demeanor and the invisible armor of a man who had seen too much. On his weary face were the unmistakable marks of his long career as a professionally compassionate man.

His career had been almost as exhausting as that of a professional lover. He was no longer young, and his health was not the best. He had been dragged from his warm bed into this cold night, he knew, for one more encounter with a despairing, angry, certainly deluded, and very likely dangerous soul. The crowd of spectators moved aside for him. Ordinary policemen instinctively deferred to him. Even the press stood back as he passed by.

The detective in charge, Simon Tobias, welcomed the weary man with obvious affection.

"Evening, Jack. Sorry to get you out at night, but this is a job for SuperShrink." It was an old joke between colleagues.

Jack Mickler did not feel he was completely awake yet, and he struggled to focus his attention. He looked up at the young man through Simon's binoculars, at his mask and cape and unsheathed sword. The outfit did not immediately spark any recognition in the sleepy doctor.

"What's the costume, Simon?"

"He's Don Juan."

"And his real name?"

"He says," Simon recounted without emphasis, improvising from his notes, "he is Don Juan De Marco, Count of Bejar, General of His Excellency's Army of the Island of Ismail, Lord of the Night, son of a famous swordsman." Simon remembered only too well how many similar street conferences he and Jack had shared. Far too many, and not all of them ended happily.

Simon continued, "Sorry, Jack, but we don't have a

clue. No mom, no dad, no fixed address as far as we know. Not even a landlady."

"Does he have a girlfriend?" Jack tried hard to get a grip on the situation.

"You're asking me if *Don Juan* has a girlfriend?" Simon laughed ruefully. Jack sighed, too tired to laugh even though he got the joke.

"What, exactly, does Don Juan want then? Do we know?"

Simon leafed through his notes and read in flat tones, all business again.

"He wishes to end his life gloriously. He asks us to send our finest swordsman to do battle with him, preferably Don Francisco da Silva."

Jack looked up at the floodlit, dramatic figure. *This is not grand opera*, he thought to himself. *This is potentially a very ugly situation and could also involve grievous bodily harm to my very own worn-out but still functioning personal ass. I'd better get myself together and figure out my next move.*

But the fire fighters, veterans of numerous crises, had already figured out Jack's next move for him. They had brought in a cherry picker, a bright yellow machine with a sort of bucket at the end of a long articulated metal arm worked by levers. As far as Dr. Jack Mickler was concerned, it resembled, only too closely, a toy steam shovel. He did not much care for the idea of getting involved with it. But Simon led him to it, showed him how to get into it, gave him no option. Jack knew he must go up in the cherry picker to the armed, suicidal boy on the billboard. He made a feeble joke, but gallant under the circumstances.

"Are you sure Freud started this way?"

Simon was sorry to have to send his old friend up there, but there was nothing he could do about it, either. Somebody had to talk the boy down or something bad would surely happen. It was Jack's job to go up there, but it was Simon's job to send him.

"What do I know, I'm only a dumb cop. Be careful, okay?" Simon couldn't help saying it, though it wasn't the kind of thing they usually said to one another. He wanted to say even more, but he couldn't. It would be too senti- mental, and time was running out. He could hardly bear to watch as the cherry picker started to take his friend away.

Jack used the time in the ascent to prepare himself for the ordeal to come. Sounds of the street dropped away as he rose higher and higher. He cloaked himself with the invisible robes of the healer, purging from his mind all ironies, all fears.

Jack had experienced such encounters so many times before, he was barely aware of the effort it took to clear his mind. He became only sensitive nerve endings, concentrated on this single moment to be shared with this stranger. He deliberately slowed his breath, relaxed his hands, cleared his face of all anxiety. His mind became calm, and the last vestiges of sleep vanished as he rose toward the boy.

By the time he reached Don Juan's level above the billboard, Jack was ready.

Don Juan was not.

Though courtly as ever, Don Juan was annoyed. He expressed his irritation by pressing the point of his sword, a light epée, against Jack's chest. Not many men can keep their composure when anything, let alone a sword, is pressed to that spot just over the heart, but Dr. Jack Mickler was as still as marble.

"Where is Don Francisco da Silva? I will fight no other."

The speech was odd enough to give Jack pause, but the purity of his concentration was such that he needed only a moment to frame a reply. He leaned ever so slightly backward, away from the point of the sword. Don Juan, as Jack had hoped, noticed but took no offense at the infinitesimal movement. He was too intent on scanning Jack's unfamiliar face.

"Don Francisco left yesterday for Majorca. I am his uncle, Don Octavio del Flores." Jack adopted a faintly Latin accent and the florid gestures he supposed would be most appropriate to a romance language. He hoped his imitation of a Spanish grandee would be good enough to establish a cultural rapport without exciting either rage or ridicule in the boy.

Don Juan put up his sword.

"This is very disappointing."

Improvisation was everything in such situations. Jack was encouraged, especially now that the point of the sword was directed away from his chest. He slipped as skillfully as he could into the role of the moment. He hadn't been a psychiatrist for thirty years without learning something about deceit.

"Something came up at the last minute. Don Francisco sends his regrets. I think perhaps we might postpone the matter until he returns?"

The feeble excuse only excited the masked man.

"This will not do! I must die at the hands of Don Francisco! I am Don Juan De Marco, son of the great swordsman, Don Antonio Garibaldi De Marco and the famous beauty, Doña Inez Santiago y San Martine. I will cross swords with no mere ordinary mortal!"

Jack decided on a different angle of attack.

"You are *the* Don Juan?"

"Correct. At the age of twenty-one, I have fulfilled the fantasies that are the torment of men three times my age. I take it that you are three times my age?"

"And then some."

The man and the boy studied each other, each taking the other's measure as do warriors about to engage in single combat, feeling for weakness and saluting the virtues of the worthy opponent.

Jack had a job to do, though, and needed to get on with it.

"So tell me—why, with so many successes, does the great Don Juan wish to end his life?"

"Because there is nothing left to live for."

"Nothing at all?"

"Not when Donna Ana is everything."

"Aha. Her name is Donna Ana."

Don Juan was naturally most comfortable in a two-person game. The masked man began to speak more freely as he began to pace again on the narrow catwalk. Dr. Mickler was careful not to look down, and he wished the boy would stand still. Dr. Mickler suffered from a small fear of heights, apparently not a problem for Don Juan.

"Now you understand why I must die," Don Juan said. "I ask only that it be at the hand of Don Francisco, so that it may be said I died in glory, crossing swords with a famous hero."

Jack gently steered the conversation onto less violent topics.

"This young woman, Donna Ana, must be very special. I'd like so much to hear about her."

Don Juan, diverted but still wary, relaxed a little as the wind stirred his cape. His voice was low, beguiling.

"There is nothing more to say. Have you never met a woman who inspires you to love until your every sense is filled with her . . . ? You inhale her, you taste her, you feel her flesh on yours and fold into her like hot lava sliding into the sea. . . ."

Jack was instantly overcome by images of his own lost loves. He struggled against the flood of longing which threatened to engulf him. He tried to retake the ground he had lost by moving to the main business of the moment.

"I have no doubt that losing a love like that can be very . . . painful. But why lose hope along with life? Why lose everything?" Jack felt surprised to hear the grief and passion in his own voice.

Touched, Don Juan allowed himself a small display of temper to cover the tender moment.

"I have known a thousand women! *More* than a thousand! And there is only one Donna Ana!"

Jack was still very much aware of his precarious position high in the air. He was cold and tired and uneasy, but he refused to give up. He answered the boy with all the persuasion he could muster.

"Yes, well, perhaps you are right. There may be no one like Donna Ana. But then, again, there could be someone just as wonderful but in a way completely new to you. You will be pleased to know that not even a thousand women can exhaust the variety of the sex. Your second thousand may be even more delightful than your first. Am I right?"

Don Juan, a fair man, admitted that he was right. Jack felt that he was beginning to gain the respect of the young man, was starting to sense a rhythm of conversation building between them, and felt that the time had come to press the attack. He tried with all his cunning to insinuate himself into the story he knew must be playing out in the young man's troubled mind. Jack knew it was risky to appear to accept a patient's warped world view, but the wind was cold and his stamina was not what is used to be.

"You'll never know, Don, whether love might appear elsewhere, just as splendid—possibly even more splendid—where you least expect it, taking you by surprise. . . ."

Don Juan was wounded. Tears filled his eyes.

Jack kept up the pressure.

"It denies even the possibility that your Donna Ana secretly longs for your love as you do for hers, and upon realizing it, will return gratefully to your arms." Jack knew that he may have gone too far. For all he knew, the lass might be married or dead. Still, he had to keep going.

"You must not forget, my friend, that the power of

your love, the power of the great Don Juan's love, is eternal and will not be denied."

Don Juan was vanquished by emotion. Tears leaked from under his mask, streaking his downy cheeks. He was utterly undone and sobbed quietly for a moment before he was able to reply.

"I apologize for this unmanly display, Don Octavio. But the heart is like the sky . . . a part of Heaven, heated by the sun, penetrated by the stars, and after being scorched and pierced, clouds cover it, storms expire in water droplets . . . and the eye pours forth at last the heart's blood turned to tears."

Jack seized the moment, holding out his arms with an elegant, welcoming gesture. He was simultaneously inviting Don Juan into his imaginary hacienda and signaling the cherry-picker operator to get ready to bring them down.

Don Juan, tears flowing, stepped lightly across the abyss to join his newfound friend in a triumphant descent. They embraced, the slight young man and the burly psychiatrist, with formality but with evident emotion, like Frenchmen at an awards ceremony. Policemen, firemen, and spectators cheered as the two men, arms around one another, returned to earth unharmed.

Don Juan sniffled just a little, still apparently overcome. Presently, Jack heard him whisper in a surprisingly unweepy voice. . . .

"Oh, God, to love like that again . . ."

Yearning, like cold steel, ran through Jack's heart. The duel between them had turned out to be a tie, after all, with losses on either side. Jack knew that the pain he felt in his heart was only a signal of the struggle yet to begin. The battle to save Don Juan would not be easy and Jack could not expect to emerge unscathed. He thought, *I will save this young man, even if it is the last thing I ever do as a doctor.*

4

Marilyn

*

In which Don Octavio del Flores returns to Earth.

Dr. Jack Mickler drove home slowly through almost deserted streets, still keyed up from his encounter with Don Juan. He spent most of the trip home in an exalted state of ambivalence. He found himself alternately awarding himself a very handsome imaginary trophy for having handled a tricky situation so well, and giving himself lectures about the dangers of getting too attached to a patient. Not only did he realize the pitfalls of counter-transference, he was considered something of an expert and frequently counseled other doctors on methods for resisting the alluring patient. On the other hand, he was singularly affected by the encounter with the young man and felt an unusual rapport with him, rare enough to warrant further exploration. After he drove into his own driveway, he realized that he hadn't been this excited or exhausted in a very long time. He had been avoiding the difficult cases and the midnight crises ever since he had decided to retire early, partly just because of this kind of post-crisis stress. The muscles in his back, even in his hands and face, were knotted and tense. He was too tired too eat and too jumpy to sleep, but Dr. Jack Mickler was home at last.

He went to his bedroom to put on his pajamas. His wife always bought him the same kind of pajamas, balloon-seat drawstring cotton jammies in navy blue with white piping around the collar. They popped up without fail every year on his birthday, in bigger and bigger sizes. But they were comfortable.

The bedroom was his wife's territory. The brass bed with curlicued posts, the frilly bed skirt, the pastels and the etchings on the wall reflected her taste. Half the medicine bottles were his, an assortment to lower his blood pressure and his interest in life. Half the pillows were his, half the king-sized comforter with the buttoned duvet. It was a nice room, but it was not a lair for the male animal. Often, in this tasteful room he had experienced the discomforting thought that he was the only jarring note, like an old broken-down chair kept around for sentimental reasons.

On other occasions, he felt alarmingly appropriate, as if he had been fitted for a dust ruffle. At those times, he sensed a confusion of persons in this room, as if he and his wife had shared not only sex but gender over the years. He sometimes came close to thinking that marriage might make a man something not quite purely male, as he suspected that his wife was not quite wholly female anymore. He also knew all about the effects of changing levels of testosterone and estrogen on the middle-aged, but he never expected to experience it firsthand. The whole thing about middle age, old age, had always been that it was completely theoretical, like puberty for a normal eight-year-old. It was just a bizarre and uncomfortable prospect off in the distance. Now retirement was only days away. He preferred not to think about it. The doctor was in denial most of the time these days.

However, after jolting around in a cherry picker in the early spring chill, after engaging in a verbal duel with a well-armed man, after enjoying a rare moment of self-satisfaction and after, finally, having gotten back home in one piece, he was in an unusually contemplative mood. He sat on the side of the bed in his boxer shorts and shoes, thinking about his own life.

I love my wife, he thought. *I love my kids. I love my house, sometimes. It is a large house because I am a successful man, Dr. Jack, SuperShrink. It is a beautiful house because my wife knows how to make it so. The belongings we have accumulated over the years are not fine but they are mine. Ours.*

He looked at the spot in front of the fireplace. It had been a cold winter but they had not built a fire in that fireplace for years. His wife probably made sure it was properly maintained. He never really knew all the details of their domestic affairs, although she carefully informed him whenever anything was fixed, cleaned, installed, or, in the case of the chimney, swept. He always tried to listen, but he seldom remembered and never understood the nuances of the house and its needs.

There used to be a fur rug in front of the fireplace, but it had disappeared years ago, victim of his eldest daughter's tenderhearted concern for the wolves. He missed it. He and his wife were probably never going to roll around on the floor like amorous puppies anymore, not in this lifetime, but sometimes he thought it would be nice to do just that. Photographs of his children sat like trophies on the mantelpiece. They hadn't been children for a long time; they had children of their own. It had been difficult for Jack to accept the role of grandfather at first. Pater familias, head of the tribe, maybe. Grandpa, no. Lately it had begun to seem more natural to be addressed that way.

His mind continued to churn. He ascribed his hyper state to leftover adrenaline plus caffeine from the coffee Simon had provided to warm him up. He was no longer allowed to drink real coffee, so the effect on his unhabituated brain was remarkable. He smiled and looked over at his wife, his partner of thirty-two years, Marilyn. She had become more, not less, mysterious to him over the years, like a puzzle he had tried and tried to work out but which had worn him out instead. He felt, when he stood beside her, like an ancient, clumsy buffalo beside an antelope. She had always been quicker than he was, even in college.

My wife is beautiful, he thought. *She is blond and takes care of herself and I never see the changes in her until she shows me. My own changes are bewildering to me. I sometimes wonder how she sees me.*

He muttered aloud, "I am so tired." And thought to himself, *I am so old. Not old. Middle-aged.*

Marilyn was on the phone to her friend Marjorie. They were like two of the incomprehensible teenage girls of his boyhood, sharing secrets on the phone. She was sitting at her dressing table. Her ashen blond hair fell forward over the phone and he could see the nape of her neck, so slender and alluring. She looked around and waved hello to him. She didn't stop her conversation with Marge. He listened to her, pleased with the sound of her voice if not with what she said.

"My body is like an alarm clock. Every morning at exactly three-twenty, I wake up with the flashes and prowl around for an hour, looking for a cool spot. No, no, I'm *taking* estrogen. It should kick in any time now. It had better. I'm worn out already and it could take years. Yes, years."

She smiled at him, maternal and distracted. She walked over and patted him on the hand, pacing the length of the telephone cord, then returned again to the mirror and the table. She combed her hair and shook it, then removed her earrings. Marital radar spun her around to inspect him just as he threw his shoes more or less into the closet. She looked at him speculatively, as if she were glad to see that he was not upset or angry, but as if she would still like to feel his forehead for signs of impending flu. She fidgeted a little, twirling a lock of hair around her finger, watching him. She continued to talk on the telephone. He guessed that she talked partly for his benefit.

"Yes, well, how come nobody warned us about this? After breasts, sex, childbirth, they should have said, will come another great event. You will lose all ability to regulate your own body heat and you will start to look like the Queen Mum. Your skin will no longer adhere to your bones, your waist will rise to your shoulders, and your hips drop to your knees. There will be those flaps on the undersides of your arms, even if you exercise every day with ten-pound weights. Doesn't matter. Your breasts will look shyly at the floor, no longer perky though they are twice as big as they used to be. Great, now when nobody cares you get to have a gigantic chest. Like being pregnant, but no payoff. You will look . . . different. That's what they should have told us, but then they barely bothered to tell us about the first change, did they?"

Dr. Jack absentmindedly dropped his boxer shorts and reached for his pajamas. He was, in truth, exhausted. He was no longer listening to Marilyn. She realized that she had lost Jack's attention. She knew very well, at least she used to know, how to get it back if she wanted it. None of her wiles had worked very well lately on her distant, unresponsive husband. She still employed them whenever it looked like she might be able to stir the embers.

She spoke into the telephone. "Hold on, Marge, Jack's here."

She moved closer to him.

She covered the mouthpiece with her hand so that Marge could not hear and looked straight into Jack's eyes. She smiled at her husband in a secret, intimate way, paying complete attention to him while her friend continued to talk to her through the phone. There was something just faintly racy in her manner, nothing crude or overt but powerful, nevertheless. Jack didn't understand all the implications, but some of them got through to his weary brain.

She whispered to him, her voice low and sultry, lovely. "A fork got caught in the drain inside the dishwasher and there was a flood, soapy water was everywhere. I got the floor cleaned up but I couldn't get the fork out. Could you take a look at it when you get a chance, sweetheart?"

Jack thought, *She is adorable. I do not in the least understand what she is saying. I am too tired and too entirely captivated by the curve of her thigh under the thin nightdress.* Jack was suddenly aware that while he might be old, he wasn't entirely dead yet.

He winked at his wife. She looked at him and almost laughed out loud. She was still on the phone. She did not take her eyes off her husband as she started talking again to her friend.

"Yes, I am still here, Marge. Jack just winked at me. Nothing. That's the sum total. Jack winked. At me. The last time Jack winked at me, I was straightening the seams of my stockings. Yes, in my garter-belt era. Don't tell me you didn't have one. . . . Well, I'd better get off, now. Talk to you tomorrow."

Jack was suddenly on a new train of thought. *Like lava flowing into the sea, that's what Don Juan said. I would have said something else. Like a sailor coming into port, perhaps. Like coming home. But what do I know, I'm only a man, not a teenaged cultural idol.* He smiled and looked a lot younger, happier. *A thousand women. Or one. I am possibly not as tired as I thought I was.*

But, in fact, he was much more exhausted than he had realized. He lay down to wait for Marilyn and fell fast asleep long before she could climb in beside him. She was awake for a long time, thinking about her husband and his curious lack of interest over the last year. And his absolute refusal to discuss his own retirement. Finally she went to sleep, too, and they drifted separately onto the vast ocean of their dreams.

5

Asylum

*

*In which the struggle of Don Juan and Don
Octavio del Flores moves to new ground.*

Early the next morning, Dr. Jack's car nosed through
the iron, guarded gates of Woodhaven State Mental
Hospital in Queens. He parked next to the superintendent's gaudy turtleback Porsche and walked toward the
building which contained his office. He looked up at the
gray stone and gothic, barred windows, at the winter-
damaged ivy swinging in the cool, early spring breeze. The
hospital used to be a haven for him, as much a refuge from
the world for him as it ever was for the disordered souls
who came there to find peace or escape jail. People knew
his name and his wife's name, even his children's names.
He wore a photo-ID badge clipped to his shirt collar,
proving him one of those privileged to come and go at will.
The square of laminated plastic was like the key to a
walled city.

As he walked through long corridors to his office, he
threaded his way through patients he no longer cared to
notice. He had a reputation as an uncannily accurate
diagnostician. He used to be able to watch patients move
through the ward, drowsy with drugs and immersed in
their own sorrows, and know at once the names of their

afflictions. Now he remembered their names and their histories, but no longer wished to remember their faces. Jack had practiced at the hospital for more than thirty years and he sometimes felt he was soggy, drenched with madmen's tears. Don Juan's tears seemed to Jack to be quite different, almost magnificent. The boy might be delusional, but there was a dignity and vitality about him that spoke of health rather than pathetic sickness.

Dr. Jack was going to the regular, morning treatment meeting to report on his encounter with Don Juan. Jack was a veteran of a thousand of these meetings. More than a thousand. He was not especially thrilled with the prospect of one more. His grievances and resentments were so familiar, he barely noticed them as they accompanied him to the conference room. He thought, not for the first or even the thousandth time, about the small pleasures he had lost.

"I can't even have a cup of real coffee or, God forbid, a cigarette to carry me through. Those were the days, when caffeine and nicotine and even, now and then, a nip from a flask might cheer me up. An egg. A sausage. When was the last time I had a proper breakfast with a nice gooey egg? I will have to sit through this morning's meeting uncomforted by stimulants or nutrients."

He frowned, startling a couple of patients as he walked toward the conference room. His thoughts were dark.

"The only chemicals I get to ingest these days make everything worse. My diuretic makes it absolutely certain that I will have to piss halfway through the meeting. The rest of those people seem to have bladders of steel. The whole meeting will last too long and it will have nothing to do with the real people under discussion. Egos will clash, but not very loudly. Everyone will want to get on with it except Paul Showalter, my boss and a prime horse's ass if there ever was one."

Jack sighed heavily as he took his place at the table. He drifted until it was time for him to talk. Then he gamely struggled into harness one more time and began to give a bald, dry report, reading from the standard admittance form.

"White male—" It struck him, as it always did, as an irrelevant, even stupid, way to start. "Why white male? Why white? What does that have to do with anything? White, brown, green . . . Jeez." Jack gave the same speech, on average, every third time he had to do a report.

Superintendent Paul, prissy as ever, presided over the meeting. He radiated irritation as Jack digressed. In his opinion, Jack was always digressing. Jack stopped just short of driving Paul into hysterics. Jack hauled himself, with an effort, back into line.

"Okay, okay. White male, aged twenty-one, brought in on a ten-day paper after a suicidal gesture apparently precipitated by the breakup of a . . . relationship." An unavoidable note of mirth crept into Jack's voice, irritating the director and, therefore, his toadies. Jack had his own camp of followers, as well, and his people sensed that something good was coming. They waited with some discreet hope for a break from the dull routine. Jack, in the meantime, did his best to drone on in the approved manner.

"The patient indicates he has had no previous history of suicide attempts and no record of hospitalization or incarceration. No mother, no father, no schools, no fixed address, nothing. We have no reason to believe that he is wanted for any crime. The boy is severely delusional. He believes he is somebody else." Jack paused a moment.

Head Nurse Alvira, firmly in Jack's corner, fed him the straight line.

"Anybody we know?"

Jack took a deep breath. He was enjoying this more than he expected.

"Don Juan"—he looked straight at Alvira—"World's Greatest Lover."

Alvira and her nurses erupted into laughter and applause, cheering Dr. Jack's timing and subversive attitude. Paul grew even more annoyed. He liked everything to stay uncluttered, rather like one of his seclusion rooms. Paul was happiest tinkering with the budget. The sloppy mess of life revolted him. He had grown colder and colder over thirty years of fending off the chaotic emotions of staff and inmates. Even the politics of the place, which used to give him an occasional thrill, were now too robust for his dainty sensibilities. Once he had been a lot warmer and more curious about his fellow creatures. In the last ten years it had grown increasingly easy for him to regard the unfortunates in his care as an unsatisfactory representation of raw material to be processed as efficiently and as neatly as possible. Jack annoyed him, presented at some level an unspoken reproach. Their long association had only sharpened the differences between them. Paul had long suspected, with profound disapproval, that Jack harbored an unseemly, mutinous tendency to laugh at his boss.

"Don Juan. Who wants him?" Paul put the question as crudely as possible, rebuking Jack. The nurses stared; this was cold, even for Paul.

"Actually" said Jack, surprising himself, "I do."

That was the third time in forty-eight hours that Jack had surprised himself: on the cherry picker with Don Juan; for a fleeting moment with Marilyn; and now, against all reason, requesting a difficult case at the very last minute in his career.

Paul could not believe his ears.

The two men did not much like each other. In one of those vagaries of hierarchies everywhere, Paul was the superior in rank but much the lesser man. He was not only much less intelligent than Jack, he had been born without a scrap of humor. While Jack had sailed through medical school, charming teachers and patients, Paul had plodded, barely making the cut. He had worked extremely hard at making friends in the right places and saying all the right things so that he could be the boss. Even though Paul had achieved all of his goals, and Jack was only an ordinary underling on the organizational chart, Paul still had the maddening sensation, daily, of being left in the dust by this man and he, for one, would not weep to see the last of Dr. Jack, SuperShrink.

Paul adopted an offensively fussy, patronizing tone like a schoolmaster to a naughty toddler. "The boy is delusional. You said so yourself. There was a weapon involved, I seem to recall. Possible hallucinations. Threats to himself and others. Very serious disturbance. It will take more than ten days. I am giving him to Bill."

Bill was one of Paul's baby-faced favorites. "You have the time, Bill?" It was not really a question. If Paul said so, Bill would have the time.

Jack wanted to deck both of them, but realized that losing his temper here in front of Alvira and the nurses and the staff, while it might be fun, would lose him Don Juan.

"Can we talk privately, Paul? After the meeting?"

In the hallway after the meeting they were like a couple of bulldogs on a disputed patch of alleyway. Paul was trapped without his entourage. On the other hand, Jack was beginning to care about the outcome, a disadvantage in this kind of duel. Paul and Jack bristled quietly at each other as a stream of patients and staff swirled past them. Jack made the first move.

"I want this patient, Paul."

"Be reasonable, Jack. The guy is really sick. You're leaving in ten days."

"So is he. He's in here on a ten-day paper, don't forget."

Paul slipped back into his schoolmaster role. It was his favorite.

"A delusional patient like this does not get cured in a week and a half. The instant his ten-day paper expires, he'll be committed. You'll be gone, and we'll have to give him to Bill anyway." Paul considered that he had scored a lot of very good points with this speech and the subject was closed.

Jack, on the contrary, believed that the preliminaries were now over and the main event was about to begin. He moved a little closer to Paul, invading his territory. He looked deeply into Paul's eyes as he towered over him. He was determined that the Pipsqueak Paul would not get away with anything, not now.

"A year ago, if I'd said I could get a patient out of here in ten days, there would be no question about my taking him on. That's not the reason you're giving him to Bill."

The truth was not something Paul cared to handle. Professional cant and euphemism came easily to Paul, as they did not to Jack. Caught off guard, he attacked.

"You're right. That isn't the reason you don't get him. It's a good enough reason, but it isn't the main reason. I didn't want to have to discuss this with you"—Paul got his anger under control and continued—"but you've been doing it by the numbers for months now, and you know it. You're burnt out, Jack. That's why you asked for early retirement." Paul's face was devoid of any recognizable human expression, but his voice held a note of pleading. "You didn't really need more time for your personal affairs, did you? So please, don't make my life any harder than it already is."

Paul had drawn first blood with that remark about Jack's failing powers. Jack's reply was an involuntary cry from the heart. In spite of everything, Jack still wanted the approval of his fellow psychiatrists, even Paul's. "I've been here thirty years, Paul."

Paul sensed an advantage and moved in for the kill.

"Yes, you have been here for *over* thirty years and, until recently, you were the best damn clinician this place has ever seen. But now you're burnt out. Time to go see the pyramids."

Paul was trying, unsuccessfully, to be nice. He and his wife, Bernice, had enjoyed a very memorable guided tour in Egypt three years ago. He became almost animated. "The pyramids are terrific things, truly. You saw my slides. All that sand, vistas, sunshine, palm trees, camels . . . the Valley of the Kings." He then returned with difficulty to the topic at hand. "Nobody could deserve it more than you do, Jack. I'm giving the boy to Bill Dunsmore."

Jack had to retreat, but he had one last round to fire.

"That kid is going to eat Bill for breakfast and dance the fandango on his bones." Jack laughed with genuine amusement at the thought of Don Juan and Dunsmore locked together in a one-sided contest. "You go right ahead and give him to Bill. But don't forget that I told you so when your pal comes back with fandango marks all over his little pointy head."

Paul took the remarks and the laugh as the feeble attempt of a thoroughly defeated man to go down with at least a tiny scrap of dignity. But Dr. Paul Showalter, Horse's Behind, had calculated without the power of Don Juan De Marco, General of the Army of the Opposition, and one hell of a dancer.

Within the hour, Don Juan, in full regalia but without his mask or sword was, sure enough, dancing a ripe flamenco before Bill Dunsmore's baffled eyes. Bill threw out a cautious line of inquiry. "Would you like to talk about why you attempted to kill yourself . . . ?"

The don stopped dancing and strolled over to Dunsmore. The mousy clinician tried not to flinch. Don Juan saw at once that this pale imitation of a man was no match for even a modestly skilled adversary. Don Juan was amused rather than offended, like a cat with whom the rodent wished to box. Don Juan decided to play with the creature. Educate it a little.

"*I* talk to *you*? You want Don Juan De Marco, the world's greatest lover, to talk to *you*, an insignificant peasant? What do *you* know of great love?" Don Juan bent over the young doctor, so that his fragrant breath actually warmed the slack lips of the bewildered physician.

"Have you ever loved a woman until milk leaked from her as though she had just given birth to love itself and now must feed it or burst?" Bill Dunsmore involuntarily shook his head, as he timidly flinched away from the looming young man. Dunsmore appeared to be trying to bury himself in his chair. Don Juan licked his lips delicately.

"Have you ever tasted a woman until she believed that she could be satisfied only by consuming the tongue that devoured her?" Don Juan moved even closer to Bill, whispering, "Have you ever loved a woman so completely that the sound of your voice in her ear could cause her body to shudder and explode with such intense pleasure that only weeping could bring her full release?" Bill was rendered temporarily speechless.

Don Juan stepped back and smiled his most affable, noble smile. No need to be cruel. He never acted without mercy. He asked the cowering doctor a straightforward question.

"Where is Don Octavio del Flores?"

Dunsmore, stunned by the fangs still plunged deeply into his limbic system, did not comprehend the question.

"Who?"

"My host at this villa."

"Your host at what villa?"

"This villa. I must ask that you attend to my question. Now, where is Don Octavio del Flores, my host at this villa?"

Bill Dunsmore finally caught on. "You mean Dr. Mickler?"

It was Don Juan's turn to be confused. "Who?"

They both started to sink deeper into confusion. Dunsmore made an effort to salvage the situation. "Why do you think Dr. Mickler is Don Octavio del Flores?"

Don Juan also made an effort. "Because that's how he introduced himself to me. Why do you think Don Octavio del Flores is this Dr. Mickler?" Don Juan, ever courteous, was losing patience. "Now you must allow me to talk to Don Octavio."

Dunsmore clutched at the few rags of logical certitude he had left. "And why is that?"

Don Juan was perfectly willing to instruct him. "Because he is a lover and you are not. You are a delusion, an hallucination, a phantasm, a mind without a body. I mean no offense, but obviously, where physical love is concerned, you have the featureless presence of . . . mist. Very nice, but you wouldn't want to tell it your deepest secrets."

No more than an hour later, a recovered but still shaken Bill Dunsmore stormed in Jack Mickler's office. Dr. Jack was not entirely surprised to see him. Dunsmore babbled, his voice shrill with wounded pride and outrage.

"Don Octavio del Flores! You told him you were Don Octavio del Flores! You told a *delusional* patient you were a seventeenth-century Spanish nobleman?" Dunsmore sputtered. Jack remained calm, even regal, but he enjoyed an unfamiliar moment of unalloyed triumph.

"I needed to get him into the bucket. Haven't you read the file?"

Dunsmore was less than noble in defeat.

"Well, he's all yours, *Don*." Bill started to leave. Jack was not quite through with him.

"You tell this to Paul?"

"You bet I did." Bill's voice was spiteful. Even so, he was more bearable in a high dudgeon than he ever was as Paul's meek little sidekick. Jack was amused.

"What did Paul say?"

"His exact words were 'Jack broke it, let him fix it!' " Bill scampered out of there.

Jack said to the closing door, "Yes! Yes! Yes! I can fix it! Me, Dr. Jack SuperShrink, I can fix anything!" He laughed wickedly at the retreating Dr. Bill. Then, seized by successive waves of admiration for his own accomplishments, his own vast reading, and excellent history of skillfully handling difficult patients, Jack began to feel that his boast wasn't far off the mark. Psychiatrists, even brain surgeons, weren't supposed to brag. They were supposed to be modest about their own achievements. But just at the end, here, with his very last patient, Dr. Jack felt the need to blow his own horn a little.

Little did he know that within the hour he would learn that adjusting Don Juan to the real world, even acquainting him with it, was far easier said than done.

6

The Chessmen

*

**In which Don Juan and Don Octavio
consider a wager.**

Jack waited in his office an hour later, fiddling with paperwork and only mildly curious about who his next visitor might be. It did not turn out to be Paul the Warden, as he expected, but Don Juan the Chivalrous Inmate. Gloria, a luscious but very proper young nurse accompanied Don Juan into the office. To Jack's practiced eye, Gloria looked somewhat too radiant for the occasion. A bit too innocent, a shade too rosy. And just a foot or two farther into Jack's office then she needed to be.

She said, "I brought Mr. Juan for his appointment."

"Thank you, Gloria."

"I can come back at the end of the hour and take him back."

Jack watched her watching Juan. She was enthralled. She was not about to leave the office of her own free will. Jack tried to give her a hint.

"That's okay, Gloria, I'll take care of him." She knew she ought to leave, but she just couldn't quite do it.

"It's really no trouble. I'll be passing this door in exactly one hour, right on the nose. I can come on my break. No problem, really . . ." A soft giggle escaped her, the last straw for Jack.

He put on his doctor-knows-best voice: "I can handle it, Gloria. Could you shut the door? Please?"

Gloria bowed her head in resignation, though her radiance was undiminished. She smiled once more at Don Juan. He saluted her with a gracious nod and wave. Her knees buckled slightly. Then she pulled herself together and vanished out the door, a new lilt in her step.

Jack scrutinized Don Juan, who, in the light of day, looked very much like a slightly scrawny teenage boy in fancy dress. Like any good psychiatrist, Jack started the session by stating the obvious.

"You seem to have quite an effect on the ladies . . . ?" Jack made it sound like a question.

"You've noticed." Don Juan was so pleased with the observation he all but patted the doctor on the head. The young man did not choose to regard Jack's observation as a query, but as a tribute to his art.

Jack was temporarily stopped in his tracks as he judged the young man's tone. There was no hint of boasting or overcompensation. Don Juan simply regarded the adoration of women as nothing less than his due. He was quite used to remarks about his effect on the ladies, that was obvious. But there was nothing obvious about what to say next.

Don Juan could see that Don Octavio was not ready to begin, but there was no rush. The courtly youth allowed his friend a few moments to gather his thoughts. In the meantime, the young man amused himself picking up Jack's antique Peruvian flute and playing a haunting folk melody, something really more suited to the panpipes, but Don Juan knew how to improvise on any instrument. As he played, he studied the older man. They already had some satisfactory history together. Jack, in his turn, contemplated the boy as he played the wooden flute.

Jack decided to try a more concrete inquiry.

"You slept well?" Jack asked, knowing that half of his patients slept hardly at all and half were asleep most of the time. He intended to find out in which half Don Juan belonged. It would tell him a great deal about the tactics the young man used to combat his demons. The wakeful patients fought against the foul terrors of the night by refusing to close their eyes; the somnolent ones sought to evade the furies by hiding under the covers. If he were a fighter, the doctor could become a comrade at arms; if Don Juan liked to hide, the doctor could protect him and reassure him, building a fortress. Whether he had to plan for a siege or a formal battle, intelligence was everything to Dr. Jack.

Don Juan stopped playing the flute and took charge of the conversation. The vital matters before them had nothing to do with sleep. He spoke forcefully but without rancor.

"They have taken my mask, Don Octavio. They had no right to do that! I never remove my mask in public! Do you understand the consequences of this?"

Jack's technique, whenever he encountered a really florid adolescent fantasy, was to adopt an initial coolness, a faintly ironic, yet never chilly or sarcastic, tone. It sometimes enticed his young charges to even greater heights of rhetoric and exaggeration, but sometimes it encouraged a more adult exchange of information. Whichever response was elicited, Dr. Jack would end up with more clues to the nature of the young creature. He said to the agitated Don Juan, "Not really. Tell me."

"I will be cursed" replied Don Juan, as simply as a child of six.

Dr. Jack, the certified SuperShrink, moved confidently forward to Technique Number Two. This technique was particularly useful for appearing to understand completely baffling statements. The doctor calmly reflected the patient's expression of strong feeling by paraphrasing it into an utterly bland declaration followed by a validation of his feelings. The technique not only made the doctor seem wise and insightful, but the doctor who used it well generally drew out additional information from the patient without seeming to pry. Jack could make it sound good, too, as if he were a long-lost buddy. He nodded his head and said, "You feel you will be cursed for having removed your mask. Well, I can certainly understand how angry that would make you."

Don Juan, a sophisticated and sensitive young man, recognized instantly that he was being patronized. He had no reason to tolerate such an attitude. The blade of his stunning wit was drawn once more.

"Well, yes, think how angry *you* would feel if someone made *you* take off *your* mask," he said, smiling sweetly to soften the blow.

The remark hit home. Dr. Jack's patients were usually too intent on their own troubles to listen very carefully to anything he had to say. He feared that his execution of Technique Number Two must have been faulty. He decided to abandon the more rigid, formulaic approaches in favor of free-form responses.

He acknowledged the patient's feelings and his own. "Yes, well, our masks are always a problem, aren't they?"

He looked at the smiling boy and wandered, lost in thought, over to his desk. He opened an unlocked drawer and started turning over a jumble of medicine bottles and shrink-wrapped packages of sample pills. He realized that he shouldn't keep the drugs in his office. They should all be locked up and accounted for, and he had been meaning to take care of that. He had, as Paul had pointed out, gotten a lot looser than he ought to be. He spent a couple of minutes accusing himself silently of sloppiness and bad technique, forgetfulness and carelessness, as he stirred the mess in his desk. He finally selected an assortment of gaily colored psychoactive pills, which he counted out into the palm of his hand. His mind was still on himself as he poured a glass of water from the pitcher on his desk.

In the meantime, Don Juan was perfectly content to wait. He reclined gracefully on the leather sofa as he scanned the room for clues about Don Octavio. The office overflowed with books. In an inadequate bookcase Byron and Berryman leaned unsteadily against the *Neurologist's Handbook*; the *Rubaiyat of Omar Khayam* and *King Lear* flanked Rollo May. *Seven Pillars of Wisdom* kept company with William James and Oscar Wilde slept uneasily with Harry Stack Sullivan.

An artistically inclined secretary had arranged all of the books in some private order of her own and they had stayed that way, gathering dust. Jack hadn't actually touched any of them in over a year, but he didn't realize that. Don Juan, seeing the dust, understood. He also understood the hopeless piles of papers which would never be filed. Knowledge was ammunition for them both, and Don Juan's intelligence was as keen as the doctor's.

The young man roamed through the room, gently touching Cycladic and other island representations of the mother goddess, small souvenir carvings of camels, a tiny brass telescope, and an astrolabe from the Azores. Although all of the artifacts were as dust covered as the books, they indicated to Don Juan a certain encouraging degree of interest in foreign countries and women.

Don Juan also noted with approval the doctor's choice of Impressionist prints, in which rosy women danced in the arms of shy men, and ballerinas put slippers on their beautiful feet. Don Juan was especially appreciative of the Degas and Renoirs.

The office was the kind of place to smoke a pipe in, if people still smoked pipes. Dr. Jack also kept a chess set on a special inlaid game table. The set was modeled after the famous medieval Lewis chessmen, brave little men in ivory and ebony. Don Juan roamed back to lean against a bookcase. He looked expectantly at Dr. Jack.

The doctor held the pills and the glass of water, trying to judge how to engage the young man without exciting any negative emotions. He wanted to establish some trust before he jammed the drugs into the boy's system. The

mask seemed to be a central, important object, and the
doctor decided to venture a question about it.

"So, how long have you worn the mask?"

Don Juan was glad to resume their conversation. He
seated himself gracefully and answered the question.

"Since I was sixteen. I placed the mask on my face
and vowed never to remove it in public. That was the day
I left my mother, the dark beauty Doña Inez Santiago y
San Martine."

Jack hated the current hospital policy of drugging
every new patient as soon as possible. He regretted having
to persuade the boy that it would be in his own best
interest to take the heavy chemicals. The newer drugs
were truly remarkable, but Jack did not believe they
should be given to every patient, and never until the
patient's problems and strengths had been carefully explored. Paul, the Boss of the Place, believed otherwise.
For Paul, it was a matter of avoiding mess and ambivalence. Drugs were quick. Drugged patients were easy to
handle, and Paul's policies were increasingly enforced
without the option of dissent or exception. Jack wondered
why he had stayed here so long, in a place where he
disagreed with just about every rule and custom. He
couldn't remember.

In spite of his doubts, Jack offered the pills and the
glass of water to Don Juan. Not only did he feel obliged to
medicate the boy, but Jack knew that he could learn
something of the young man's previous experience with
the system by displaying the pills. Veteran patients either
flinched or glowed at the thought of chemicals. Some of
them were experts in side effects and symptoms. Only the
first-time patients were baffled or puzzled by an offer of
capsules. Careful observation of Don Juan's reaction
would help to establish whether he was familiar with the
hospital routine, and would add to the doctor's store
of clues.

Don Juan did not even glance at the pills. His eyes stayed on the doctor's face.

Jack held out the medication and said, with some insistence, "Pills. They will help you."

Don Juan peered at the pills.

"They are to stop delusions?"

"Yes. They will stop delusions."

"And what delusions are the ones you wish to stop?"

"That you believe that you are somebody you are not, namely the legendary figure Don Juan."

The young man said, "Then we must take them together, Don Octavio, because you are also severely deluded."

"How so, Don Juan?" The doctor was caught off guard.

"You have this persistent fantasy that you are someone named Dr. Jack Mickler."

Jack had to admit to himself that it was a good point. He probably shouldn't have perpetrated a lie in order to persuade the boy to come with him. Deceit was not a good psychiatric strategy, not in the long run. The pigeons almost always came home to roost, just as they were doing now.

Don Juan jumped up out of his chair. He quivered with justifiable outrage. He clenched his fists and pushed aside Jack's hand, rejecting the pills.

"I am very disappointed in you, Don Octavio! Very disappointed! You don't believe that I am truly Don Juan De Marco, the world's greatest lover, do you? And you have not been honest with me."

"Does it matter what I believe?" Jack's voice was calm and sad.

"No, Don Octavio, it does not." The young man answered with dignity and courtesy. He was willing to forgive the doctor his unfortunate lapse. Dr. Jack stared back, unsure whether to explain his reasons for deceit or to let it alone. Jack decided to level with Don Juan. It was a strategy of last resort.

"You know," Jack said, "they can make you take the medication. You're here on a ten-day paper. During those ten days, they can do whatever they think is appropriate."

Jack was surprised that he had so easily revealed his lack of identification with the institution. By rights, he should have said "*We* can do whatever *we* think is right." In his whole career, he had avoided phrases attributing sinister motives to unspecified third parties since a lot of his patients were already convinced that nameless but numerous unseen agencies were wickedly responsible for personal troubles and world wars.

Don Juan did not appreciate any of the nuances in Jack's speech. Instead, he started to draw his sword, remembering only at the last minute that he no longer wore it. He shouted, his face dark with rage, "*I am not deluded! I am Don Juan!*"

Jack plodded on, feeling worse every second. "If, after ten days, they decide that you are not able to live safely on your own, they can make you stay here for a year. A whole year."

Don Juan was astounded by this injustice, but he did not doubt the veracity of Don Octavio's message. He searched for an escape route. His only hope was to win his new friend to his cause. He scooped up a handful of ebony chessmen.

Then the young man modulated his voice and unclenched his fists. Brute force would never win this fight.

Don Juan said to Dr. Jack, "I have a proposition for you. Here's my proposal. Ten days. Ten chessmen. I'll remove one a day. If you don't make me take the medication, before the last is gone, I will have told you everything you have wanted to know about loving a woman and my own remarkable, heroic story of love, shipwreck, eunuchs, and pomegranates."

Spellbound, Jack drank the glass of water intended for his patient.

"I will begin," said Don Juan, "by telling you how I came to wear my mask—and of my mother, the dark beauty, Doña Inez. She was a goddess, a woman of divine loveliness. I remember her always as bathed in a golden light, naked and unashamed, combing her hair before a mirror. Rubens, Rembrandt, Renoir, all have painted beautiful women but none as glorious as my mother. When I have finished, I will remove the first chessman. A pawn."

Jack was determined to follow through as if this were a normal conversation. He asked, "And when the last man is gone and you have finished your tale, then what?"

"Then you will know that I am really Don Juan. I will leave, wearing my mask and sword."

"And if I don't believe you, what then?"

"If you truly don't believe that I am Don Juan De Marco, the world's greatest lover, then I will take my medicine and you may keep me for as long as you like."

"I cannot accept your wager, Don Juan," Jack said, "The ethics of my profession prevent my betting on your health and sanity. But I will listen to every word you say, and I will try to act in your best interest. That I promise you."

Jack leaned forward in his chair to study Don Juan's eyes more closely. For an instant he could see an apparition reflected there. He could almost share the boy's vision of Doña Inez, naked and serene, swaying gracefully as she combed her long dark hair by lamplight.

Don Juan seized the moment. "Are we in agreement? I have these days to tell you my story?"

Jack nodded, unable to speak for a moment, then shook himself out of the trance into which he had been cast by the image of Doña Inez.

"Yes. That much I can accept. I agree that I will listen

to your story until your ten days are up. That will be on next Monday. That is all I can promise."

Don Juan smiled. He was, as ever, gracious in victory. With the preliminaries understood by both sides, they prepared to move on to the heart of the matter. Jack felt sure this would be an exceptionally productive first session.

7

Doña Inez

*

The tension between Jack and Don Juan was much reduced. As they prepared to resume their discussion, Jack noticed the same strange sense of harmony and brotherhood he had felt on the cherry picker, when the boy had stepped across the abyss into safety. The doctor busied himself with pouring out water, which Don Juan accepted with a small bow, as if it were the finest champagne. They toasted each other, smiling. Man and boy, patient and doctor, then settled in for a long afternoon's session.

Dr. Jack said, "You were going to tell me about your mother. . . ."

"It became evident from a very young age that there was something different about me. My memories of my mother start when I was very, very young, no more than two. In my favorite, and earliest, clearest memory I see my mother, Doña Inez, in all her splendor, standing naked as a goddess before her mirror, combing her long dark hair." Don Juan wove his tale unencumbered by any false modesty, a cheerful Oedipus singing the praises of his beautiful mom. He said, without a trace of unseemly pruriance or apology, "Her rippling tresses cascaded almost to the poignant curve of her flawless, pear-shaped bottom. She worked the comb through one shining lock which had been thrown over her shoulder to brush the delicate tip of her left breast. She hummed to herself, an old Spanish lullaby."

Jack was surprised at how vividly he could imagine himself in the richly panelled bedroom of Don Juan's lovely young mother, complete with delicious details. He decided to enjoy the sensation and analyze it later. Don Juan continued, in a tone of affectionate nostalgia.

"Don Octavio, you will believe me when I tell you that I was a singularly attractive infant. My mother has told me so, and showed me pictures of myself naked in a hip bath. I well remember the glorious view of my mother's splendid form which I enjoyed as I bathed. As I splashed merrily in the hip bath, I stared at my mama with exalted admiration. A grin of toothless delight animated my adorable chubby face. I cooed and gurgled. I splashed. I worshipped my mother."

Dr. Jack recognized the family romance at once. However, the tenderness and reverence with which Don Juan recounted his crush on his mom was completely new to him. Even the most sophisticated and depraved grown men, even the youngest and most innocent boys, and certainly most adolescents, were shy and reticent about their earliest attachments to their mothers. Not a trace of shyness or reticence could be detected in Don Juan's voice. Neither was he boasting. He appeared to be telling the truth as simply as he could.

"My mother has told me that on one such occasion, she sensed the warm rays of infantile masculine attention beaming her way from me, her innocent son. She turned and looked me in the eye, then reached instinctively for a robe to cover her glorious nakedness from neck to knee. It is one of the family stories at which we used to laugh together."

Dr. Jack, careful to conceal his continuing surprise at this description of blithe frankness between mother and son, nodded to indicate that the young man should continue.

Don Juan indicated with a wave of his elegant hand the passing of blissful time. In his most charming voice, he painted for the silent doctor a landscape with figures, the flower-filled, dusty street of a small Mexican village, a street filled with barefoot nine-year-old boys, wild as wild ponies in the sun.

"I began to realize," said Don Juan to Dr. Jack, "that I was not like the other boys. When I was eight, I became the object of a sort of cult, unknown to the other boys or the adults of the village. Day after day, I stood like a maharajah in the shade of a lemon tree. Young girls waited in line before me. Each virgin in turn gently placed a flower at my feet, then received my tender kiss on her lips. They placed hundreds of red and white flowers at my feet each day. The next day there would be another hundred blossoms. Not a garden in the village that had not been ransacked for my pleasure."

"No latency period," thought Dr. Jack, "no scorning of girls, no chums. 'Curioser and curioser,' as the old saying goes."

Don Juan smiled at the memory of so many devoted girls, then went on. "By the time I was ten, the attraction that females felt for me, and I for them, was becoming of some concern to my mother, the dark beauty, Doña Inez." Dr. Jack could well believe that Doña Inez, however candid her approach to matters of infantile sexuality, would have experienced some worry over all those adoring maidens.

"So my mother presented me to God and asked the Lord to save me before it was too late. The village was poor, but the church was richly baroque. It gleamed with twisted golden columns. The languid marble figure of San Sebastian glowed in the light from the rose window. The affectionate, forgiving statue of the Madonna held her hands out to comfort her wayward children. I appreciated, you understand, the more sensual aspects of worship."

Don Juan recognized the look of a nonbeliever on Dr. Jack's face and decided to elaborate on certain aspects of his religious studies.

"I remember especially a Sunday when I was ten. My face was scrubbed. My hair was combed. I wore the red robe and elaborate embroidered white bib of the altar boy. The air was full of the scent of holy incense and the heavenly music of the organ. I carried the silver chalice to the priest and then looked out at the congregation."

Don Juan's voice held a hint of laughter in it.

"The front row, Don Octavio, was packed with nuns, sitting shoulder to shoulder in their black habits and white wimples. They had angelic smiles on their virginal faces, and their eyes were fixed only on me, Don Juan. Even the eyes of the Mother Superior. Apparently, it was already too late."

The doctor could not help but recognize the threads of a story even older than Chaucer, of an age and moldiness comparable to the farmer's daughter's fable, but he did not care to point this out to Don Juan. He was not all that sure he was still capable of pointing anything out.

"When I was about thirteen, Doña Querida, another dark beauty, stood before a different mirror in a different bedroom, undressing by firelight. She was down to stockings, bra, underpants, and a slip made of the most delicate Chinese silk. The bushes outside her low bedroom window rustled and shook with more than the very light summer breeze." Don Juan smiled as he remembered the luscious Doña Querida and her inadequate window shades.

Dr. Jack recognized the voyeuristic tone, but did not care to interrupt the story. Don Juan recounted his early exploits with such a shameless simplicity of manner that the doctor could not see that anything would be gained by trying to elicit more insight from the boy. Besides, he was enjoying the story. "The rustling grew louder as she moved into a pool of bright lamplight. The bushes rustled because they concealed a clutch of nine- and ten-year-old boys. The other boys all stood on tiptoe to peek into Doña Querida's private sanctuary. I rested in the shade of a lemon tree, proud of my young comrades."

"By the time I was that old," Don Juan said piously, "I understood the obligation the Lord places upon us, to share one's blessings with those less fortunate. But I digress. Let us return to the generous and lovely Doña Querida."

Don Juan invited the doctor to imagine the delight, the wonder, with which the boys discovered the generosity and beauty of women, a discovery which would always be remembered with nostalgia by men even in their eighties. Dr. Jack found a need to shift slightly in his seat, as the combined force of Don Juan's narrative and his own memories of love worked certain changes that required adjustment of his posture and some of his clothing.

"Apparently unaware of the baby voyeurs, Doña Querida slowly undid the snaps on her garter belt and, with agonizing deliberation, peeled a sheer, dark stocking from her well-turned leg. A worshipful sigh arose from the impassioned bushes. She smiled to herself."

Don Juan folded his hands in a prayerful attitude.

"Ask and it shall be given you; seek and ye shall find; knock and it shall be opened to you." There was not a trace of blasphemy in Don Juan's soul as he quoted from the evangelist. "Matthew was no fool.

"Doña Querida finished removing the first stocking, then went to work on the second, rolling it deliciously down her downy leg as the eyes at the window grew more and more enthralled. At the very end, as she slid the stocking off her toe, the immaculate white cotton of her panties, covering the very gates of Paradise, briefly revealed itself to the audience. A collective gasp of delight went up from the boys at the window.

"The gorgeous and generous Doña Querida suppressed a smile. She had known all about the boys in the bushes. She enjoyed holding their small and passionate hearts in her power. It was a harmless game to her, and instructive to us, her acolytes. She began to remove her brassiere, cleverly unhooking it without taking off her slip. Nothing was revealed, though a very great deal was implied."

Don Juan and Jack considered for a moment the great power of implication in such matters. Don Juan continued.

"A loud groan of disappointment escaped from the younger boys. The groan was too loud for Doña Querida to ignore. She resumed her modesty. She was as coyly surprised as a milkmaid caught bathing in the farm pond on a September morning. She chased my friends from her window. The show was over for most of them.

"It was over, that is, for all but one of the youngsters. I watched from the shadows under my lemon tree. Doña Querida, alone, as she believed, opened the window again to breathe in the heavy fragrances of night-blooming jasmine and moonflowers."

Don Juan savored the intoxicating power of the unseen watcher.

"I stood that night and watched Doña Querida at the window in her slip. It was like catching a glimpse of a panther in the darkness, like being allowed to see, for just an instant, the secret world it inhabits at night, how it moves and hunts and loves. You understand that she knew, I am sure, that I was watching her.

"Soon Doña Querida moved her hands to the nape of her slender neck, lifting her heavy dark hair from her shoulders. As her arms came up in a lazy stretch, her breasts rose under her slip and pulled the thin material taut over her, clearly outlining the darling bumps of her nipples as the cool night breeze played over them."

Don Juan's voice was heavy, golden, perfumed, as he recounted the first of the many lessons he had mastered in his study of the arts of love.

"I noticed for the first time how the underclothing a woman wears barely touches her skin, how it rides on a cushion of air as she moves, how the silk floats about her body, brushing her flesh like an angel's wings. And I understood how a woman must be touched."

Don Juan paused, allowing the sensuous image to hover in the doctor's mind for a moment.

"Doña Querida at last removed her slip and bent forward from the waist, leaning into the night air, her ripe young breasts swaying in front of her like two large bells ringing for Christmas morning. I was more than impressed by this magnanimous display of feminine charms. I slumped against the lemon tree, utterly undone."

Dr. Jack was similarly unstrung, staring in stunned silence at the completely composed young man before him. The imagery was so vivid, the tale so preposterous. He grasped at a straw of ordinary reality.

"Are you Mexican? Spanish? Italian?"

"That's all you have to say? You want to know my *nationality*?!"

Jack realized that his question was ridiculous but he forged ahead anyway, trying to sound professional. "I'm confused about your name and nationality. De Marco is Italian, isn't it? But we're in Mexico, aren't we . . . and your accent sounds Castillian, from Spain."

Don Juan regarded Jack with a judicial eye. The man was not as advanced as he had thought.

"Very well. I'll answer your question. My father was born in Queens, New York. His name was Tony De Marco. He was Italian. The family was originally from one of the Venetian Greek islands. My father was the Dance King of Astoria. My mother was Mexican, the only child of a wealthy landowner. Her maiden name was Doña Inez Santiago y San Martine, as I have told you before."

Basics provided, Don Juan began to cast his spell again.

"Both her parents were killed by a sickness, a rare form of bubonic plague. My mother was stronger and survived. She took over the operation of her father's coffee plantation.

"When my father met her she was clothed in a sparkling white peasant blouse, a deep pink hibiscus tucked behind her ear, and she was barefoot in the clean white dust of a sunlit Mexican road. As he arrived, she was instructing her foreman in one of the many tasks to be performed in the harvesting of the crop. The foreman touched his cap, nodded, and left. Her authority was absolute in this realm. You understand that no man in the village, let alone her foreman, would ever have dreamt of touching her."

Don Juan looked to see if Dr. Jack was back on the beam. He was.

"My father had come to Mexico to work for a pharmaceutical company. He had just gotten off the bus and was walking to a house where he had rented a room, when he passed my mother standing in the sunlight, the bright rays of the sun lighting her hair as if she were a saint at the doorway of Paradise. She was a vision so beautiful that, at first, my father did not believe that she was real."

Don Juan sighed at the sweetness of it all before going on. "It was love at first sight. They stood there in the moonlight, kissing and touching each other, dancing a slow and tantalizing tango until morning."

Dr. Jack had an objection.

"I thought you said that your mother was standing in the sunlight?"

Don Juan was amused by Jack's dull devotion to boring facts.

"That's my father's story," he said. "My mother says

it was at night." Undaunted by this interruption, Don Juan took up his story once more.

"They were married the next week. My father took the name Don Antonio and became el patron, running the coffee plantation. Their love was like a perfect prayer. Even God could not deny it.

"I was born exactly nine months later."

Jack looked thoughtfully at Don Juan.

"I'm afraid our hour is over. We have to stop now."

"But I haven't told you about my first love, the gentle Doña Julia, and how I came to wear this mask . . ."

If Jack knew anything, he knew how to tie off a session. In his opinion, no patient was ever really finished at the end of the hour. Most of them were only getting up a good head of steam just as he had to usher them out the door. The last few moments of an encounter, as the patient tried to bargain for a little extra time, always held a mixture of relief and unsatisfied curiosity for the doctor. After thirty years, though, he was tired of saying what he always said. He found his own voice dull and cloddish as he steered the young man toward the door. "You can tell me tomorrow. Our time is up for today."

Don Juan accepted the tone of courteous affection in the doctor's voice. He walked back to the desk. He took one of the bishops and replaced him on the inlaid board.

"*Hasta mañana!*" said the young man in a cheerful tone as he bowed and stepped lightly out of the office.

His departure left Dr. Jack alone with the task of making sense of the session. He needed to figure out which parts of the story were fable, which truth, and if any, what kind of truth. Some patients spoke only in metaphor, and some believed, with painful and unshakable loyalty, in the literal truth of impossibly false legends concocted by their own feverish psyches. Jack reached for his familiar tools of rationality and habit, though he was starting to doubt their power to protect him from Don

Juan's musical and enchanting storytelling. Jack began to dictate his session notes.

"Don Juan De Marco. First session. Patient related details of early childhood. Adolescent erotic themes. *Vivid* adolescent erotic themes."

Jack paused, remembering the beguiling beauty of those themes.

"No medication at this time."

Medication had become so routine that almost no patient at the hospital was completely free of chemicals. Superintendent Paul had embraced the idea of the psychoactive substance with a zealot's fervor, since it relieved him of the burden of thinking very deeply about the personalities of the inmates. Jack was not quite so convinced. He regretted the inevitable loss of passion and individuality caused by the medications, yet they also stilled the boiling, unruly heart and soothed the terror of confused and exhausted minds.

Jack decided that there wasn't much to be gained in debating the issue with himself. He shrugged off his doubts and soldiered on, chanting into the machine:

"Preliminary diagnosis: bi-polar depressive disorder.

"Manic phase?

"Rule out brief reactive psychosis.

"Rule out delusional disorder.

"Rule out narcissistic personality.

"Test for substance abuse. Voyeuristic tendencies. Grandiosity. Strong attachment to mother, with unusual Oedipal aspects."

Dr. Jack considered the enormous stream of jargon he had poured into his machine over the years. He also thought about the cheerful, healthy, and gentle way that Don Juan had revealed himself in the past session. He also reviewed his own surprising personal enjoyment of Don Juan's stories. The doctor spoke into the machine again.

"Delete all that. Change to . . . 'Diagnosis undetermined at present.' "

8

Nurses

*

*In which Don Octavio catches his breath
and a mild case of spring fever.*

Jack was tired after his session with Don Juan and his unsuccessful effort to summarize that session. He stared out the window, unseeing, until it was time to go home. After he got home, he wandered around the house in a distracted way, still trying to understand the effect of his mesmerizing patient on his usually impervious self.

Marilyn fixed him a nice wholesome dinner. She even broke out the good china and crystal, noticing that her husband seemed to need a little special treatment. In spite of her efforts, he seemed even more inattentive than usual. He didn't even nod at intervals as she talked, but appeared to be completely wrapped up in his own world, which he did not remember to share with her. Even so, she had things to report, the mundane content of their lives together. She used to have more exciting things to report—children's crises, conversations with various branches of the family, plans for vacations, gossip about the neighbors. Now her list of shared topics was considerably smaller, but she did the best she could with it.

Jack plucked a fresh rose from the centerpiece and held it in his enormous hand. He toyed with it, brought it close to his heart, brushed it against his lips, a faraway look in his eyes as she rattled on.

"So I said to him, let me see if I understand this." She was recounting some adventure of the day, something that might even have been important. Jack would never know. "You've been exploring our car for six days now and still have absolutely no idea why the radiator keeps running out of fluid. This means that we get the car back just as broken as when we brought it in. Except now, I said, now you want us to pay you four hundred and thirty dollars for the time it took you *not* to fix it?"

Jack continued to drift, engrossed in the flower. Marilyn continued to talk. He thought, "Her hands are so elegant, her body so familiar. Yet there are newly prominent veins marking her hands; her body cannot help but change." He felt a new tenderness toward her, as if she were very young, trembling on the brink of womanhood.

"So, you know what he says? He says, we can keep looking, Mrs. Mickler, but it will still cost you sixty-five dollars an hour. Jack . . . Jack . . . Earth to Jack . . ."

Jack came out of his trance and shrugged.

"Pay him," he said.

"Pay him?"

"It's only money."

Marilyn studied Jack for a moment. He was either coming down with a cold or something was up. He looked pretty healthy to her.

"Jack . . . where were you just now?"

"Mexico. I was in Mexico."

Marilyn's eyes opened much wider as she stared at her husband. She played to his playful mood.

"But, honey . . . you *hate* Mexico."

Jack laughed with delight.

"I know. This was a *different* Mexico."

Jack was still in a good mood when he arrived at the hospital the next morning, ready for his last week of work.

The vernal equinox was right around the corner, and there were King Alfred daffodils in shoals beside his feet. He could not help picking a bunch of the sweet-scented blossoms. He was going to see Paul Showalter, and he remembered that the man once had some humanity. They had even been friends, in a casual way, a long time ago. He could not recall when that went away. Paul was getting old, too. They all were, he thought. Might as well go easy on the poor bastard. He decided to make an effort to be decent to Paul.

Jack strolled into Paul's office. He bowed, smiled affably, and handed the daffodils to him. Paul put the flowers in a nice blue jar he had brought back from Egypt. He frowned, fearing that his colleague was pulling some kind of practical joke on him.

"It's very kind of you to give me flowers, Jack. What's the occasion?"

"It's spring."

"Yes, I know. So, tell me, Jack, when exactly do you plan to start Don Juan on medication? You *do* intend to give him medication?"

"He's extraordinary, Paul. In thirty years of practice I've never seen anything like it. Love is perfect. Sex is never a problem, always sublime, almost religious in its intensity. He related comic sexual adventures of early adolescence without bitterness or embarrassment. His mother is a magnificent beauty, deeply religious, full of unblemished maternal love for him. He is untroubled by conflict, untouched by shame or guilt."

Jack looked out the window to the new green grass and to two fresh young nurses, prim in starched white uniforms.

"I've heard these fantasies before, Paul. We all have, in bits and pieces, from one adolescent or another, but never all of it from one kid in less than an hour."

Jack never asked favors, but this morning he didn't care whether he seemed foolish to Paul or not. He planned to plead shamelessly on behalf of the boy, planned to barter his own honor if necessary. He just wanted to protect Don Juan until he could understand him better.

Jack looked out the window again, trying to frame his next sentences. Suddenly he noticed that the nurses on the lawn looked somehow transformed, laughing, their bodies more than voluptuous beneath their professional garb. They appeared to be hearing secret harmonies and even dancing to them. Jack shook himself free of the mild illusion. Paul, in the meantime, was cautiously trying to refrain from stirring up any nasty scenes on this glorious morning. He was not entirely without sensitivity.

"What are you saying, Jack?"

"What I am saying, Paul, is that the pain he's covering must be remarkable."

Showalter was impressed by Jack's passion and unexpected friendliness, but he had a hospital to run. He tried to be as gentle as possible.

"Then why don't you start him on his medication, Jack?"

"Because if I give him medication, I won't be able to get into his world. It's a wonderful world, Paul. I need to learn more about it. I have to get into his world to understand it. You know as well as I do that any hope of interpreting emotional tone or complexity goes right out the window when we pour on the meds." There was a tiny new flame in Jack's eyes, a newly seductive tone in his voice. The superintendent gave in against his better judgment.

"All right, Jack, have it your own way. No medications for now, but do me one favor."

"What's that?"

"Do something about the effect that Don Juan's magnificent adolescent fantasies are having on the female staff in this hacienda. We've got more nurses than patients on Valium at the moment."

"I'll see what I can do."

Jack wandered out to the nursing station, where women in white were bustling around. They knew it was up to them to keep the place running and the doctors in line. They were busy women, usually; today they were . . . excited. Jack was genuinely sorry to have to dampen their ardor, but he'd made a deal with Paul and intended to keep his word.

He said, "No more meds for you. I've got strict orders from the top. You are going to have to cool it."

The women knew exactly what he meant. They broke into a chorus of soprano and contralto protest.

"Ah, Jack, he is so . . . cute."

"He really is, Jack. Every time I see him, I feel like I just want to take him home and . . . well, you get the picture."

"What I haven't gotten, he's filled in for me." Jack's voice implied a lot of forbidden secrets. He was teasing them. They didn't mind.

"Really? What did he say about . . . me?" The luscious Gloria could not help asking. She did not expect an answer.

Jack arched his eyebrows and made a comic face at her. He was still in a good mood. He took out his notebook and jotted down a list of names. He tore the page out and handed it to the senior nurse.

"Okay. From now on, these are the only members of the nursing staff assigned to him. All the rest of you will have to keep your dainty mitts off the merchandise. Do I make myself perfectly clear?"

They allowed him to get away with this kind of stuff only because they liked him and figured he didn't know any better, an old dude like him. The old dude was too busy to stay and chat with them, anyway. He had other fish to fry and a young caballero to tame.

Don Juan, meanwhile, waited for the arrival of Gloria, his escort from the day before.

Instead of Gloria, he found at his door a truly enormous young black man wearing a sharply pressed immaculate white uniform and a no-nonsense expression. He introduced himself, leaving out the part about the varsity football at Harrison High and the stint in the army. He was three times the size of the slender Don Juan, and he had been filled in on the patient's claim to be the world's greatest lover.

"I'm your new nurse. I'm Mr. Compton. But you can call me Rocco, Casanova."

"I'm not Casanova! I'm Don Juan! Don Juan! Got it? *Don Juan!*"

Rocco did not smile. "Yeah, right," he said. "Come on, man." And he moved his charge right along to the doctor's office.

Don Juan was Jack's only patient, his last one before retirement. Jack was free to give his full time and attention to the young man—who, by the time he reached the office, was clearly not pleased with the change in his nursing care. He intended to bear up without whining, though not necessarily without retaliation.

Jack started the session with a standard inkblot test.

"Tell me what you see . . ."

Don Juan saw a great deal more than was comfortable for the doctor.

"Here are her nipples and here is her pubic area. Her lover is kissing the contours of her bottom, where it folds into her upper thighs."

Jack pretended to note the response in his notebook. Then he took back that card from Don Juan and selected the next card in the well-worn pack. Unfortunately, the next card's inkblot clearly depicted two women making love. Jack had used that very same card a thousand and two times. It had always looked like a shapeless blur before. He decided to give up the inkblot test for the moment.

"I think," Jack said, warily, "we should move on to something else."

"What do you have in mind, Don Octavio?"

"Well, for instance, why don't we talk about whether you know who I am?"

"Yes, I know who you are." Don Juan was tired of the game. He, too, wished to move on to something more . . . interesting.

"Who am I?" Even as he asked, Jack realized that this was a dangerous question.

Don Juan was happy to oblige with the answer.

"You are Don Octavio del Flores, uncle of Don Francisco da Silva."

"And where are we?" Jack probed carefully.

Don Juan answered this boring question, too.

"Well, I haven't seen a legal document, but I assume this villa is yours."

"And what would you say to someone who suggested that you are a patient in a mental hospital and that I am your psychiatrist?"

Don Juan smiled his gracious, feline smile and answered the question. "I would say that such a person must have a rather limited and uncreative way of looking at the situation."

Don Juan stood up, flinging his cape to the floor. He paced the room, trying to decide how to get his message across to the doctor.

"Look, you want to know if I understand that this is a mental hospital? Yes, I understand that. But then, you will ask, how can I say at the very same time that you are Don Octavio and that I am a guest at your villa, right?"

Jack nodded.

"By seeing beyond what is visible to the naked eye."

Don Juan continued. "There are those who do not share my perceptions, it is true. When I say that all my women are dazzling beauties, they object. No, no, they say, the nose of this woman is too large, the hips too large of another, the breasts of a third too small"—Don Juan shrugged at the pettiness of such objections—"but I see these women for how they truly are . . . glorious, radiant, spectacular, flawless . . . because I am not limited by my eyesight."

The young man looked into the older man's eyes and spoke quietly, with great sincerity.

"Women react to me the way they do, Don Octavio, because they sense that I search out the beauty that dwells within them until it overwhelms everything else. And then . . . they cannot resist their own desire to release that beauty and envelop me in it." Don Juan was quite close to Jack, speaking very softly.

"So . . . to answer your question, I see as clear as sunlight on the water that this great edifice in which we find ourselves is your villa. For thirty years you have dwelt here, they tell me. I can see your mark everywhere. It is clearly your home and, as for who you are, you are a great lover like myself, even though you may have lost your way, Don Octavio del Flores."

Unexpectedly, Jack's eyes filled with unshed tears.

"And now," Don Juan seated himself on the sofa and lightened his tone, "if we have settled this matter of identity, I am prepared to tell you how I acquired my mask, if you are prepared to listen."

Jack took a deep breath. *Centered and ready and calm,* he reminded himself. *If I don't stay on track, who's going to help this boy? And if I don't stay clear of emotional entanglements here, who is going to help me?* A confused and vulnerable expression flickered over Jack's normally controlled face.

Don Juan looked at Jack with real affection, sensing the struggle within him. Struggle was an excellent sign of progress. "Good. Back to Mexico. . . . *Olé!*" And Don Juan moved on to more important matters.

9

Doña Julia

*

The young Don Juan receives his initiation into the deeper mysteries of women. Don Octavio gets to watch.

"My mother," Don Juan said, "God bless her, did not give up easily. When I was sixteen, she made one last attempt to instill in me the virtues of a good Christian by finding me a religious tutor. She selected Doña Julia, a dark beauty with a heart of fire, but pious, a blameless young wife." He chuckled at his mother's naive attempts to steer him into chaste habits.

"My mother's judgment may have left something to be desired."

Don Juan savored the memory of his delectable tutor. The image of the beauteous Doña Julia gradually materialized for both the doctor and the patient, as Don Juan continued to speak.

"Doña Julia was the most devout of matrons. She read to me from the lives of the saints and from holy scripture. I particularly enjoyed her reading of the 'Song of Solomon,' but even the begats were beguiling in her dulcet tones.

"She was twenty-three, the faithful wife of Don Alfonzo, a man of fifty. It was no secret in our village that Doña Julia would have been much better served by two men of twenty-five. Be that as it may, every word that she spoke to me has been burned into my memory. Some of her favorite passages remain with me, intact, and delight me still."

Don Juan's voice took on the grandeur of a bishop as he rolled out the sacred passage: " 'What? Know ye not that your body is the temple of the Holy Ghost which is in you, which ye have of God, and ye are not your own?' "

Don Juan sighed as he contemplated the completely appropriate sentiment. "I was, indeed, not my own. I was Doña Julia's, her slave, her lapdog, hers to take or throw away. I wished to be her glove, her shoe, her camisole. I was smitten."

Jack remembered suddenly what it was like to be smitten, as Don Juan recounted the delicious ache of young love. Jack's own first real experience of love had been with a girl two years older than himself, a cheer-leader, who, while not exactly married, did have much more extensive experience than Jack at fifteen. *Follies of youth, where are you when I need them?* he thought, tempo-rarily losing focus on his patient as his own delicious past and drab present troubles distracted him. He shook him-self and concentrated again on the young man's story.

"I felt within me a torment, a burning wound, an inarticulate yearning combined with the most indescrib-able pangs of bliss, a pain too sweet to endure. But what was it?"

"You had no idea what it was?" Jack inquired, in a voice carefully cleansed of all irony.

"Well, I had an *idea*, but nothing definite. . . ." Don Juan smiled at the memory of his initial perplexity, and went on.

"I was given the freedom of Don Alfonzo's house. I ate dinner with the two of them, picking at the steak, ignoring the wine. I could think of nothing but my beloved, not even dessert, not even whipped cream. I lost about fifteen pounds during the course of that summer and have never regained it. Sharp pangs of hunger consumed me, but my hunger was to devour the lovely Doña Julia. Yet I was still not certain how such a consummation ought to be accomplished."

Jack remembered the rural nature of the village Don Juan had described. Considering the candid behavior of farm animals, lack of information on the basic mechanical procedures seemed unlikely to have been the source of the difficulty. Young boys did sometimes misinterpret or fail to connect their observations of nature with their own perturbations. On the other hand, Don Juan might be emphasizing his innocence for other reasons. Jack reserved judgment and allowed Don Juan his claim to ignorance, as he continued to describe the slow process of enlightment.

"I had certain indications. The heat I felt when her glance met mine, the sensation as a straying tress of her hair brushed accidentally against my cheek as we studied the gospels together. What could these signs mean? I had no clue to follow but the silken thread she might someday throw to me. I was drowning in uncertainty."

He regarded his own past innocence with amusement and sympathy. Dr. Jack and Don Juan displayed identically rueful expressions as they both recalled the universally baffling puzzle presented to the young male as he approaches his first experience of love. No matter how many observations have been made of other species or how much theoretical knowledge has been gleaned from novelists and encyclopedias, the application of theory is never completely without its perilous aspects. Jack and Don Juan both sighed as they recalled that bittersweet moment just before the arrival of certain knowledge. Don Juan pulled himself together and went on with the story.

"My father, understanding that manhood was nearly upon me, took it upon himself to teach me to use my sword. We spent long hours in the garden. He taught me the decorum of swordplay, the ritual and courtesy of the encounter, as well as the usual thrust and parry."

Jack had a question. He tried not to sound too skeptical.

"There was a lot of swordplay going on while you were growing up, was there?"

Don Juan was unperturbed.

"It was a small and isolated town that resisted modern technology."

Having settled that, Don Juan plunged back into his story.

"As Doña Julia passed through the town, carrying fresh melons and mangos to market, I noticed her usually happy expression had been replaced by a sadness even more enchanting than her smile.

"I sensed that Doña Julia was having a struggle within herself. Doña Julia was seen by the priest to dash into the cathedral. She threw herself to the floor in front of the Virgin Mary, where she repeated at least seven iterations of the 'Ave' and some hushed petition which the priest did not understand. This was not, you understand, a confession. The priest saw no harm in sharing his bewilderment at her behavior, even with me, his favorite altar boy."

Jack did not seem to be completely familiar with the rosary, so Don Juan recited the words for him. He wished to make sure that his friend understood the beauty, power, and aptness of Doña Julia's prayer to the Virgin. Don Juan recited the prayer slowly, lingering on each of the syllables.

" 'Hail Mary, full of grace, the Lord is with Thee. Blessed art Thou among women, and blessed is the fruit of Thy womb, Jesus.' "

Don Juan's voice reverberated with reverence for the sacred words. " 'Holy Mary, Mother of God, pray for us sinners now and at the hour of our death. Amen.' "

Don Juan was much affected by the sonorous power of the prayer, but he needed to move on to other matters. "My own situation was becoming no less difficult than hers. I could only think of Doña Julia. Just to keep myself from going mad, I turned into a metaphysician. I considered the meaning of truth, of existence, of God. I thought of the timetable for the sun's demise . . . and then I thought of Doña Julia's eyes. . . ."

Don Juan was almost overcome by the thought of her eyes and the memory of the first evening when Doña Julia found him reclining on the flower-strewn riverbank.

"On that blessed evening, Doña Julia sat down beside me on the grass. She touched my fevered brow with her cool, soft hand, and smoothed my hair as she spoke of her sorrows.

"She said that a virtuous woman should face and overcome temptation rather than take the coward's way by fleeing from the occasion of sin. She said that a test of virtue could only be valid in the very presence of desire. Her conclusions bathed me with metaphysical, intoxicating bliss. She said that she was a very virtuous woman, with only the greatest respect for her husband, the highly regarded Don Alfonzo. She swore never to disgrace the ring she wore.

"Some primeval instinct urged me to grasp her dainty hand, press it to my lips, and kiss it tenderly. Tears came to her beautiful eyes. Overcome by an emotion she could not control, she reclined, half-swooning in the moonlight. She still held my trembling hand in hers. I began to rain light, adoring kisses on her half-revealed bosom. She protested. I persisted. She said that she would never consent . . ." Don Juan was lost for a moment in the memory of that sweet encounter and its delicate progress toward consummation.

"But somehow she consented," Jack said, remembering his own first love with fond gratitude.

Don Juan said simply, "She did.

"Then suddenly," he continued, "I was hit with a revelation. The way a woman's body is made, the way a man's body responds to it, the fire burning in my loins, the intense desire to merge as one . . . it all came together in a single brilliant flash.

"Doña Julia's ecstasy was such that she tossed her head like a racehorse and purred like a lioness. I kissed her neck. Her skin was so much warmer than mine, so soothingly soft, so delightful as I kissed her everywhere, maddened by my proximity to her inmost secrets."

Don Juan considered the greater mysteries.

"Would we love if we had never heard of Love? If the word 'Love' had never been spoken by anyone? Is all art imitation, including the art of Love?" He returned to the memory of his first beloved.

"I kissed her toes, her ankles, her round, rosy knees, her thighs, her everything. Is Love a sickness? Or is it not rather an all-consuming fire which warms the heart and then burns it to a crisp? Can there be inspiration without Love? If no woman ever touched a man as Doña Julia did me, never caressed a man's calves, thighs, buttocks, his chest, his shoulder, his lips; if there were no experience of unfettered passion in this world, would there be any painting? Any music? Any poetry? Art of any kind?

"I think not, Don Octavio," he declared. "I am sure that my own interest in the arts was born that evening, as Doña Julia threw herself over my willing body, mounting me. I was more than happy to play her humble beast of burden, as she guided me with her hands and her thighs and her incomparable passion. That evening was when my first love taught me all I would ever really need to know of Love.

"Women are the closest any man will ever get to God. Sex, my friend, is the ultimate form of worship. It is the hymn of life itself, the immortality we are granted on this earth, union with the stars, with all creation. There can be no greater expression of the wonder and majesty of God than in the process of love which creates and gives meaning to life, the moments which lead to ultimate bliss as two people perform the act of love as my Doña Julia and I did that evening on the riverbank."

Jack, in his youth, had often noticed the same sublime connection between celestial and earthly fires of love. His notion of God's nature since then had been mostly as the author of disasters, like age, pain, death, floods, earthquakes, and hailstorms. The beauties of the universe had escaped in the daily sadness of loss and fear and effort.

Don Juan's devotion to the truth might be suspect, but his passionate appreciation of the grand moments of manhood was evidently sincere. In Dr. Jack's experience, patients were seldom able to find any comfort or beauty in the world at all. They were not prone to sing such hymns to the pleasures of love. Love, in Jack's experience, was not usually one of the happiest topics in patients' lives. This patient, however, was resoundingly an exception, as he went on with his paean to Love. Even Dr. Jack, no theologian, noticed a certain joyous pagan tint to Don Juan's story.

"There is, in truth, nothing sweeter, Don Octavio, than first and passionate love," said Don Juan. "It stands alone in a man's experience like Adam's recollection of his fall. All of his life, all of my life to that moment was poured like a libation to the goddess of Love. The fruit of the tree of life had been plucked. Life could never yield anything more worthy of praise than this ambrosial act.

"The very first woman I ever loved fully, with all my body's power and my heart's delight, revealed to me the smiling secrets of the universe. I learned from her the answers to the only four questions worth asking:

"What is sacred?

"Of what substance is the spirit made?

"What is worth living for?

"And what, when all is said and done, is worth dying for?"

Don Juan paused for dramatic effect.

"The answer to all these questions is the same. The answer, Don Octavio, is Love. Only Love."

The doctor's office grew totally silent.

Then Don Juan stood up and put his hand on the doctor's shoulder. He spoke very gently but with great firmness.

"Doña Julia was my first love. I will never forget her. Now I believe our time together for today is finished, Don Octavio."

He walked over to the desk and took up the second chessman, a black bishop, replacing it on the board. Jack watched Don Juan without speaking. He needed to stop this nonsense about a wager, but felt that he had lost his compass and was in the hand of the god, a sailor in unknown waters. He had no idea where to go next.

He struggled to regain his bearings while Don Juan put on his cape and quietly left the office. Jack called out to him, "And the mask? What about the mask?"

But the young man had already vanished into the corridor and could not reply.

The chessmen were still lined up on Jack's desk. He stared at them for several moments as he collected his thoughts. He began, out of habit, to dictate session notes into his tape recorder.

"Initial diagnosis, obsessive-compulsive disorder with libidinal exaggeration. Strongly self-referential erotomanical features with some distorted religious elements. Rule out delusional disorder. Rule out . . ." Jack paused, unsure of what to say to the machine, feeling that he ought to say something more.

"Rule out . . . depression with obsessional features, narcissistic personality, possible. . . ." Jack, stuck for possibilities, looked idly out the window. On the lawn below his window, Don Juan, wearing his Spanish hat and his flowing cape, was teaching Rocco, the male nurse, to dance. The two men whirled together, executing the intricate and sensuous moves of the tango. They were having a wonderful time.

Jack was shocked. "Possible hysterical personality! Possible acting out! Possible sociopath! Oh, Christ, who knows . . . !" Jack erased the entry from his recorder and buried his head in his hands, exhausted and confused. Outside the window, Rocco and Don Juan practiced their dance steps blissfully, as the men of the Argentine did when the tango was first invented.

Jack knew it was time for him to go home for the day.

10

Marilyn

*

In which Don Octavio repairs to the marital couch.

Jack drove home from the hospital with the radio tuned to an all-traffic station. He was tired and needed some serious quality time to recuperate from his session with Don Juan De Marco, King of Sexual Innuendo. Jack was not, however, as exhausted and downhearted as he had often been after a hard day at the office. His hard days had been filled with confused and unhappy patients, tragedies and torn lives. He felt refreshed and somewhat renewed and did not know whether it was because of his encounter with the don's reminiscences or because of his own memories of the magnificent generosity of the women in his past. He hadn't thought of those sweet girls in a long time, and it cheered him to remember their laughter and their frolicsome games.

After a nice healthy dinner devoid of red meat or butter, Jack lay down on the living room sofa to listen to a CD he had purchased on the way home. It was *Don Giovanni*, conducted by Karl Böhm, who, at an advanced age, remarked that Mozart's music had the effect of a fountain of youth.

The CD came with an extensive booklet of notes and

a libretto. The cover featured a lurid painting of Don Juan being consumed by the fires of Hell, but the frontispiece showed Mozart himself in pigtail and ruffled shirt, looking very pleased with himself and not at all worried about the flames and torments.

Jack held the booklet in front of his eyes, but watched Marilyn. He looked at her as she moved around the room, touching and straightening things, picking up and tidying, bending her body gracefully, fluffing pillows, patting the room into shape. She did not look at him, but sensed his gaze. It had a quality of lascivious appreciation she had not received for a long time. But it was familiar. *He's undressing me with his eyes!* she thought. *That's what we used to call it, anyway. Making sheep's eyes at me! The man is flirting!*

She felt as if she had been transported back to Italy, the summer she spent in Florence during college, when she felt the warm regard and whispers of Italian men following her everywhere. She blushed. It was not, she thought, a flash but a blush. *Well, well,* she thought. *Virginity can strike at any time.*

Marital love, in Marilyn's opinion, had a tidal quality. It ebbed and flowed, and lately she had wondered whether the tide had gone out for good. Apparently not. She sat down beside Jack where he lay on the sofa. She gently touched his cheek.

"I take it," she said, "you might like to go upstairs?"

Jack smiled happily. Marilyn, with some curiosity, took the booklet from his hand and read the cover. "*Don Giovanni?* Why this opera? Why any opera? You hate opera! Or is this like Mexico?"

Jack looked at her. He did not really know the answer. He reached up and ran his hand over her silky hair, looking into her eyes. They were the color of cornflowers, of blue bonnets, of summer skies.

He said, "You have beautiful eyes."

She enjoyed the compliment but it irritated her a little.

Her husband sounded just a trifle confused, as if he thought he was talking to some strange woman. She shook off his hand, offended, but not very seriously.

"Yes, Jack. Thank you very much. Now, if you will excuse me, I am going to go upstairs and take my calcium so my bones won't break into little pieces, my aspirin so that my heart doesn't clog up, and put on my estrogen patch to convince my body it is still twenty-three."

She went upstairs, and Jack climbed after her as the opera continued to fill the house with music. He noticed, not for the first time, that when she was irritated but not angry, Marilyn tended to exaggerate the sway of her hips. Especially on the stairs. Especially when he was right behind her. He smiled to himself. She was really a wonderful woman.

He got under the covers before she did. He lay in the bed listening to the woman perform her evening rituals of cleansing and tidying herself. She was taking her time about brushing her teeth. *How maidenly*, Jack thought, *as if she were my blushing bride again*.

Marilyn came out of the bathroom wearing her best silk pajamas. She slipped under the covers right away, stricken by ridiculous modesty. Lately she had found it difficult to be naked when she was completely by herself, let alone in front of Jack. It was like being fifteen, though now her shyness arose not from inexperience but from fear of ugliness and the shame of a declining body. She could not bear even to glance at her own neck in the mirror, let alone her breasts. Jack appeared to be staring at the ceiling. She calculated the odds of their performing an act of love together. In her opinion, passion was not likely to overtake them, and she hesitated to make any overtures. She was afraid of rejection, of indifference, of the unreliable state of Jack's libido lately. She decided to cool the situation.

"Why don't we take a rain check, darling?" She didn't

really know what kind of an answer she would get, or what kind she wanted.

Jack did not answer directly.

"You know," he said, musing aloud, "I've been thinking about our adolescence. That was such a great transitional battlefield, full of storms and doubt and beauty and sudden discoveries. Now nothing's left in front of us, except death itself. We've gotten gray and we've changed. I feel like Rip Van Winkle. I wake up and I wonder where I am. There are whole countries I knew the names of which no longer exist. There are regions of pleasure which haven't been heard from in months. What happened to all our passion and our sexual frenzy? What can we use to fuel us for our next maybe twenty years on earth? Human beings were designed to be dead at fifty and we're not."

Marilyn murmured, as tenderly as if he were a wounded child, "It's all right, dear, we don't have to make love tonight. It's okay. Really."

Jack was unstoppable in his urge to tell her his thoughts.

"It's not about sex. It's not a question of that. I feel like we've surrendered our lives to the momentum of mediocrity. I've worked at the same damned place for thirty years. I've forgotten what it is to want anything, to follow the wayward light of desire. What happened to that celestial fire, that consuming flame that used to light our way?" It was a real question, and Marilyn thought for a moment, composing a real reply.

"I think that what we have learned, Jack, is that fires cause a lot of trouble. Fires are really hard to control. They flare up, use a whole lot of energy, then suddenly die."

"Bullshit," said Jack succinctly.

Marilyn had more to say. "A good, steady, warm glow does the trick over the long run. Keeps the dark and the cold and the dangerous animal at the back of the cave all at bay. We need that glow, Jack."

Jack was not ready to accept the concept of a nice warm glow. He rejected it completely.

"No fire, no heat. No heat, no life. That's the equation, Marilyn. That's what we're up against. We can't live on embers forever. We have got to stir it up sometimes. Mix it up with the saber-toothed tiger, build a bonfire and dance naked around it!"

Marilyn began to get the drift of his discourse.

"May I assume that the upshot of all this is that you will not be easing gracefully into retirement?" His theme was not unfamiliar but his joyous tone was absolutely new to her. He had been without signs of happiness for a long time, obviously dreading his retirement so intensely that he hadn't even spoken of it to his wife. She had filled out and sent in the forms, signed his name to the papers, taken care of all the details that surrounded his retirement from a state agency. His passive, stubborn refusal to talk about it had frightened her. He had made no preparations that she could see, and she worried that when he got to the actual day, it would be for him like falling off a cliff into the sea. So a mention of his retirement, even obliquely, was very welcome. And he seemed to be happy.

"You're damned right, I'm not." Jack shook his fist at the bedroom ceiling. He put on his tough-guy tone. "You and me are in this for the full twelve rounds, sweetheart! We are going to go out in a blaze of glory, like Halley's comet. That I promise you!" Marilyn briefly wondered whether Jack knew that comets were utterly devoid of heat. They reflected light, but they were only ice balls, she'd heard. And Halley's comet wouldn't be back in their lifetimes. Before Jack had gotten so remote, she would have told him that she had no intention of traversing the heavens as a gritty snow ball. But now she was so relieved that he was talking to her again that it didn't matter much what he said.

But she did remember 1986 when they had driven out to a narrow, south-facing pit of land and looked out over the bay, searching the night sky for Halley's comet with hundreds of other people. A local traveler, that comet, fighting the solar winds, marking lifetimes. Most people would see Halley's only once. She shivered at the thought that her one glimpse was long past.

Jack fetched her hand from beneath the covers and kissed it tenderly, paying especially close attention to the texture of her skin, the sensitive tips of her fingers.

Marilyn was worried about him and had been for at least a year. Yet there seemed to be something new this week, a break in the endless wall of his dreary, unexpressed misery. Not just restlessness or confusion as age gripped him. Something else. Like a dead willow sending up a shoot. He sounded positively tender and new, hopeful. She cautiously tried to reach him without driving him back into silence. "Listen to me for a minute, Jack. Be serious. What's going on? You've been acting . . . funny . . . lately. What's the matter?"

"I'm treating this kid who thinks he's Don Juan. He's got a costume. A sword. A mask. Everything—"

"Who is he, really?"

"I don't know who the hell he is." Jack was finally ready to admit it. "I haven't a clue. There's something about that kid, though. He's getting to me."

Jack suddenly kissed Marilyn with great passion. She kissed him back with equal fervor. She turned out the lamp on the bedside table. In the dark, in the bed they had shared for decades, grown shy of each other in a year of failing love, they struggled out of their pajamas and enacted the heartbreaking comedy of middle-aged passion in a domestic setting.

Marilyn said "Wait, wait, there's a book in the bed. . . . Okay, I've got it. . . ."

Jack said "Wait, wait, I've got a cramp in my foot! Wait! Wait! Just a minute!"

Marilyn said, "Wait, wait, I am not ready!"

They were awkward with each other, as clumsy as seals on land.

Then, like seals at the edge of the sea, at the time of the fullest moon, drawn by the celestial, cool fire of lunar gravity, they were borne away by tidal waves of passion. Like seals, once they reached their own familiar element, they were beautiful and graceful. The sounds they made were wordless cries of pleasure and love.

For just a moment in the midst of everything, Jack thought he heard the juvenile voice of Don Juan De Marco saying "At every instant we fell into each other's arms. . . ."

11

Don Antonio

*

In which Don Octavio enjoys the benefits of the rejuvenating power of Mozart as Don Juan reveals the secret of his mask.

In the morning, Jack remembered with shy amazement and some pride the marital pleasures of the night. He tuned the radio to a classical station and hummed along with Puccini. The weather was soft and the trees were swaying and streams of warm spring air washed over him as he walked into the hospital. Unnamed operatic melodies wafted through his mind. He thought of Marilyn with tender gratitude as he settled down to await his young patient.

Don Juan seemed to be very much in tune with the beautiful morning as he instantly resumed his narrative of blissful but adulterous young love.

"Time stopped for us. During the scant four months Doña Julia and I were together, eternity was all around us. There was neither day nor night . . . just my love and hers. Neither of us slept much. We flew from one passionate encounter to another. All the world was dim and blurred compared to the moments of our love. My virginal awkwardness disappeared as new possibilities opened to me."

Dr. Jack raised his eyebrows at the thought of new

possibilities opening to the don. He remembered his first giddy months with Marilyn, when they lived in a state of perpetual passion, before the children came. They made love in every room of the apartment. They could not bear to be apart for an hour. He smiled at the memory of himself striding like a young god home for lunch and love. Don Juan described a more romantic setting, but a similar flood of delight.

"We took long walks in the moonlight," Don Juan remembered, "making love in the welcoming shadows of a ruined abbey. We borrowed her father's white stallion and rode bareback through the desert, flying naked over the mesquite, as if the horse beneath us had wings. Doña Julia would sit before me, my arms around her, my hands on her breasts. We made love all the time . . . even on the horse, a singularly well-trained beast."

Don Juan checked to see if Jack was following all this. He was. Don Juan continued, enchanted by the powerful memory of first love, illicit though it may have been.

"As for Don Alfonzo, her aging husband, he spent so much time away handling the details of his trading business that I almost forgot his existence, though I had eaten his food and been a guest in his house. I was able, practically speaking, to live in Doña Julia's own home. Her own bedroom. I will never forget those endless afternoons in the shuttered, shadowy bedroom of Doña Julia, making wild, passionate love beneath the religious icons she displayed on her bedroom wall."

Jack thought uneasily about the pictures of his children on his own bedroom wall as Don Juan dismissed any religious qualms with a shrug.

"The eyes of the Virgin seemed, Don Octavio, to follow me with understanding if not approval as I worshipped at the shrine of the divine Doña Julia. I was bathed in her scent; I carried her perfume with me wherever I went. Of course, I seldom went anywhere in those months, only on infrequent picnics. My days and nights were spent exploring the nature of Love with Doña Julia. I truly believed that I had found everlasting paradise, until late one night—"

Don Juan, playing with the story, stopped for a dramatic pause and a short drink of water. When he continued, his voice was full of naughty delight.

"I heard the dreadful sound of footsteps outside the bedroom door! It was none other than Don Alfonzo, Doña Julia's aging husband!"

Dr. Jack resisted, with difficulty, an urge to laugh. A cardinal rule of psychiatry suggested that the doctor should never laugh at his patients' jokes, even when they were telling ribald and comic antique stories. The bawdy stories covered like fig leaves the awful inadequacies of their love lives, allowing them to avoid painful insights. Still, Jack was in an awfully good mood, making it hard not to chuckle a little. He composed himself with an effort. The decorous conventions of professional compassion had to prevail, no matter what.

Don Juan, fully aware of the comic nature of the incident, went on with it, like a vaudevillian telling a mildly spicy joke.

"Don Alfonzo was just down the corridor, calling to Doña Julia! He called her his sweet little canary! He was coming closer every minute! The door opened! Don Alfonzo saw only Doña Julia, alone in her rumpled bed but he was not fooled! He shouted as he advanced on the bed, crying 'Where is he? Where have you hidden him?'

"My Doña Julia knew how to think quickly in a crisis. She decided that the best defense was a good offense. She shouted back at her enraged husband. 'For God's sake, Don Alfonzo, what sort of drunken fit has seized you? How dare you suspect me . . . me, for whom the thought of any sort of infidelity is anathema, whom the mere thought, let alone the deed, would surely kill? Search the room if you must! Look into every nook and cranny! Under the bed! Heap insult upon insult, wrong on wrong! You

ungrateful, barbarous, insensitive man! Was it for this
kind of treatment that I married a man more than twice
my age? I expected more wisdom than this from you,
Alfonzo. If you continue to insult me like this, our marriage is over for good, I hope you realize that! I mean it! I
don't care! Go ahead and search!'

"Don Alfonzo said he would. He did. And found me,
naked as a tuning fork, hiding among Doña Julia's frothy
and fragrant petticoats in the wardrobe.

"But not immediately."

Don Juan drew a deep breath as he remembered the
scene. His face showed the ambivalent expression of a
mature man remembering the follies of youth, rueful but
secretly proud of himself.

"Doña Julia's speech had not convinced him. He tore
the bedroom apart. He looked under the bed and in all the
closets. He cursed in a most indelicate manner. It was
only a matter of time until he remembered the wardrobe,
the last piece of furniture untouched as he ransacked the
room. Doña Julia continued to implore, Don Alfonzo
continued to search, and I began to worry.

"Fortunately, Don Alfonzo felt the need to retrieve his
sword, which he had left by the front door. We knew it
would take him three minutes, tops, to fetch it and get
back to the bedroom, having made the trip in some haste
ourselves lately."

Jack understood. He had once had to flee from a
girlfriend's enraged boyfriend, and no weapons were involved, but he remembered that night as one of truly
amazing record speed as he sprinted out the back door
while the Visigothic beau lumbered in the front door.

Don Juan sensed Jack's sympathy to his plight.

"You can imagine my state. I was in fear for my life.
Total terror. Doña Julia fetched me out of the wardrobe
and pressed a big rusty key into my hand. 'Quickly, my
darling,' she said, 'run quickly! Out the garden gate!' But
before I could move, Don Alfonzo returned! His sword

upraised! His eyes aflame! Bellowing like a wounded bull! I could only call upon the saints to preserve me."

Don Juan paused again, a slightly less comic expression on his face.

"It was a bad moment, Don Octavio. But fortunately, Don Alfonzo had for many years overeaten and failed to take any exercise. He was not only enraged, but his anger led him to lunge toward me too impulsively."

"He lurched toward me at as great a speed as he could muster. It was not, Don Octavio, as fast as your average rhinoceros. More like a Zeppelin. At any rate, I stepped deftly aside as he neared. His momentum carried him all the way through the French doors to the balcony, where his progress was stopped by the balcony railing.

"Thus saved from disaster, at least for the moment, as Don Alfonzo lay in a heap on the porch, I was suddenly filled with bravado.

"I seized the adorable Doña Julia by her waist, bent her to my will one last time, and kissed her thoroughly. I then seized my cape and sword and bowed to her. I cried, '*Adios, mi amor!*' Then I ran like the wind, the slow but determined Don Alfonzo and his sword right behind me!"

Jack contemplated the image of the overweight, out-of-breath, fiftyish man chasing the slender, athletically inclined, surefooted boy. Suppose he ever found Marilyn . . . The idea was too terrible to contemplate.

Jack said, "What happened to the girl?"

"That last hurried embrace in her bedroom, spoiled by the rude intrusion of her red-faced husband, was the last of her kisses I ever enjoyed. It was my last glimpse of my darling tutor, the lovely Doña Julia. Overcome by remorse, she left the village that very night. I wrote to her, but I never received any reply. Yet I bear the greatest respect and love for her to this very day."

Jack got up and stretched, sure that Don Juan had come to the end of his story. He was wrong. There was more. Don Juan, with an imperious wave of his slender hand, indicated that the doctor should sit. The doctor sat. The boy continued.

"Don Alfonzo was humiliated that he had been made a cuckold by a sixteen-year-old boy. To retaliate, he announced publicly, in the village square, for all to hear, that he and my mother had been conducting a clandestine and illicit affair for many years.

"Don Alfonzo spoke in the crudest possible terms of women's most intimate, secret parts. He described in ugly words the act of love and its cruelest variants. All the time he spoke the name of my lovely mother with scorn and filthy contempt. The riff-raff of the village began making obscene gestures and shouting bawdy insults at my mother as she passed them on her way to church. Old women whispered her name and laughed as they stared at her. It was, of course, a terrible lie that Don Alfonzo told. He spoke only to gain revenge, only from a mind poisoned by hatred and envy. The situation was unbearable."

Don Juan spoke with restrained anger as he recalled the ugly stain Don Alfonzo had tried to put on his mother's good name. As he described the shameful, lewd words of the wronged husband, he was once more acutely aware of the injustice of that man's speech.

"When he attacked my mother like that, he was attacking a completely innocent party. It was me, Don Juan, he should have been denouncing, me he should have slandered in the square. I had eaten his food, slept in his bed, made love to his wife. I was the one but he was too cowardly, too stupid and too determined to harm my whole family. He did not even try to punish the truly guilty.

"My father was outraged. Though a man of peace, he was quick to defend my mother's virtue and reputation. On a brilliant, sunny day in the middle of the plaza, my father slapped Don Alfonzo in the face with his leather glove. The two men moved to the center of the plaza to fight. The lounging men and the gossiping women formed a ring around them. Their weapons were sharp as razors and flashed in the sunlight as they saluted each other before the duel.

"A friend ran to our house and fetched my mother and me. When we arrived, the battle had already started. They tested one another, feeling for weaknesses. Don Alfonzo, though nearly ten years my father's senior and slowed by age and obesity, had been trained by the great swordsman Don Jesus de Tolosa. Don Alfonzo's rage and hatred helped him fight much harder than anyone expected he could. Even worse, by a tragic stroke of fate, it turned out that Don Alfonzo was left-handed, making defense more difficult for my father.

"Even with Don Alfonzo's superior training and defensive advantages, my father would have prevailed easily, were it not for a momentary but fatal lapse. My father looked away from his enemy for one instant . . . he looked away to search my mother's eyes, her beautiful eyes . . ."

Don Juan could hardly bear to describe the end of the swordfight. His words came slowly. Jack could hardly understand him, his voice was so broken as he continued to speak of that terrible day in the village square.

"And in only a flash of time, it was over. That moment when my father's attention was distracted by love, that single instant, cost my father his life. He fell to the ground as Don Alfonzo looked around him, bewildered. I could never afterward remember the exact blow that killed him. I only know that I ran to him, I knelt beside him on the ground. I cried, 'No, No, Father, don't die!' But his life blood was pouring out into the dust of the plaza. His breath was rasping and his eyes wandered, unseeing. I fell into a rage to kill the man that had caused such disaster. I grabbed my father's sword, ready to defend his honor. . . . My mother cried out, 'No, No! Oh, God, now I will lose them both!' "

Jack was old enough to have seen a few deaths, some of them violent. He had sat by his own father's bed as his father struggled to die. He had seen his mother's face bewildered by pain and fear as she watched by the death-bed. He had long smothered the memory of that death and the death of his mother only three months later. And Marilyn's father only a year ago, after surgery that did nothing but harm. Marilyn's face had been burned by her tears, as if she wept acid. Nothing was easy about death, and nothing quaint or charming no matter where it took place.

Don Juan's voice became resigned, somehow older and full of regret. "I was very young, Don Octavio. I had seen my father attacked, my mother's reputation ruined while I stood by, powerless to prevent the disaster. I felt I must fight, though my opponent was skillful and murderous. In the end I killed my man. That foolish lumbering man was soon bleeding to death in the dust near my father and crying out for his wife and his mother. His wife had fled and his mother had died long ago. Then his voice stopped in a gush of blood and he was gone.

"I do not remember many details of the fight, only the surprised look on Don Alfonzo's face as he fell, slashed many times and stabbed to the heart by my hand, then his lonely, fearful cries until he died. I discovered that there can be nothing glorious about killing. The man was a fool and may have deserved to die. I do not know. But I do know that there is no elation in seeing a man's breath fail, his heart cease beating, his eyes stare into eternity. Death awaits us all, but the man who becomes Death's servant dies along with his victim. Nothing he does from then on will ever be pure."

Jack had treated killers and had seen the monstrous scars of such a crime, even when the killing itself was accidental or imaginary. The boy's recognition of the damage seemed to Jack to be a hopeful sign that Don Juan had reserves of health.

Don Juan continued to dwell on the day of his father's death. He said, "I staggered, stunned by grief, over to my father and dropped to my knees on the ground beside him.

My mother cradled his head in her lap and spoke his name softly, trying to call him back from death, smoothing his forehead with terrible tenderness. My father rallied briefly. He seemed to be looking at me with eyes that accused me of causing his pain. I begged him to forgive me, I begged him not to die. My mother shouted for the priest, people in the crowd were shouting. I never knew whether he heard me. He seemed to murmur something, a blessing, a sign of forgiveness but, to my sorrow, I cannot be sure. His breathing was labored and harsh, his voice was low. I tried to staunch his wound with my shirt, tried to shield him from the crowd that pressed in on us. And then he was dead. His breath stopped as I wrapped my arms around him and cried useless, hopeless tears. My mother kept calling to him for long moments after his spirit had left us."

Don Juan tried to return to his earlier tone, making his father's death into a legend. But the pain was too personal. Jack noticed that the boy was trembling as he spoke. "And so it was that my father, the great swordsman, Don Antonio, died in my arms in the plaza as my mother wailed her widow's song of grief and despair, and the women of the village took up the chorus of mourning. But finally the other women led her away, and the men took my father's body to be prepared for burial."

Don Juan's voice was tired and strained. He looked down at the floor.

He said, "That evening, to hide my shame, I placed the mask on my face and vowed never to remove it in the presence of another human being. It is an executioner's mask. If it were not for my misdeeds, my father would still be alive and Don Alfonzo would be, too. I regret them equally. One gave me my own life, and I stole the life of the other. I caused my mother terrible grief, and my sweet first lover was lost to me forever. My mask is the mask of shame."

Don Juan wept bitter tears as he remembered that

terrible day. Jack instinctively reached out to the young man to comfort him. Don Juan covered his face with his hands and murmured the words of his tragic sorrow.

"My father left me too soon, Don Octavio. I was too young. I never had the chance to know him."

Jack saw on his office wall dusty photographs of himself with his son, of himself with Marilyn. Of himself with his own father, their arms around each other, so many years ago. Jack realized that he was now older than his father had been when the picture was taken. He thought, *we are always too young. We never know our fathers.*

Don Juan, his face wet with tears, slipped out of the office to return to his room. After he had left, Jack looked at the brave little chessmen on his desk. Jack's cheeks were wet with his own tears, whether for himself or Don Juan he had no way to tell. Both he and Don Juan were wrong, he thought. The ten-day paper had started to run the minute the boy was brought in. Counting the weekend, the time of the temporary writ was already half over.

Jack thought about the boy's defiant, almost gallant attempt to gamble with his freedom. Jack took away chessmen until there were only five left, the king and queen, two knights, and a pawn. He looked down at them, thinking how few days were left to help the boy. He thought, too, not for the first time, how little help one human being could be to another in healing the fundamental wounds of grief and guilt.

Later that night, Jack toiled over textbooks and case histories in the hospital library. He needed to find an answer, some way to help Don Juan. His eyes were tired and gritty. He found it difficult to focus on the pages. His joints ached from sitting still at the library table for so long. He had skimmed hundreds of sad stories, studied dozens of pages of numbers and graphs and plowed through mountains of inane theory. He had reviewed potential medication protocols and his own session notes from other cases. He was no nearer to having an answer than when he began.

He finally put the books and papers away and walked through the deserted corridors to Don Juan's room. Don Juan was rolled up in a ball on his hard, narrow bed, hugging his pillow. He was wearing gray hospital pajamas that were too big for him.

Jack stood for a few long moments, looking down at the tear-stained face of the sleeping boy. He thought the boy looked very much younger than twenty-one. Without his brave manner and his fine clothes, he looked more like fourteen. Jack pulled the covers up and tucked them around the boy with a father's practiced hand. Then he turned and walked out, his heart full of love and sadness. It had been a long day.

12

Catherine

*

In which Don Octavio meets an obstacle.

𝔇r. Jack Mickler drove home that night much later than usual. The streets were empty. The house was dark as he drove up to it. It felt cold and he felt empty. He was too tired to sleep. He ate a cold leftover quichelike thing and drank some cranberry juice, then wandered into the living room. He turned on the lights and stayed downstairs for a while, haunted by the vivid memory of Don Juan's words and his own remembered losses.

He was surprised to find himself contemplating, with a high degree of personal interest, the image of the lumbering man and the fleet-footed boy. For the first time, he realized that he no longer qualified as a fleet-footed boy. While he had no reason to suspect Marilyn of any dalliances, he was wounded by the thought that if, such an occasion arose, he would wheeze and plod. In his current deplorable condition he would never be able to catch up to the slowest, fattest, fleeing boy. After a while spent in regretting his girth, he noticed one of his wife's catalogs on the dining room table. As he leafed idly through it, something caught his eye. He got out his wallet and got on the phone.

"Hello, my name is Jennifer. How may I help you this evening?"

Jack told her how she could help him and supplied his credit card number. He and Jennifer the operator concluded their transaction. Jack sat beside the phone for a while, mystified by his own actions and by the general feeling of happiness which had descended upon him during his conversation with Jennifer.

Shortly after that he went to bed and slept peacefully until the alarm went off.

Early in the morning, but after his wife had already departed for the grocery store and the library, there came a loud knock at the door. Jack was still in his balloon-seat pajamas and his old terry-cloth bathrobe when he walked to the door. His heart beat faster as he anticipated what awaited him.

Two men, a very large carton, and a van waited outside his door. The younger of the two men said, "Dr. Mickler? Sign on line thirteen."

The delivery men looked at Jack with interest. Not everyone received such a package. It was the heaviest they had ever delivered, and there were three more of various sizes, all heavy, in the truck.

It took all three of them to get everything up the stairs into the spare room in the attic. The delivery men were trained to assemble the equipment they delivered, and they were done in no time. They waved to Jack as they left. "Good luck," said the younger delivery man.

"You're going to need it!" said the older delivery man.

Jack shut the door behind them and raced upstairs to his new toy. He read the instructions, he dressed himself carefully, he set to work on his new project just as Marilyn, cool and beautiful, arrived home from the stores and the library. She followed the sounds of panting, groaning, huffing and puffing up the attic steps, fearing some catastrophe had befallen her husband.

It had not. She found him, to her profound astonishment, enmeshed in a weight machine. He was wearing new sneakers and straining against the resistance bars. She feared for a moment that he might kill himself. She knew that before starting any strenuous exercise program you were supposed to check with a doctor. Her darling husband *was* a doctor and he never checked with anyone. He was red in the face and barely able to make any part of the machine move. He couldn't budge the springs with his legs or the pulleys attached to his hands. He was so weak that his efforts did not even register on the computerized dials of the instrument panel. On the other hand, he had a great big grin on his face.

Marilyn's heart almost burst with love for him. "Jack?" she said, almost timidly.

Not timidly at all, but grandly, Jack answered between huffs: "The journey of a thousand miles begins with a single step."

He tumbled out of the machine to give her a sweaty, breathless hug, and went off to take a shower. Marilyn looked at him as he walked down the stairs, still panting but with a new spring in his step.

Maybe it will kill him, she thought, *but I'll never stop him.* There were tears on her cheeks. Her heart was full of love and sadness.

By the time Dr. Jack had put in a couple of hours at the hospital, shuffling papers and thinking about packing up his belongings and his books, his knees and shoulders were complaining. The barometer was dropping, rain was in the air, and all the little aches and pains, old injuries and new, made themselves known to him. His mood was not as bouncy as yesterday. He had agreed to have lunch with Paul Showalter, to talk about Don Juan. He was not looking forward to it. Jack looked at the mountain of books in his office. They would all have to be packed up by the end of the week. He couldn't deal with them. So he wandered off to the cafeteria, not at all pleased with his day so far.

Dr. Paul Showalter was having an equally unsatisfactory morning. On his way to the cafeteria, he had been greeted by the spectacle of Don Juan De Marco sweeping down the corridor in caped splendor, escorted by the delectable Nurse Gloria. Paul was incensed. *Rocco* had been assigned to escort Don Juan. Don Juan was not supposed to be left in the care of any females, let alone the young, impressionable Gloria. Paul stepped toward them, ready to take executive action.

Don Juan bowed low to the superintendent. *"Buenos noches, el capitán."*

The delectable Nurse Gloria repeated, *"Buenos noches, el capitán."*

Paul asked, controlling his annoyance, "Where's Rocco?"

Don Juan was glad to pass along the news. "Rocco has moved to Madrid." And the pair of young people moved out of sight around a corner. Paul didn't have enough time this morning to deal with the problem himself. He had other problems. One of them was already waiting for him, in the person of Dr. Jack Mickler, an imminent retiree directly responsible for the disgraceful behavior of Nurse Gloria. And Nurse Rocco for that matter. Something had to be done.

Paul and Jack met in the cafeteria, both out of sorts, both tired, both wishing they were somewhere else. They selected salads made of anonymous green things, leaves of a special Cafeteria Salad Plant. Neither man was hungry enough to eat the salad. They concentrated on each other while the salads went on wilting and the ice cubes in their diet sodas melted under the blue florescent lights of the cafeteria.

Jack told Paul about Don Juan.

"And then," he said, "after having killed Don Alfonzo, he returned to his father who was bleeding to death in the street, and cradling his father in his arms, asked him for forgiveness, which his father granted. To hide his shame, Don Juan placed a mask on his own face and said he would never take it off as long as he lived. It's the perfect myth, Paul."

Paul was carried away by the story, just as enchanted by it as Jack was when he first heard it. He started at once to tame it by surrounding it with other stories and dogma from the canon of psychiatry.

"Wonderful. You're absolutely right, Jack, it's a marvelous story. It's like a Greek myth. The son becomes potent, sexually active, which leads directly to the destruction of the father, who he replaces, since, of course, he must someday become the father himself. But the guilt of replacing the man who loved him and gave him life, that guilt is too great. It's enormous. He must hide it with a mask."

Paul was proud of his explication of the mythical elements in Don Juan's story, but he hadn't lost sight of his main objective.

"It's time to put the kid on medication, Jack."

Jack was stunned. He had for a moment believed that Paul was won over, that Paul understood Don Juan's unique case and accepted the reasons not to put him under medication. He had overestimated Paul's flexibility and underestimated the effect that Don Juan was having on the entire hospital. He recalculated quickly and started out again, with less confidence.

"Are you kidding, Paul? You've got to be kidding, right? Is that all you have to say? Let me tell you something, Paul, and you know this as well as I do, if you want to see a real nut cake, just give a nice, big, healthy dose of anti-psychotic medication to a kid who is perfectly normal or even just a little bit off-center."

Jack then played his only card. "And this kid is perfectly normal, Paul."

Paul looked at his subordinate with amazement and even a little concern.

"What is happening to you, Jack? This kid is schizophrenic. He is not Don Juan. His world is confused. He needs to get into the real world. Our world."

Jack sensed something wicked on the way. "How do you know that?" he asked. "How do you know he's not Don Juan?"

Paul was happy to reply. "How do I know? I have been the head of psychiatry for this hospital for twenty-five years, Jack. He did not materialize from the head of Zeus and neither did I."

And then Paul played his trump. It was a winner. He said, with a snide smile and a superior tone, "In any of these sessions with you, Jack, did Don Juan ever happen to mention that he's been living right here in Queens with his grandmother? Did he mention that to you?" Paul pulled a slip of paper out of his pocket and looked at it. "His grandmother reported him missing last week."

Jack was devastated.

"Where did you get that? How do you know?"

"Simon Tobias from the local precinct called us about an hour ago. Now please, Jack, go put him on medication."

"I can't do it, Paul. I can't. I won't. It would interfere with whatever treatment I might otherwise provide. It just isn't right in this case, Paul." Jack's voice was starting to get louder. Paul looked around to see if anyone else was listening.

He said, "Okay, Jack. Keep your socks on. You've got five days left to do what you want. He's your patient until the paper runs out, and I'm not going to argue with you anymore." He suddenly lost all tolerance for the situation. He stood up, abandoning the wilted salad and his stubborn colleague.

"Just one thing, Jack. I can understand that you may want to shield the boy from the same reality the rest of us have to face. But who are you saving? Who really benefits, your patient or yourself?" Paul turned to leave.

Jack shouted, "Wait a minute! Are you accusing me of exploiting a patient for my own psychological advantage? Is that what you're saying? That's completely unfair. You haven't been listening to me, have you?" Jack knew he was blustering, but he couldn't help it. Paul's accusation had contained just enough truth to hurt, and yet Jack knew he really did have the boy's welfare at heart. He started to follow Paul out of the dining room.

Paul was not about to entertain any more arguments. He stomped out, the picture of righteousness, proudly trailing clouds of certified sanity.

Jack called hopelessly after him, "Paul, Paul, wait a minute . . ." but the conversation was over. Paul had pointedly left the piece of paper on the table. Jack picked it up, knowing what he had to do.

An hour later Jack found himself in a neighborhood he had never before visited, though, on the map, it did not seem very far from the hospital where Jack had worked for so many years. The address on the slip of paper was on a rundown street which vibrated with menace. Strange music poured from open windows and boom boxes. Small dim stores advertised palm reading and herbs. He parked his car at the curb and wondered how much of it would be left when he returned to it later.

Young men, lounged casually in expensive leather coats at every street corner. Mercury street lamps, turned on even in the afternoon gave the pavement a sulphurous glow. Women, their faces hidden by untidy hair and their bodies hidden by shapeless, colorless clothing, scurried past, carrying packages and wailing infants. Other women, brazen in metallic miniskirts and spike heels, stared at Jack and whispered suggestions as he passed. The street smelled of uncollected garbage. At night, there would be rats.

Dr. Jack, eyes fixed straight ahead, marched to the address which he had memorized on the way over. He tried to look as though he knew where he was going. He suspected that nobody on this street was fooled for a minute by his act. The best he could hope for was to pass for an undercover cop. He reached the door to Mrs. De Marco's building. It was painted a glossy black. He could see his own reflection in the paint. The door was unusually large, and the building had once, evidently been more elegant. There were grinning marble gargoyles in the shape of imps and griffins at the corners of the building above the filthy third floor windows. He pushed a button on the intercom.

A hoarse voice crackled out of the wall.

"Yes, what is it?"

"Mrs. De Marco?"

"Yes?"

"It's Dr. Mickler, Mrs. De Marco. I spoke to you on the phone about coming here to talk to you about your grandson." Jack found he was trembling. *Tired*, he thought, *I'm still tired.*

He was visited briefly by the thought of Don Juan and the beautiful Doña Julia naked on horseback. And the father dead in the plaza, the dust soaked with his blood.

Mrs. De Marco buzzed him in.

He opened the big door with difficulty. The foyer was lit by a yellowish bulb and the floor was covered by broken, unpleasant red and yellow tiles. He climbed a long, long dark staircase, but he felt as if he were falling. The walls were painted a shiny brown. The paint was chipped and peeling. He heard an infant's inconsolable cry from behind one of the triple-locked and chained doors. By the time he reached Mrs. De Marco's door, he was out of breath. He stood and panted for a moment, hoping to get his composure and his breath back before meeting Don Juan's grandmother. She must have heard him on the steps, though, and opened the door before he was ready.

"Come in. I am Catherine De Marco. Come into my kitchen, we'll have coffee."

Jack crossed the threshold into the stuffy little living room. The walls were covered with pictures of saints—and not the more charming saints, either. These were martyrs being burned at the stake, roasted on grills, broken on wheels, impaled, eaten by lions, and pierced by arrows. Even St. Nicholas appeared to be boiling little boys in a bathtub of scalding water. It was a grisly array of religious pathology and Dr. Jack involuntarily shuddered as he glanced at them, and at the particularly bloody crucifixes pinned above each lintel as they passed through from living room to dining room to kitchen.

A foul-smelling pot was bubbling on the stove. *Lord,* thought Dr. Jack, *it smells like eye of newt!* He didn't even want to think about it and would have been far happier not to smell it, but he couldn't help glancing at it. Mrs. De Marco went over to stir it, humming to herself. Then she picked up a crusty old coffeepot and a stained, chipped cup.

She poured thick coffee into the cup and set it in front of her visitor. She moved heavily in the kitchen, a crone in an apron. Jack looked for any trace of the grace he had seen in Don Juan. There were resemblances. He and his grandmother shared the angle of their jaws, the shape of their eyes, the long, slender hands; but her hands were crooked, grasping. Her fingernails were like claws painted red, and in her left hand she held a plastic flyswatter.

She brought Jack a singularly ugly ceramic thing in the shape of a sheep. The sheep had a red stain on its front. Catherine De Marco removed the thing's lid to reveal brownish powder. Jack knew he looked confused.

"Sugar. It's a sugarbowl. The lamb of God. I bought it at Our Lady of the Mills Sodality Church Bazaar when I was a girl. Gave it to my mother on her name day." Catherine De Marco picked up the lamb and laughed. "My mother always hated it." The old woman was obviously glad to have it back. A prized possession. Probably poisoned her mom with arsenic in the sugar, just to get it back. Odd hostile thoughts tripped through Jack's brain, but he fought them. *She's just a pitiful old woman. Keep telling yourself that*, he thought. Just to prove to himself that he had control of the situation, Jack spooned up some sugar from the lamb of God while he tried to carry on.

"Mrs. De Marco . . ."

"Call me Catherine."

"Catherine . . . I'm wondering whether you could help me with some information. . . . If you could answer some questions for me . . . about your grandson—"

"Johnny? You mean Johnny?"

Catherine De Marco jumped up, surprisingly agile, and smashed a fly which had settled on the table. Jack, startled, thought he really ought to award her the ears and the tail as they do bullfighters. He cleared his mind again and looked at the old woman as neutrally as he could. *She isn't necessarily evil*, he thought. *She's just old and maybe what my mother would have called peculiar.*

She smacked another fly. She crossed herself as if the fly's death were a man's. It was awfully early in the year for so many flies. They were all flying in the direction of the stew pot. Jack shuddered again. There was no screen on the kitchen window and it was wide open.

"Would you like me to shut the windows for you? Keep the flies out?" Jack asked.

"No."

They looked at each other, the aging doctor and the aged woman. Jack accidentally took a sip of the hot, bitter coffee. It tasted as if it had been boiled for a week, then burned for another week. It was so strong that Jack feared for his heart, which had been known to flutter when he drank too much caffeine. The old woman smiled an evil smile. Jack had the sensation of falling down a well as he looked into her eyes. He tried to move right along.

"His name is Johnny, then?"

"Yes. His full name is John Arnold De Marco. Arnold after my father, Armondo. What did you think his name was? He's not still doing that Don Juan business, is he?"

Jack suppressed a groan. He guessed what was coming.

"I'm surprised you know about that, Mrs. De Marco."

Catherine swatted another fly. The air seemed to be thick with flies and the reek of the stewpot. She crossed herself again.

"I'd have to be deaf, dumb, and blind not to. It's all because of that damned centerfold, Donna whatever the hell her name is." Catherine positively cackled. Her voice was like a handful of brass fingernails being dragged over sharp rocks. Jack felt despair.

He said, against his own better judgment, "Donna Ana . . . she's a *centerfold*?"

Catherine whispered, radiating malevolent satisfaction, "You want to see something?" She clutched at his arm, and pulled him into what she said was Johnny's bedroom.

All four walls of the tiny room were covered with carefully trimmed magazine pictures of a young woman in various poses, nude and seminude. The young woman was well-developed, with big breasts, thin waist, and pretty in a bottled blonde, generic way as far as Jack could tell. But in every picture her face was covered with a black silk mask just like the one Don Juan—Johnny—wore. In one picture, she also had on a Spanish hat and Spanish boots, if nothing else.

Jack stared at the pictures. A huge avalanche of disappointment crashed down on him. He felt he had been a fool. An old fool. Conned again. Disenchanted.

The crone fully appreciated and enjoyed his distress. Men, in her opinion, were all fools. She was delighted to see this specimen properly humbled. She killed some more flies.

"The boy is convinced that he's found his one true love." Catherine's voice was heavy with sarcasm. "He's worse than his father . . . Tony, better known as Antonio, the Dance King of Astoria. He was a dance king like I'm the Queen of Sheba."

Jack, brokenhearted, tried to salvage something.

"Didn't his father win a prize for dancing?"

"You heard of him? Yes, and it's about the only thing he ever did right. You want to see his picture being the great dance king?"

Jack nodded, feeling like a dazed buffalo, mortally wounded.

Catherine showed Jack her proof, a photograph of her son Tony dressed up in a vaguely Latin ballroom costume, a tinfoil crown on his head. Jack, resignation and defeat written all over his face, decided to get as much as possible out of the unpleasant old woman. He carefully erased all traces of disappointment from his voice. He had come all this way to get information, and he was not going to leave without the goods. *If you're going all the way to Hell, you might as well come back with Eurydice. Or at least a pomegranate.* He stuck with his interrogation, concentrating on details.

"His father sold . . . pharmaceuticals, I believe?"

"Is that what Johnny said? His father couldn't sell a boat to a drowning man! He worked for a dry-cleaning shop—sofas and drapes. He only got that job because my brother's father-in-law took pity on him."

"Is his father still alive?"

"Didn't Johnny tell you anything at all? Tony died in a car crash five years ago."

"In Mexico?" Jack still had one thread of hope.

"In Phoenix." Catherine De Marco neatly severed the thread.

"Are you telling me they never lived in Mexico?"

The man was not as quick as she had thought. "Never. When they first got married, that Latin tramp wanted to take him to Mexico. It wasn't enough to marry him, or to spend all day and all night in the bedroom banging up and down like sexual intercourse came with an expiration date. Oh, no, that tart wanted him to go live in Quack-awhacka or wherever the hell her family came from. But I told her, I said, you go down to Mexico and I'm coming with you. So she settled for Phoenix."

Jack pursued the facts doggedly, sure now of what kind of answers he would get.

"Where is his mother now?"

"That I couldn't tell you. We were never . . . what you might call close."

Catherine was on the brink of another cackling attack. Jack hurried onward. "Mrs. De Marco . . . how often did you see Johnny when he was growing up?"

"Only once."

"You only saw your grandson once in his life?"

"Once. That was the only time they ever invited me. I traveled to Phoenix by bus. I hated it. I refused to fly—"

"—and I don't like trains, but that bus was the worst. Johnny was six. They put me up in a fancy hotel and took me to the world's biggest hole"—she threw up her arms in disgust—"the Grand Canyon!!!"

Jack walked over to the bed and picked up the two leatherbound books lying on the cheap bedside table. The books were *El Burlador de Sevilla* by Tirso de Molina, the original telling of the Don Juan legend; and *Don Juan*, the long, long poem by Byron. Somewhere in this place if he looked long enough, he was sure, he would find a cassette tape of *Don Giovanni*. The highlights.

"That was the only time you ever saw John?" he asked Mrs. De Marco, sadly, and sat down on the narrow bed. Above the headboard, pinned by four red thumbtacks, was a spectacularly large and graphic centerfold of the masked woman, with her name in the corner. Her name, it said, was Chelsea Stoker.

Catherine was talking again. "That was the only time I ever saw him, right, until three months ago, I opened the door. And there was Zorro."

13

Voyagers
*

In which Don Juan sets a new course.

Jack left Catherine De Marco's apartment a weary and damaged man. The whores and pimps and drug dealers on the sidewalk seemed to be mocking him, whispering insults at the big fool lurching past them. The only good thing about the situation was that his car was still there when he returned to it. He got in it and left. The radio was playing a sultry version of his favorite Cole Porter song, "I've Got You Under My Skin." But Jack's bruised eardrums and psyche could not bear the sound of sentimental crooning.

He switched the radio to an all-news station, where the usual suspects were being rounded up. Weather and traffic were bad. Murder, riot, parricide, and suicide were, as usual, on the rise. Jack took a bitter pleasure in punishing himself with reality.

The thought of the weight machine intruded itself into his mind and caused him to utter a string of drab curses. He felt sure that he would never use the damned thing. It would only take up space in the attic and Marilyn would laugh at him forever for buying it. Maybe he could send it back. Probably not. Self-pity and disgust at his own folly overwhelmed him. He recognized in his own aching heart the terrible impact of the toxic grandmother. After all these years of dealing with malevolence in one form or another, he thought he should be immune. "You are never immune, never safe, never far enough removed. They can spit venom thousands of miles. Think of talk radio. Poisons all over the landscape."

Jack despised himself for losing track of the realities. He had definitely located a possible source of Don Juan's elaborate fantasies. A grandmother, a toxic granny. Well, it was a common enough story. Jack had heard variations over and over again. Only this one hurt a little more than usual.

And at the heart of his misery, like a gigantic cement toad in a bleak suburban garden, was the fact that he had an afternoon session coming up with "Don Juan," king of the centerfolds. Paul Showalter would be so pleased, damn it. Jack's bad mood worsened as he drove through twisted, ugly streets, getting lost and frazzled.

Jack arrived back at the hospital, carrying one of the centerfold pictures of the masked pinup. It showed her naked on a white horse, wearing spurs, and carrying a whip. How appropriate, he thought, how very apt. He was overtired and he was late, too, so that even though he had hurried, the boy was already in his office when he arrived. Jack struggled to act professionally, but there was a cool edge to his manner as he tossed the picture of the girl into Don Juan's lap.

Jack had decided to confront the boy directly with the facts and his own lies. "I spoke to your grandmother this afternoon. She says you grew up in Phoenix, Arizona. She said your name is John Arnold De Marco. She also told me your dad died in a car crash." Jack couldn't keep an accusatory, whiny note out of his voice. He knew he should be ashamed of himself, for behaving in an unprofessional way with this patient.

Don Juan was untroubled. "Interesting fantasy. But I suppose, if it makes her happy, it is harmless enough."

"You're telling me that *none* of what she told me is true?" Jack's attitude wavered between hopeful and skeptical.

"Correct," said Don Juan, "Aren't you relieved?"

The young man had hit the nail squarely on the head. Jack unconsciously squirmed and wriggled in his chair. He fidgeted, not able to get comfortable as he tried to find the right line of attack in his treatment of the boy. Suppose his patient had lied? A lie could be as revealing as the truth. It directed the observant doctor to what the patient wished to believe. Dr. Jack knew all that. He also knew that he really wanted to believe in Don Juan. He wanted the story to be literal, verifiable truth. *I want to touch the wounds,* he thought. *I want to see the angels.* Right. Some of his patients claimed that they had done exactly that. Plus heard the voices and, some of them, even smelled the terrible fires of Hell. Verification wasn't always easy for the overloaded brains of physician and patient. Jack knew he had allowed himself to be drawn into an alternate and incorrect version of reality. But he was too tired to pull himself together and stop. By rights, he shouldn't even talk to the boy anymore, but turn him over at once to another doctor. He didn't want to do that, not with his very last case.

Jack was troubled as he continued to question Don Juan. He felt that his questions were inappropriate. But he wanted the answers.

"She told me something else, your grandmother. She told me that your father worked for a dry-cleaning establishment."

Don Juan shook his head sadly.

"Lies, all lies."

Don Juan jumped up and began pacing. The situation was beginning to concern him. Jack could see that he was earnestly weighing the best way to cancel his grandmother's spell. Or erase the facts.

Don Juan spoke earnestly. "Look, you want me to give you some crazy story like my grandmother's so you'll think I'm sane? If that's what it takes for me to get out of here, I'll be happy to do it for you. But there is a rumor that you are a psychiatrist."

Jack had to smile. "I've heard that rumor myself."

"Well, then, can't you tell when a woman is insane? Totally, completely, undeniably, obviously *insane*?"

"Are you telling me that everything your grandmother told me is not true?" Jack almost whimpered, he was so tired and confused.

Don Juan whirled. His cape flew out around him, and his bootheels clicked together. Then he bowed to Jack, a sardonic expression on his usually gentle face.

"In so many words, yes. She hated my mother. This, in itself, was not unusual, because my grandmother hates everybody, without exception. She hates not only my mother but her mother, her two sisters, my father, me, and a whole string of strangers, because they won't live the way she wants them to live."

Jack remembered the cackle of the venomous old woman.

"How does she want them to live?"

"Without sex. The idea of a woman actually desiring intercourse with a man drives her out of her mind. She believes that all men are fools and knaves and criminals, that what they steal and trample upon and ruin are women, and they do this invariably with the tool with which the Devil, not God, provided for that special purpose. Need I name the tool to you, Don Octavio? At any rate, it is that specific organ, and the women who weakly fall prey to it, that excite her most terrible rages. She is also upset to consider the offspring which are produced from such a source. If my grandmother had her way, the generations would not continue. All propagation would cease except that carried out discreetly by plants. She is a madwoman."

Jack had encountered similar cases of all-encompassing hatred of life. Such people were like saints or artists of destruction, single-minded and unstoppable in their devotion to a single aim. Jack did not doubt that Mrs. De Marco was one of those. They were not uncommon. He nodded to the boy that he understood.

Don Juan said, "My grandmother believes that she is a religious woman. But she does not have the truth of God. She believes only in the truth of her own hatred of life, her own hatred of God's most beautiful works."

Don Juan considered the awful insanity of his grand-mother.

"She went so crazy whenever she believed that my mother and father were having sex, that she broke windows and crockery and called for the priest to perform an exorcism. She was sure that my mother and father, full of passion and love, were possessed by Satan. Also all that crockery smashing and all those tantrums were extremely unpleasant, even frightening. She called my mother ugly names and whispered foul lies into the ear of my father.

"So," said Don Juan, reasonably, "we stayed as far away from her as possible."

"In Phoenix, Arizona?"

"In Mexico. But my grandmother couldn't handle it. She went around telling all her friends and her weird sisters, my aunts, that my mother and father had moved to Arizona. Mexico was, for her, a personal insult. But she believed in Arizona. She could tell her friends that her son had to move there because of a high-paying, powerful new job."

Jack was surprised by Don Juan's serene, tranquil, and thoughtful calmness. Usually the relatives of people like Mrs. De Marco were full of rage when they talked about their efforts to struggle free of the web of hatred. But there was no frustration or anger in Don Juan's tone as he talked about his grandmother, only sorrow for her foolish and unhappy delusions.

"My mother and father would write to her from Mexico, and she would not answer. Then my father found out from his uncle, my grandfather's brother, about her Arizona story. He had an idea. He got a forwarding service in Phoenix to take care of the letters. My grandmother was happy to stay in touch once the address was in Phoenix."

"You never lived in Phoenix, Arizona?"

"I have never"—Don Juan was kind about this, but firm—"lived in Phoenix. I was in Phoenix for exactly one week in my whole life. That was the week my grandmother came out to Arizona on the bus. She spent the whole time complaining. We showed her some sights, bought her some souvenirs and took her out to dinner, attempted to make her happy—not very successfully, I must say—and so we shipped her back home."

Jack slumped deeper into his armchair. He felt a little dizzy. He tried to sort it all out. Don Juan waited for him to pull himself together. He offered Jack a drink of cold water. It seemed to help.

"What about your father's death, then?"

Don Juan spoke very quietly and simply.

"I have told you how my father died, Don Octavio."

Jack was impressed by the sadness and dignity of Don Juan's eyes, his quiet voice. Jack sighed, not fully recuperated from his confusion.

Don Juan looked carefully at the centerfold. Jack, reminded of that photographic proof of deception, said, "It says right there, her name is Chelsea Stoker. Her picture was plastered all over your bedroom walls."

Don Juan was amused by the doctor's naivete.

"Tsk, tsk. Don Octavio, you know they never use their true names. She is really my Donna Ana. She's trying to teach me a lesson. And that was not my bedroom. It was only where I was temporarily hanging my cape. And my hat. Do you think I, the great Don Juan, would be so foolish as to eat anything that noxious woman cooked? Do you think I am so lacking in a proper man's pride as to share quarters with her? I was only being polite to an elderly relative, sleeping there infrequently whenever I passed through town."

There was a long, gravid pause. Jack remembered the smell of the stew Catherine De Marco had been cooking, the fly-specked squalor of the apartment and the obvious evidence of a quirky religious fervor. Don Juan had a point about his grandmother's cooking and her unsuitability as a guardian for a young man.

Even if Don Juan's grandmother was absolutely crazy, which she surely was, that didn't mean that Johnny was *not* crazy. They might both be insane. Jack decided on one last stab at professional control. Nothing like this attack of irresistible transference had ever happened to him in thirty years of practice. He was astounded at his own incompetence and the risk, to his patient and himself, of his own behavior. He needed to get grounded, right away. No excuses.

"You know," Jack began, thoughtfully, quietly, "I once treated a young man about your age who had fallen in love with a poster, a very attractive poster. He had always felt awkward with girls . . . and the girl in the poster was a knockout, a true beauty."

Don Juan listened intently.

Jack watched the boy, trying to gauge what effect his words were having. Jack went on, still very quiet, very sincere and dignified, very kind. "He did everything to try to contact her. Called the magazines where her picture appeared, the poster company, everyone he could think of, hundreds of calls. He even hired a private detective."

Jack took a deep breath. What he was trying to do was dangerous; it could drive the boy deeper into delusion. It could make him harder to reach. Or it could bring him back to earth. Jack's voice was soft, almost a whisper.

"Finally, someone at the magazine took pity on him

and gave him her telephone number. He called her. They talked for a minute and she said good-bye. He clearly got the feeling that there was never going to be any reason for him to call her again."

Jack stopped. He looked into Don Juan's eyes for a reaction, hoping for the best.

Don Juan said, "And then what happened?"

The doctor took a deep breath. "And then he tried to kill himself."

Don Juan saw that he had been led into a trap. He was calm, but he refused to stay ensnared. "Donna Ana is real, Don Octavio. Would you like me to tell you about her?"

Jack felt that he had no choice. "I suppose so," he bleated. His exhaustion seemed to be boundless. He could not formulate any kind of plan. The boy had politely rejected every inconvenient facet of reality. He was not defensive, not even seriously offended. The don had simply stepped aside, a fencer's elegant step, and let reality recede as it rushed past him. Jack wondered if anything he could say would ever reach the boy.

Don Juan looked cheerful as he continued. "Shortly after the death of my father, in Mexico, my mother decided it would be best to send me to Cadiz. She herself had decided to take the veil. She was well on the way to permanent vows in a cloistered order near the village and worried that there would be no one to look after me once she had taken up residence in the convent. She had considered the situation very carefully, with great love and tenderness. She informed me that she felt that a sea voyage might purify me . . . as though the Spanish freighter were Noah's ark and I was the dove, being sent out to bring back the twig of peace."

Jack objected. "I didn't know Spain had a merchant fleet—"

Don Juan was ready for that. "It didn't. The crew was Spanish. The ship itself was officially registered as Liberian. My mother also informed me that I had a substantial inheritance from my father, enough to support me in comfort for the rest of my days. Funds would be forwarded to various ports. I was to become what I believe they call in England a 'remittance man.' I would not have to work for my living as long as I was moderate in my way of life.

"And then, my mother, the beautiful Doña Inez, and I, we said our tearful good-byes on the pier. She was dressed in the deepest mourning, which concealed her lovely face. I wore my mask. We sobbed as we embraced each other for the last time.

"You can imagine the scene, Don Octavio. The whole village turned out to bid me bon voyage. My mother and the other women of the village had prepared a trunkful of embroidered wool shirts and warm socks in case Cadiz would prove to be less tropical than Mexico. I tried to convince myself that I was starting a new life abroad. But my heart was heavy as I waved farewell from the deck of the freighter. All of the world that I had ever known grew smaller and smaller as the ship pulled away. Soon I could no longer see the familiar shore and the lights of my village were lost to me in the gathering evening mists."

Don Juan paused to see if Jack had any objections. He did not. All boys, if they were to become men, must leave home, even if only in their dreams. It was well-documented in every culture's mythology as well as the most elementary of psychology textbooks. Jack, therefore, expected a voyage of some kind. Not, however, the kind that Don Juan began to recount.

"Of course, what my mother never knew was that the ship was run by scoundrels. By rascally, bloodthirsty, heartless . . . pirates."

Jack still had no objections that he cared to voice. *In for a penny, in for a pound*, he thought, hoping he'd never have to explain all this to a symposium on deluded docs. Jack was tired after his long day, but most of the awful self-loathing and despair he had felt at Mrs. De Marco's had dissipated. In fact, he noticed a restful, warm sense of relaxation and peace in his weary body, as he allowed himself to be carried away by Don Juan's story.

Don Juan continued in a pleasant, matter-of-fact voice. "After a long, tedious and choppy cruise, during which I suffered every hour from the most violent pains of disappointed love, longing for my home, and seasickness, those devilish pirates changed course. In truth, I barely noticed, incapacitated as I was by my assorted maladies.

"Instead of sailing for Cadiz, they made for an obscure sultanate, landing at a well-defended, ancient, busy but nameless Arabian port city, where"—Don Juan peered closely at Jack and spoke very quickly, looking Jack right in the eye—"all the passengers were immediately sold into slavery."

Jack was tired and not tracking too closely, but even so, he couldn't help yelping as if bitten by a very small dog. "You were sold into slavery by *pirates*?"

"Yes. Absolutely. I was sold into slavery, and certainly by pirates. And tomorrow I will tell you the details of all that transpired." And, with an air of bravado and nonchalance, Don Juan stood up, bowed courteously to his doctor, and left Jack whimpering in his chair.

14

Bernard

*

Don Juan visits Paradise.

The next day was a gorgeous spring day in Queens. Touches of green softened the tender tips of the trees. Gentle zephyrs blew through the weeping willows on the grounds of the hospital. Robins and wrens, swallows and swifts, pigeons and squirrels raced and pecked and sang and carried on, driven by the warm current of life renewing itself at the equinox. Cheerful citizens came outside their houses to converse with each other on the sidewalks. Jack bounded up the steps to his office, feeling better than he had in at least a year. He stared out his office window at the flowers and people. They all looked beautiful to him.

Jack had a hard time convincing himself that life was real and earnest. It seemed to him to be bubbling up like fountains of soda water all around him. *Lemonade springs are all very well*, mused Jack, *but if I don't think of something, Don Juan is going to be locked up here for a very long time.*

He stopped looking out the window. He turned his mind, with difficulty, back to the business at hand. He bent over his skimpy notes. He searched for clues in his vast memory of psychopathology. He was still pondering all this when Don Juan, the very embodiment of spring itself, swept into the office. The young man was capeless and hatless. His shirt was unbuttoned and his hair had been tumbled by the warm wind. He got right down to work.

"If you will recall, Don Octavio, when we last met I had been carried off by pirates and sold into slavery."

Jack said nothing, but it occurred to him that he really did not need reminding. The last session had been more than memorable. Don Juan's pleasant voice took on a highly confidential tone.

"I must tell you, Don Octavio, I was frightened as I shivered on the dock. It was, you understand, a temperate, even warm island on which I had landed, but the thieving pirates had stolen most of my clothes as well as my sword. Fear for my future caused ice-cold chills to run through my veins. I wore only the briefest of loincloths, and my mask. I had been chained, hand, waist, and foot to a signpost which I could not read. It was in Arabic, a graceful script, but unknown to me."

Jack nodded agreement and folded his hands into a steeple, trying to look wise, not seeing where this could possibly lead.

Don Juan went on, his voice turning somewhat nostalgic as he began to recount the charms of that ancient port city.

"A spice-laden wind blew from the green hills and I could see date palms in the distance. Clear water lapped at the wharf pilings, musical and gentle. The sky above the city was as blue as lapis lazuli. A vast white translucent palace was visible halfway up a small hill above the town. I could see that it was the abode of a great king. Near the mouth of the harbor, lacy white towers kept watch above the ancient wall, gleaming as if made of ivory. The city gates appeared to be made of gold—dazzling even to a wretched, shivering prisoner like me."

Don Juan discreetly inspected Jack's face for signs of

disbelief or inattention. He saw neither. Jack was carefully maintaining the bland, neutral mask of unconditional regard which he had donned some thirty years ago.

"Yes . . . go on. . . ."

Don Juan sailed onward, describing the scene on the dock. "Not only was I chained to a signpost, I was tied to my fellow passengers by a long rope. I was the last in line. After me was only the post and the water. The harbor was full of splendid three-masted sailing vessels and small, fast clippers. All of the boats had eyes painted on their prows, which seemed to be looking at me."

Jack remembered the fishing boats with eyes he had seen on his trip to a professional conference a year ago, where he had delivered a paper on the role of pseudo-paternal transferrance in the treatment of severely depressed postadolescent males. The conference had been held at a luxurious seaside resort on the wonderful island of Rhodes. Jack suppressed a small nostalgic smile as Don Juan described his predicament.

"Although the boats only seemed to be looking at me, a crowd of richly dressed citizens were, in plain fact, looking right at me. They were dressed in multiple layers of silk in vivid colors, some even sporting tissue of gold and ropes around their waists. The contrast just made me feel more naked and extremely pale.

"Unfamiliarity with the customs of dress of that place left me unsure of the genders of individuals in the throng. I assumed that the ones with knives were men, and the ones with ropes of pearls around their waists were women, but they were so cloaked and veiled that details were hard to determine.

"My fellow passengers were carted off one by one. Only I was left. This may sound unlikely to you, Don Octavio, but I swear it is the truth. Though I was nearly naked, chilled with fear, and incredibly hungry, having digested nothing whatsoever throughout my journey, the deepest pain of all was that no one appeared to have any interest in me as a slave. Finally, I was the last passenger left. The pirates were boarding their vessel, laughing like a bunch of mangy hyenas. The auctioneer, like all of his ilk, was annoyed to have one last trinket remaining at the end of the day's bidding.

"The crowd was dispersing and night was falling over the splendid city. I was beginning to worry about what would happen to me if I *weren't* sold. Just then a long shining limousine, a Rolls, pulled up on the wharf. It was flying two tiny pink flags with gold crests. The crowd parted before it. The windows were, of course, made of smoked glass. I could see nothing of the interior of the car.

"The driver got out of the car. He was spiffily dressed in a gold-braided, semimilitary, soft-booted, baggy-pants uniform. He wore a gleaming scimitar at his side. He strode over to the auctioneer. They had a conversation which I could not overhear, though I tried. The driver pointed to me and said something. The auctioneer shook his head and started to walk away. I was afraid the deal had fallen through. The driver shrugged and said something else. The auctioneer replied. The driver nodded; the plumes in his turban nodding with him. The auctioneer cut my ropes and unlocked my chains. The driver and the auctioneer shook hands.

"With that handshake," said Don Juan, "I became the property of the Sultana Gulbeyaz."

Jack could not help himself. He began to smile, then covered it quickly with a cough. Don Juan noticed and resumed his talk with amusement. "And then what happened?"

"Her driver was named Baba, short for Bernard. I later learned that he was a eunuch. His situation, a matter of some distress to him, was, in fact responsible for his meteoric rise to favor at the Sultan's court."

Don Juan, bemused, took a sip of water as if it might fortify him for what he had to say next. Jack was surprised to detect a faint blush on the manly cheek of the usually unflappable Don Juan.

"Baba, I would learn later, was actually a very fine fellow. At that time, however, he was a stranger to me. His appearance, especially around the knife, was not reassuring. When the auctioneer cut me loose from the signpost and Baba led me to the limousine, I had no idea what might await me. Baba put me in the backseat of the car, my hands still tied, though the harsh nautical rope had been replaced by a soft silken tie.

"I noticed that there was a vase with a fresh red rose bolted to the side door, but the inside door handles had been removed. It occurred to me that the limousine had been used before to transport wretches like me.

"Baba thoughtfully tucked a crocheted lap rug, a sort of light Afghan, around my thighs, then locked the doors from the outside and drove swiftly through the winding streets of the Old City.

"The limousine windows were darkened so that commoners could not look in, but passengers could see out. As the enormous car turned this way and that, I could see that I had entered a magnificent city, as old and even more splendid than Constantinople. Geraniums as big as trees blossomed in pots on scrubbed and gleaming front door steps. Whitewashed walls reflected the headlights of the powerful limo. Intricate blue tiles glowed softly on the domes and spires of innumerable buildings obviously dedicated to the glory of God.

"Beautifully dressed, handsome people strolled through the well-lit streets. Polite vendors offered passersby lemon ice, rose tea, and something that looked very much like a tortilla. I was hungry and thirsty, as well as being in desperate fear for my life. The rest of the trip passed as if in a dream. When we reached the palace, Baba had to guide me by the elbow, I was so exhausted and unnerved. As we went through the magnificent, carved bronze doors,

I was most aware of cool tiles under my bare feet and then the welcome softness of deep, silky carpets.

"Baba, while maintaining a dignified silence, was not unmindful of my needs. He led me to a small sitting room where, on an antique table, delicate plates were covered with delectable, dainty cakes and cheeses. I fell upon the food, eating, I am afraid, noisily and greedily. A bracing mint tea quenched my thirst. When I had eaten my fill, my next request was for a bath. The peril of the sea voyage and my ordeal on the wharf, had taken its toll. Baba led me to a small room with a bath already drawn.

"Clouds of scented steam went up from the marble tub. The faucets were gold, in the shape of dolphins. Sheepskin rugs lay on the intricately tiled floor. Precious oils and essences in ruby and emerald glass jars were arranged on a small marble-topped table. Bars of sandalwood soap, scented shampoo, and large sponges rested invitingly on a shelf above the faucets. Snowy white, thick, luxurious Turkish towels hung from a heated towel rack, and a handsome, fur-lined bathrobe hung from a hook. I somehow expected Baba to leave while I bathed. He did not. He waited discreetly outside the door of the bathing chamber. When I was finished, I felt much, much better and went out, wrapped in the long, sumptuous bathrobe, to get some clothes."

Don Juan was definitely blushing. Jack thought he ought to say something to reassure the boy, but he couldn't think of anything soothing. Before he could murmur "There, there," Don Juan spoke again.

"Baba went to a large closet and returned with what I could clearly see was a feminine outfit, complete with a waistband of pearls, a diaphanous veil, and a long black wig. Baba spoke to me, not unkindly. 'You must put these on.' I refused, of course.

"Baba said, more insistently, 'You must put them on. There are worse things that can happen to a man here than dressing as a woman. Think it over.' Baba showed me an alcove with a small but richly draped bed. He told me he would be back in the morning for my decision.

"I was refreshed by a long night of delicious sleep, untroubled by dreams or worries. In the morning, Baba arrived early. He brought me a breakfast of fried sardines, small grilled sausages, yogurt, grapes, and hot, sweet, strong coffee. There is nothing like a good night's sleep and a hearty breakfast to help a man make the right decision."

Jack nodded his approval of his sentiment, one which he had often conveyed to his troubled patients. Don Juan's manner became carefully matter-of-fact as he described preparations for his first day in the seraglio.

"Baba helped me to dress, providing special undergarments. He made sure that my arms and face were free of unsightly hairs. He shaped my eyebrows, using a tweezer. This was, you may imagine, a painful procedure. I endured it all with, if I may say so myself, stoic fortitude. Baba then arranged my wig, settling it in long curls on my shoulders. He gave me an especially useful lesson in the skillful handling of my veil.

"Then he taught me to apply my makeup. He provided mascara and eye shadow, lipstick in a soft pinkish red, a creamy foundation in an alabaster jar and my rouge, nothing garish or loud, just a little enhancement. Under the circumstances, I had to give up my mask, but it was soon replaced by a mask of a different sort. I reasoned that, since I had removed my mask under duress, not of my own free will, I could still contend that I remained basically faithful to my vow to hide my face."

Jack nodded. He was familiar with the deals his patients made with God and their doctors, and the extremely fine distinctions which could be made by even the least subtle of them whenever it was a choice between the full disaster of realized guilt or the mild embarrassment of a pardonable lapse. Some of them opted for guilt, but most of them preferred something milder, no matter what their crimes.

Jack turned his attention back to his patient. The young man was obviously living in the realm of runaway metaphor, and his story certainly touched on some delicate matters, but nothing about his manner suggested that Don Juan was seriously distressed by any of it. He went on describing his training in feminine behavior, employing a cool and instructional tone.

"I practiced walking in high-heeled sandals under Baba's expert guidance. It was a difficult skill, but I mastered it. Soon, after a dab of musky perfume and a last rearrangement of my gauzy veil, I was ready. For what, I had no idea."

Don Juan looked at Jack, whose face was still studiously blank. He revealed nothing, not so much as a raised eyebrow or a stray twinkle in his eye. Jack had his very best granite-jawed noncommital nonexpression in place. Don Juan absentmindedly patted his long hair into place and picked a piece of lint off Jack's shirt collar.

"Don Octavio, you must believe me. When Bernard finished with me that morning, I appeared to be a very attractive young woman. To this day, if you want to know the truth, I sometimes take up a little mascara, a little blush. . . ."

Jack said nothing, but moved uneasily in his chair, leaning slightly away from the don. Jack folded his hands over his belt buckle in an unconsciously defensive posture.

Don Juan continued with his story. "Bernard—Baba—told me about the palace, the Sultana, and the Sultan as we walked down long, sunny corridors filled with the scent of fresh flowers and the music of many ornate fountains. Baba said that the Sultan had a harem of fifteen hundred young women. The demand placed on any one of his wives was therefore, relatively minor, so the women filled their time with learning, song, gossip, and good deeds.

"Bernard revealed to me that the Sultana was twenty-six and spoke English with a charming French accent. She had been educated at the Sorbonne and at Radcliffe, and had taught all of her attendants to speak English, French, German, Spanish, and Japanese. She wore traditional garb as a tribute to her ancestress, whose name had been forgotten in the general fuss over Bathsheba and also in deference to her husband, one of the lesser Suliemans. Bernard told me that the Sultan, an old-fashioned type, preferred his women to maintain voluminous drapery most of the time. This was a preference I would soon have reason to appreciate.

"According to Baba, the Sultana Gulbeyaz held the position of Wife Number 16.2.14, having been wed to the Sultan on February 14, Valentine's Day, of her sixteenth year. The Sultan had to have some kind of filing system, after all. Her nickname was Bootsie, but the Sultan seldom remembered to look it up, and usually referred to all his wives as 'Darling.' Baba knew everything about everyone because he was responsible for all of the court's filing systems, which were vast and extremely complex."

Jack thought of his own boxes of unfiled papers, a highly distracting image. Don Juan noticed Jack's attention wandering and waited for him to get back on board. Jack shook off the thought of his rooms full of unruly paper. He was soon ready to listen again, and Don Juan took him back into the seraglio. Jack was more than glad to go.

"Baba and I traversed the great central courtyard where roses and orange trees bloomed in the sunlight. Statues of handsome boys, cherubs, and goddesses decorated the colonnaded walk. Long vines full of red flowers cascaded from upper windows. Delicate music wafted from shadowy rooms. Exotic canaries and hummingbirds flew, singing, through the courtyard. The air was perfumed with a faint scent of spice. My silk skirt played about my hips as I walked.

"Baba led me to a carved, gilded, highly decorated and well-guarded door. A demure young woman ushered us into a large, high-ceilinged room. It was filled with rich sofas, handworked pillows, and precious rugs. A large frame held an example of elaborate embroidery. The walls were covered with a series of huge, intricately worked tapestries. The topic of the tapestries appeared to be the tale of Venus and Adonis, rendered rather more graphically than I would have expected."

Jack could not remember the story, but assumed it was one of the racier classical tales. Don Juan's posture became languid, fluid. His voice was almost a whisper as he described the palace room.

"I did not have as much time as I wished to inspect the treasures which filled the opulent room. I barely glanced at the beaded curtains, the crystal lamps and ornate gold vases, the antique porcelain figurines. All of my attention was soon directed to one regal figure. The obvious mistress of the room, Sultana Gulbeyaz herself, stood on a low platform at one end of the chamber. She was a handsome woman of statuesque, even Junoesque proportions. The Sultana was clearly an imperial and powerful woman of great intelligence and wisdom, I could see that at once. I was impressed, Don Octavio, I truly was. Even to this day, my friend, I am still awe-stricken when I think back to the sight of Sultana Gulbeyaz as I first saw her, standing so straight and tall before me."

"I think we could take a short break here, if you don't mind."

Don Juan smiled and said, "Very well, Don Octavio. But I have much to tell you today."

Jack thought to himself, *I bet that's the God's truth, now. And the weird thing is, I want to hear what he has to say.*

15

Bootsie

*

Don Juan learns to compromise.

Jack and Don Juan got up and walked around the office like orbiting planets around the sumptuous vision of the palace. Jack was a little worried that he might not be able to get past the vision of Don Juan garbed as an attractive Oriental maiden. He even thought he noticed a certain lithe new sway in the boy's walk. Don Juan happily contemplated the next part of his story.

They settled back down and Don Juan began again.

"Don Octavio, you must imagine the most regal, the most magnificent, the tallest woman you have ever seen and then add inches to her stature and splendor to her figure. Also drape her in the most costly of garments, hand embroidered with gold threads, sewn with pearls and rubies. Her hands were adorned by gold and silver rings set with emeralds and sapphires. Heavy carved bracelets and armlets and even anklets exhibited the finest art of the jeweler. Large diamonds glittered from her earrings and necklace. She was obviously a woman of some influence and resource."

Don Juan said, "My new friend, Baba, dropped to his knees before her. I did the same. She extended her jeweled foot from beneath her gown. Bernard kissed her great toe with reverent gusto, then he kissed the hem of her gown. He groveled, Don Octavio, an attitude I have never mastered."

Jack still had no objection or comment, though he was highly entertained by the vision of Don Juan, dressed to the teeth in women's clothes, kneeling on the floor, but still trying to stand on his dignity.

Soft breezes from the daffodil beds blew through the open window of Dr. Jack Mickler's office, and a mockingbird flew past, singing a few Mozartian notes. Don Juan considered that his story was having an appropriate effect on Don Octavio, whose face was relaxed and serene at last. Don Juan continued.

"Baba presented me to the Sultana with a sweeping introductory gesture. I still did not understand why I was required to be in drag. The Sultana extended her elegant foot in my direction. Baba made a discreet gesture indicating it was my turn to kiss the Sultana's toes. I did nothing. Impatient, she wiggled her foot. I still did nothing. Aghast at my impertinence and foolhardiness, Baba made kissing noises and even more urgent gestures. I have never been one for ceremony. I had no intention of performing any sort of ritual obeisance to the Sultana. It was against my principles, Don Octavio, which were still quite strong, for I was a very, very young man.

"I went so far as to shake my head, sending Bernard into a frantic pantomime of waving, pointing, and foot kissing. I shrugged, and he gave me up for dead, covering his eyes so as not to be witness to my impending and gruesome fate.

"Instead of visiting a terrible fate on me, the Sultana shrugged, too, and extended her manicured, ring-covered fingers. Feeling that she had offered a satisfactory compromise, I kissed her hand. She accepted my tribute, and Baba was visibly relieved."

Don Juan, remembering that tense moment, mopped

his brow with a lace handkerchief. It was growing warmer and warmer in the doctor's office.

"The Sultana spoke then, in a deep, attractive contralto. She said, 'You may rise. And you may leave.' I rose and I turned to leave. The Sultana grasped my hand as I began to step away. 'You,' she said to me, 'may stay.'

"The expression on her face, Don Octavio, was unmistakably alluring. She smiled what even the most ignorant and distracted lout would have had to recognize as a sexy smile. As Baba and the rest of her retinue retired from the room, the Sultana drew me into her boudoir and removed my wig. She took my earrings. She took my necklace. She took my veil and my bodice. She pulled me down onto her bed and kissed me warmly, even passionately, on my painted lips.

"Don Octavio, I began to develop a theory about the reason I had been brought to the Sultana. To my own surprise, my eyes filled with tears. Bootsie was equally surprised. She put her hand behind my head to support it and kissed me again, even more firmly than before. I burst into tears."

Don Juan shook his head. He said, with evident disbelief, "I still loved Doña Julia! The thought of loving another made me cry!

"The Sultana undid the remaining buttons of my dress. I sobbed even more loudly. The Sultana unfastened some laces and snaps. I wailed. She reached for a crucial fastener, then stopped and spoke again, in her thrilling exotic accent. She said, 'Do not worry, my little bird, I will do nothing to harm you.' I confess that I was still unable to control my emotions."

Jack felt an overwhelming urge to snicker. He maintained a serious expression with great difficulty.

Don Juan went on.

"Bootsie began to realize that I was not going to be that easy to conquer. She stopped peeling my clothes away and asked me what was wrong. I said, 'Your Highness,

I'm sorry but I love another!' This put the regal woman in a high dudgeon. She stormed to her dressing table and picked up a long, sharp, curved dagger resembling the deadly kris of Malaysia. She held the serpentine knife to my throat. She shouted at me rudely, 'Undress!'

"I wept even harder. She held the snake-shaped dagger to my throat. I bent my head back so that she could cut my throat more cleanly if it seemed necessary to her to do so. I said, 'Kill me if you must. I am prepared to die for my true love!' "

Don Juan paused to admire his own steely nerves and romantic fervor, pointing out to Don Octavio that such bravado was not easy to maintain with a knife at your throat, especially a serpentine knife. Jack nodded, remembering a few awkward moments when he first learned to shave himself. Don Juan held his finger across his own Adam's apple to indicate the angle of the knife. Then he went on.

"The Sultana groaned and turned the dagger point toward her own breast. 'Why, oh why,' she said, 'do I bother to go on this way!' She looked down at the sharp point hovering over her chest and reconsidered, saying, 'On the other hand, why fret over one skinny lovelorn boy?' She put the knife back against my throat. My eyes were blinded with big, round tears. I sniffled. I said, standing very still as she held that weapon against my neck, 'I am ready to die, for I could never live knowing that I had defiled the memory of that woman who brought my manhood alive and made it sing!'

"The Sultana said, 'It sings?'

"The Sultana thoughtfully removed the dagger from my neck, intending to press it once again to her bosom. She looked into my overflowing eyes, and, to the surprise of both of us, her own eyes began to fill with tears."

Jack had a good idea of the effect the Sultana's weeping would have on Don Juan. He remembered similar occasions when his own resolve was utterly dissolved by the salt flood of a woman's tears.

"I was prepared, Don Octavio, fully prepared to lose my life rather than debase my love. How could I ever be unfaithful to my dear Doña Julia, who had as good as given up her own life to love me? How? How could I bring myself to sleep with another after I had given myself, body and soul, to sweet Doña Julia? How could I forsake the purity of the love I shared with my flower, the innocent Doña Julia? How."

Jack, no stranger to the seamier aspects of self-justification, had a pretty good idea of how Don Juan might bring himself to do such a thing. He nevertheless permitted the boy to continue to tell him exactly how he performed the necessary contortionist tricks of conscience which would bring him to an obliging state of mind and body.

"I looked into Sultana Gulbeyaz's moist eyes, and found myself drawn to comfort her. I comprehended her sadness, her disappointment, her glorious face, her moist, inviting lips. I kissed her alabaster brow, just to soothe her, you understand. Then, to soothe her a little more, I kissed her nose, her rosy mouth, her magnificent neck. . . .

"Actually," Don Juan shrugged helplessly, "I was surprised at how easily the past can be overcome when the present requires our attention." A slightly reminiscent, even sentimental expression crept over Don Juan's face. "She was ecstasy."

"Several hours later, Baba returned to the Sultana's room to fetch me. As we strolled together through the gleaming corridors of the palace, I was eager to share what I had discovered with my new friend. I told him, 'You know, Baba, until this afternoon, I have always believed that a man could love only one woman. I have been badly misled.' In my enthusiasm, I had completely forgotten Bernard's own truncated manhood. He looked at me, as he was certainly entitled to do, with disillusionment.

"A deeply polite man, Baba did not correct my gaffe and I babbled on. 'It's absolutely incredible to me,' I said, 'that only a few hours before now, Doña Julia was the only woman who existed for me . . . and now there is the magnificent Sultana, Bootsie. What a glorious body, breasts like—' Baba, driven to uncharacteristic testiness by my ill-considered speech, and by respect for his employer, requested, at last, that I shut up. Who could blame him? I hadn't considered his feelings at all. I was just trying to understand what all this could mean."

Jack leaned forward in his chair and asked, "And what *did* it all mean, Don Juan?"

Don Juan appeared transported by rapture.

"It all means, Don Octavio, that . . . life is bountiful!" Don Juan sighed voluptuously.

"Baba did not take me back to my little room. He escorted me down labyrinthine ways to a completely different part of the palace. We soon came to a pair of huge steel doors, embossed with scenes of shepherds and shepherdesses and, of course, sheep. Two large, beefy, implacable, bald men with bare chests, lances, and satin culottes were guarding the doorway. The men stepped aside, the doors swung open, and inside"—Don Juan took a deep breath before going on—"there were women! Women as far as the eye could see! Beautiful, beautiful women, all as naked as the day they were born! Delacroix could have painted them! They were splashing in a pool; they were draped over chairs and sofas and the curving staircase! Naked arms! Naked legs! Naked bosoms! Naked everything, thousands of them! Their limbs glistened in the lamplight! Drums were throbbing in the background! I was struck dumb with amazement and awe."

Jack's mouth hung open. Professional neutrality had completely vanished from his face. Don Juan looked down modestly and said, "For the next two years, my days were spent with the Sultana."

Jack croaked, "And your nights . . . ?"

Don Juan shrugged. "My nights were spent with the fifteen hundred women of the Sultan's harem."

Dr. Jack Mickler rushed out of his office, propelled by the two lessons he had just learned. Life might well be bountiful! The past might be overcome! He did not even wave good-bye to Don Juan, who stopped to comb his hair in front of the mirror and toy with the chessmen before he left.

16

Marilyn

*

Don Octavio provides a princely feast
for his lady.

on Juan wandered back to his room. Jack rushed out to get a phone book, and came back to his office to make half a dozen calls in rapid order.

He then took up his recording mike and began, absentmindedly, to dictate his session notes. The words he spoke were the names of dire illness, human catastrophe. The tone in which he spoke them was lilting, almost musical, as if they were the lyrics of an old, old song.

"Narcissism, grandiosity, obsession, hysteria, severe delusional process, poor grasp of reality, inappropriate affect." Jack began to hear himself chanting; worse, he began to hear the disastrous words in a new light. As he went on, his tone darkened and his voice slowed until he was finally silent, watching afternoon shadows lengthen across the hospital lawn.

"Multiple personality disorder possible, mania, confused sexual identification, reactive psychosis . . ."

Jack finally packed his machine into its carrying case.

"Who am I making notes, for anyway? Bill the Toad? Paul the Warden? The Borough of Queens? The State of New York? Am I making notes for God? It doesn't matter.

By next Tuesday, nobody is going to care what I think. *I* won't even care what I think."

Jack shook off the thought of his impending separation from his job, and drove on home. What he guessed was Mozart's music rejuvenated him from the car radio. He was not actually listening to Mozart. His musical education was sadly inadequate. What he listened to was "Mon coeur s'ouvre à ta voix", from *Samson and Delilah* by Saint-Saens. Softly waked his heart, indeed. Puccini would have been just as suitable for his mood. Bach would have been fine. Barry Manilow would have been okay with him. He was as tender as a newborn calf, and as full of hope.

He stopped at a small neighborhood jewelry store on the way home. He had a few plans for the night. When he got home, Marilyn would surely have heard the message he'd left on the answering machine. "Get yourself dressed up, honey," he had murmured to the machine, "we're going *out* tonight!" He had an unusual moment of shyness, thinking of the message. Maybe he could have put that a little better. Too late, too late. Damn the machines, full speed ahead!

When he arrived home, he could see right away that his message had not gone over particularly well. He had meant it to be jaunty and festive. Marilyn had heard it as a command. She was in full wifely retreat, not even starting to dress.

"Where, do tell, are we going *out* tonight?" she mocked him, but she was teasing, not trying to hurt him. "*Out* to a pizzeria? *Out* to a staff party? *Out* to what? To where? Tuxedo Junction? What, baby?"

"Oh, Marilyn, we are going out to the prom, that's where we are going. Get out your white dress and your high heels, honey, we are going to howl, at the moon."

He was so nice and so funny about it, and so wrong about what kind of shoes she'd been wearing for the last five years that she could hardly stand it. She scrambled into her married-to-the-mob, mother-of-the-bride beaded dress, known by her to be Jack's favorite because it resembled the dress she had actually worn to the dance when Jack first fell for her. He thought it did, anyway. Marilyn thought to herself, *Senior prom . . . really, really senior . . . overly senior.* She did not think that the dress with its elaborate beading, low-cut back, and attitude, was very becoming. It was fussy, not her style, not anymore.

She was willing to humor him, though. When their children were at home, they used to eat out whenever they needed neutral territory to negotiate plans and renew their conversation. It had been a long time since they had done any negotiations or conversations, let alone promenades. Jack had grown remote. He seemed so exhausted, so distant. No interest in anything. She worried about him. No way to help him unless he asked her. Unless he wanted her. And even then, even then, how?

He got into his best suit.

He's needed a new suit for a long time, she thought. *He's going to ask me for a divorce or tell me he's dying. But at least he looks happy, so it probably isn't death.* She put on her makeup and coat, ready to go out to the car.

"No, no," said Jack. He looked positively bashful. "I ordered a limousine."

"This really *is* the prom, isn't it?" Marilyn had to laugh, but gently.

"Yes, it really is."

"Where's my corsage?"

"In the refrigerator."

She was amazed by his attention to detail. She normally had to arrange everything in their life together. She would never have expected him to remember that the flowers had to be put in the refrigerator. Not only had it been ages since their last dance together, it had been ages since their son's high school prom. Corsage in the refrigerator. It made her feel at a disadvantage to have him fussing about her for a change.

He actually pinned the flowers to her coat. Then the

limousine arrived, and they were soon lounging on the velvet pillows of the long, private car.

"It's so extravagant, Jack."

"It's so sexy, Marilyn." Jack looked sidelong at her, and they both laughed. "Champagne, too, Marilyn . . . just wait! I'll have you where I want you, me proud beauty." Jack twirled imaginary mustaches in a very bad imitation of lecherous villainy. They collapsed against the pillows, laughing harder than they had in a year or more.

Problems and news of the day vanished, masked by the smoked glass of the limo. The driver handled the long car skillfully, moving swiftly through the narrow streets of the old city. Music of a classical, romantic kind played softly, and they sat with their hands entwined, as if they were being transported on a magic carpet.

Soon they had arrived at the Ritz, the same hotel in which Don Juan had loved Victoria, his nameless conquest. They passed the same doorman, paused on the same stairs, crossed the same inlaid floor, and sat at the same table. Jack ordered a bottle of Tattinger's champagne and oysters Rockefeller for two. They silently toasted each other.

Marilyn was still dazed. She looked away from Jack's eyes, which conveyed nothing useful to her, except a hunger which had nothing to do with the meal they were about to order.

"So, Jack . . . what's the occasion?"

Unfortunately, the wine steward arrived with the champagne. The steward served the bubbling wine with all the pomposity wine stewards customarily employ for lovers and tourists.

"You're the occasion, my love."

Jack held out a small, velvet-covered jewelry box and snapped open the lid. Inside were two tiny gold-and-diamond earrings in the shape of doves. They were cunningly fashioned, the sort of jewelry that even a woman who cared little for jewelry would love on sight. Marilyn took them and looked at them carefully. She had no doubt, somehow, that Jack had selected them himself, not sent anyone out for them or let some salesman talk him into them. She was touched, but caught off guard. She fastened them into her ears.

"They're beautiful, Jack. They really are. You're sure that there isn't something . . . going on . . . here? Jack . . . what is up? Please. You've always hated, and I quote, fancy restaurants with all their pretense and over-priced tidbits with fancy names and unmentionable ingredients. When did you get a taste for oysters and champagne?" She was being brave.

"To you, my dove." Jack lifted his glass and toasted his wife.

"To me, then." Marilyn sipped her champagne and nibbled on her oysters. "Please, Jack. Let me in on the secret. What are we doing here?"

"There's no special reason, honey. Except for you."

A flower girl dressed as a gypsy, or perhaps she really was a gypsy, placed a bouquet of long-stemmed roses next to Marilyn's plate. Jack, with princely abandon, paid her and gave her a large tip.

Gypsies in restaurants always recognize the lover who will buy a flower for his lady. It is a professional skill of the flowerseller to read the signs of rising passion in the way a man leans toward a woman, in the way she glances at him and takes his hand in hers. Strolling musicians, not always gypsies, but with the same keen eye for the romantic moment, were also drawn to Jack and Marilyn. A band of enthusiastic musicians soon surrounded their table, serenading Marilyn with what they firmly believed was a traditional lovers' lullaby. Jack sent them all away. They were too raucous, too many for his tender mood. When the band went on break, they were replaced by a pianist. Jack requested a great many highly sentimental old piano favorites: "As Time Goes By." "Someone to Watch over Me."

Even "Stardust."

Marilyn proceeded to drink a lot of champagne.

They had creamy, tart lemon soup. They ate succulent grilled lamb with thyme and garlic. They enjoyed a pilaf of unusual delicacy and a Greek wine with sunlight implied in its taste. They consumed an eggplant dish as light as a souffle and bearing a slightly racy name. Flavors of cinnamon, of nutmeg, of olive and pistachios surprised and delighted them. They threw caution to the winds and ended with raspberry trifle, brandy, and strong real coffee.

As they sat there drowning in romantic music, consuming intricate and seductive food, drinking strong wines, and gazing into each other's eyes, Marilyn tried to tell Jack how worried she was. She spoke tangentially about the things, the stuff, the photographs, and papers, and sets of inherited dinner plates, and books she did not know what to do with.

She knew she was babbling. Lately she had become background music in his life. They no longer had the intensely passionate shared interest of children and building a home. Jack seemed distracted, no longer interested in making love or making a life with her. She believed that she no longer knew how to reach him. He looked at her with love and longing.

He took her hand in his. He raised her hand to his lips and kissed her hand with great tenderness and sensuous appreciation. Marilyn grew quiet.

She said, "This may be too much for me, whatever it is. Talk to me. Tell me." She was still afraid, of what she did not know.

Jack spoke slowly and looked into her troubled eyes.

"What's happening is that I have come to realize, after thirty-eight years of marriage, and kids, and grandkids, and the lives of our dogs and cats, after all this time and all the disasters and doubts and tears and carelessness and, in sickness and in health, you remember, 'til death do us part, I am absolutely crazy in love with you." This sounded pretty dire to Marilyn. It wasn't as reassuring as he had intended.

She said, "You are? You're not having some kind of nervous breakdown or affair with some bimbo or terminal illness or some damned thing like that? Are you?" She tried to make it sound like a joke but she failed to disguise her real concern for him, her fear for him and for herself.

He smiled gently at her. He was glad to know that she still cared about him. She was a beautiful woman, a wonderful woman, and she was still his. A miracle. What had he been thinking this past year? Why had he ignored her, avoided her body, avoided their shared life? Why had he allowed himself to drift, to get tangled in the currents, to get lost?

He told her what he wanted her to know.

"You are the most beautiful thing that has happened to me in my life. Without you, I would be one-quarter the person I am. I adore you, with my body I thee worship, I am yours, kiddo, for good and forever. I love you, love you, love you." Jack kissed her hand again, more passionately.

Marilyn said, "You do?" And before they knew it, they were flying out of the lobby of the hotel, into their magic limo, and over the bridges to home. And to their own bed, where they slept in each other's arms, as if they were together in a small boat on a large ocean. Marilyn found that she was still wearing her new earrings when she woke up smiling the next morning.

17

Paradise

*

Don Juan reminisces; Don Octavio acts.

Wile the anonymous Victoria continued to eat in restaurants alone, hoping for a certain young man to appear, and Don Juan slept alone in a narrow hospital bed, Dr. Jack arose from the bed of a beautiful woman. His heart sang on the way to work. It sang along with one of Marilyn's cassettes, one on which she had put some of her favorites. Jack had never listened to the tape before. It was just in the car, like the ice scraper and the gloves. He seldom played any kind of music in the car. Dr. Jack thought of himself as a strictly all-news, traffic, and weather every ten minutes drive-time listener.

This morning Dr. Jack almost felt like dancing as he hummed along, a rhumba, a tango, and then a samba. The tape played a Jimmy Buffet song about fruitcakes; Dr. Jack hummed along happily. Marilyn's efforts to bring him up to date had not been very successful. He recognized none of the music he heard. Now he loved it all.

Even the hospital could not bring him down this morning. He faced his office bravely and turned on his portable radio. He searched the dial for something like Marilyn's tape. He found a salsa station and, still hum-

ming, started to take books and things off the shelves.
Someone had helpfully provided a stack of flattened boxes
and gummed tape, a hint from the person who would get
his prime location after he left. Probably Bill, that twerp.
Jack did not even flinch at the thought of Bill's twerphood
occupying his beloved office. But he called a moving
company to arrange for the removal of his big leather chair
on Tuesday. No need for Bill's behind to enjoy that much
comfort. The desk belonged to the Borough of Queens and
would have to stay. He had spent countless hours at that
desk, teasing apart the puzzles of hurt human beings,
making telephone calls to other people's relatives, filling
out endless forms, and reading endless memos. He remembered when it was new and he had just been given this
nice big office. He had been so proud of it all. And believed
a lot of nonsense that he no longer cared to remember,
among it that he could make a difference for good. And
that he was basically right about most things. The thought
of the fresh new doctor he once was made Jack uncomfortable, and he turned his thoughts once more to the shelves
and their evidence of human occupation over time.

The knickknacks would have to go home with him.
The flute. The statues of the Mother Goddess. The
guitar. The photograph of his father. The photograph of
his son. Of himself and Marilyn when very young. Books,
oh, God, the books. Jack decided, though the decision was
like a knife through his heart, to give the books away
before he left. Marilyn was so worried about the stuff
accumulating in the basement, a ton and a half of books
from the office would not help matters. He would take
home just one small box of books. Maybe two. His favorites. No old texts or handbooks. Old casebooks, maybe.

The casebooks represented people he had helped or
failed to help. Many of them were dead by now. Others
were probably all right. For a lot of them, Jack's case notes
were the most permanent record of their hopes and fears.
The hospital had its records and kept things for a certain

amount of time. Jack was not prepared to entrust copies of his notes to the tender mercies of the vast, complex, and confused filing system of the State of New York. He would take the casebooks and their stories of human misery and hope along with him for safekeeping. Maybe someday he would read them again and make better sense of it all. Or he would shred them. But he wanted the option. He threw the notebooks into boxes.

His chess table and chess set would be the last to go. It meant so much, apparently, to Don Juan. Jack felt he had to respect that, but it also reminded him that he should repeat, with emphasis, his refusal to participate in any wager about treatment. He touched the smooth chess pieces. Only two knights, a bishop, and a queen were left on the desk. He turned away and started again to sort through his books. He thought about the problem of the boy as he packed. He came to no conclusion, either with the packing or the puzzle of Don Juan.

The young man soon appeared, right on time, still jaunty, ready to spin out more of his fabulous story. *Fabulous* thought Jack, *is a word describing illness only in my profession.* In the rest of the world, "fabulous" meant "great." Well, it might be a good thing he was leaving his profession after all.

Jack settled down for the afternoon's session. Don Juan noticed the boxes and the half-empty shelves. He prowled around, poking into boxes, peering at the shelves. Normally, Jack realized, he would be bothered by such territorial infringements. This morning it did not bother him at all. His office had already begun to feel temporary. The stuff had begun to turn into trash, most of it. *That's what happens when you have to leave a place*, Jack thought. *I hate leaving places.*

The young man began to talk as he prowled.

"Bootsie, the Sultana, was a most learned and accomplished woman. She taught me courtly deportment, providing a polish that my obscure village could never furnish.

She taught me to play the mandolin, to appreciate poetry, and to sing in tune, an art for which I had a natural talent. Bootsie also tried her best to teach me mathematics, but I could never ever master the basics and finally she gave up."

Jack thought of his own recurring struggle with his checkbook and smiled.

Don Juan smiled, too, remembering the matchless refinement of his education. "We spent the days in her bedroom, surrounded by trays of delectable food and the most exquisitely illustrated books on all topics, from navigation to cooking. We never neglected the arts of love. We explored Ovid and Catullus and the *Kama Sutra*. We studied her vast collection of Japanese pillow books. And she gently led me through the most subtle and delightful experiences, exploring many varieties of human knowledge and thought, engendering in me an appreciation I have never lost."

Don Juan's voice was filled with gratitude and admiration. Jack suddenly remembered that, although the Sultana was only twenty-six, to Don Juan she was an older woman. And he remembered, with tenderness, certain of his own early encounters with instructive older women.

Don Juan went on, "She taught me more than any other woman. I like to think that I may have taught her something, too. The gifts she gave me were more precious than gold, for I carry the memory of her lessons with me every day."

He took a deep breath. "So my days were filled with the most demanding, though charming, education. And my nights were spent within the very heart of feminine bounty, the sleeping quarters of the Sultan's concubines."

He indicated with a grand wave of his hand the huge extent of the dormitory. Jack could almost see the tangled heap of round and delicious femininity. In fact, he was pretty sure he had actually seen the exact picture Don Juan described on one of the visits he and Marilyn had made to the Metropolitan Museum with the kids. Jack didn't mind being treated to another view of it. He had always liked those alluring steambath paintings.

The don's voice dropped to a whisper, as if he feared to wake the women he remembered. "The young women slept with their delicate limbs tucked under them like feathered wings, a thousand bosoms beating for love like caged birds for air.

"Many and beautiful, they lay about in the deep silence of the enormous room like flowers in an exotic garden. Their collective scent was of jasmine, cinnamon, carnations. They were orphaned princesses, and they all knew how to dance. The sound of tambourines and finger cymbals, lutes and mandolins followed me everywhere. Olives and tangerines and dainty sweetmeats were provided to me, and stronger fare three times a day.

"One of the orphans, named Lola, would smile in her sleep like the moon breaking a cloud. I kissed her as she slept, to make her smile. Then I would move on.

"I crawled from bed to bed, from one image of loveliness to another. Among my favorites, certain of them were especially wonderful. Dheaudeau was as dusky as India and as warm, a kind of sleepy Venus of the subcontinent. She would sleep with her lips parted, her soft breath on my cheek as she pulled me to her without even awakening from her dreams. We would make love and she would never admit to waking until the very last minute. . . ."

Don Juan savored the memory of their games.

"And then there was Katinka, translucent, as if she were freshly carved from Parian marble. She would lie as still as a statue, in breathless, hushed, and stony sleep . . . white, cold, pure . . . and then, like Pygmalion's statue waking, the mortal and the marble still in conflict, she would timidly expand into life, an ice maiden no more.

"These women counted on me, Don Octavio. I say that some were favorites, but they were all favorites. They needed me. They needed me every night. Sometimes more than once every night.

"And at the same time, you understand, Bootsie needed me every day. If it hadn't been for the stalwart Bernard's help, I could never have managed to comb my hair, let alone maintain my other grooming and my costume.

"At the end of two years, I noticed that I didn't have the same enthusiasm as before. The ladies didn't complain, but I was, I confess, beginning to wear out. I remember one awful morning. I had been up all night with the orphan princesses, about six of them, when the Sultana called for my services. I hadn't even had breakfast. My wig was a mess. I could barely hobble down to the Sultana's boudoir. Bootsie murmured, 'Come to me, my little cockatoo,' and beckoned in the most alluring way, pointing to a particularly difficult passage of one of the more arcane treatises. . . . Well, my friend, when I tried to rise to the occasion . . . so to speak . . . I collapsed in exhaustion, limp as a noodle in the Sultana's gorgeous bed. That was the beginning of the end, Don Octavio."

Jack decided not to say that it happened to the best of men occasionally. He did not even mention the deleterious effect daily multiple relationships could have on a man's constitution. He merely waited for the rest of the story.

"Shortly after my embarrassing lapse in the Sultana's boudoir, I was walking down the corridor, my wig awry, my veil askew, my gait unsteady, accompanied by the faithful Bernard, when who should appear but the Sultan, followed by his extensive retinue.

"Bernard whispered to me, 'This could be a problem.'

"I looked around in panic for somewhere to hide. Baba grabbed my elbow and steered me straight ahead. 'Act like nothing is wrong. Behave!' I tried to look invisible but as the Sultan came nearer and nearer, I fell to my knees.

"It was not, you understand, an entirely voluntary fall. My knees were like jellies. My heart beat faster and

faster. The Sultan stopped in front of me. I could only see
his feet. I was afraid to look up. I kissed his plump toes,
the hem of his garment, his ankles, trying to work my way
past him. . . ."

Jack was startled. He thought, *The return of the Father
Figure! Freud may have been right after all!* He accidentally
chuckled, and didn't even feel guilty. Juan looked at the
doctor sharply. He preferred his doctors serious.

"The Sultan, rather than continuing with his progress
down the corridor, reached down and gently tilted my face
up so he could see it.

"He smiled. He winked. He said, 'You may rise, my
little dove!' and then he said something privately to Bernard and winked ominously at me."

Don Juan sighed. "Oh, well, all good things must
come to an end.

"Baba, sensing the danger to us both, and with the
help of the equally guilty Sultana, arranged for me to
depart poste haste . . . within that very hour. The ladies
of the Sultan's court came down to the dock to wave good-
bye. Bootsie's eyes were filled with tears. Baba's were, too.
They all waved their silk hankies and made the curious
ululation of grief and joy common to all that island's
natives at moments of strong emotion. It sounded to me
like the cheers of a vast throng as I whipped off my wig
and put on my mask, waving a fond farewell as the ship
pulled away from the dock. I kissed my hand to all the
ladies, and to Baba."

Don Juan sighed again, remembering the colorful,
affectionate crowd on the dock.

"No woman, Don Octavio, is like another, and yet
they are all the same. Each desires to be touched with
understanding, with compassion, encompassed by tenderness, guided slowly to explore the depths of her own
passion, nurtured and studied, adored." Don Juan went
on more firmly. "For this I have come to understand

above all else, Don Octavio. There is no loving without knowledge, none. I know . . . because I have loved them *all*!"

Jack said, "We have to stop now."

Don Juan said, "But we haven't gotten to the part about Donna Ana yet! I just wanted you to know that Donna Ana was not just someone I picked up on the rebound from Doña Julia! I'm not *finished*!"

Jack said, "Never mind. I would like to hear this all in its entirety but I have to do something right away. It will be all right." And he rushed out of his office, still talking over his shoulder to the don. "I'll . . . see you later."

Don Juan murmured, "Of course," and removed a chessman from the desk. Just two knights and a queen were left.

Jack, meanwhile, drove like a madman over hill and dale to his own home, where Marilyn was sitting at the kitchen table in her old pink shirt and denim skirt, reading the newspaper.

"What's wrong, dear?" she said, "This is awfully early for you, isn't it?" She sounded worried, startled, but gracious, as if one of her married children had popped up without warning.

Jack had a plan, but it seemed a little stupid to him now that he was actually home. He suddenly felt unsure of himself. He wanted to run out the door, back to the hospital instead of taking the chance. He didn't want Marilyn to laugh at him, though she must, he knew very well, know all about his follies and weakness by now. He stepped toward her.

She stood up, thoroughly alarmed by his expression. She thought he might be about to faint or cry.

"Marilyn . . ." Jack's voice faltered. Marilyn braced herself to handle whatever he would say or do.

"Marilyn, how would you feel about . . ."

"About what, Jack?"

"About coming upstairs with me?" he spoke all in a rush like falling down a well.

His request was so unexpected and such a tremendous relief that she took him by the hand and led him, without further ado or ceremony, to their bedroom, where her old pink shirt and denim skirt, her undies and her socks, joined his trousers and his shirt, his undies and his socks in a tumbled heap on the bedroom floor.

Jack and Marilyn made love with a poetry that had long been lost to them. Marilyn was enraptured by the tenderness with which he handled her body, the reverence with which he kissed her breasts, the longing with which he cradled her head in his hands. His hands were sure and skillful. He savored every nuance, every secret, every shadow, looking at his bride, his beloved, in the afternoon sunlight, in the bedroom which had become a garden, a palace, a monument to their love.

Together, they set sail on that ancient course from which no traveler returns unchanged. Nothing remained to hurry or trouble them except their own passions. By the time the sun set that evening, they were two old friends and lovers, serenely together in Paradise.

But still alive and eating popcorn in bed.

18

Retreat

*

*In which Don Octavio learns the value of
strategic withdrawal.*

When Jack arrived at his office that afternoon, he closed the door behind him. He wanted very much to be alone for a few moments. He noticed the three chessmen on his desk. "Today, tomorrow, and Sunday," he said to himself, "Not much time left, not much at all."

He started to put less-favored books in a box. He got a marker out of his desk and carefully lettered on the side of the box: DR. JACK'S FREE BOOK SALE! SPECIAL! TAKE ONE, GET TWO FREE! He carted the box down to the library and left it on a table. He did this twice more before the meeting. His bookshelves were almost empty. Only Byron, Berryman, and other lightweights left. He decided he would buy some new books and read them as soon as he was free of the hospital. It had been over a year since he had been in a bookstore, although Marilyn was always suggesting something for him to read. He needed new glasses, too.

Now, he thought, *I will have plenty of time*.

The thought didn't exactly thrill him.

He preferred to think about his patient. He even preferred to think about the meeting Paul had called on this, Jack's last full day of work. The topic of the meeting was to be the disposition of Don Juan's case. It was Paul's warped idea of courtesy to make him defend his opinions, even though Paul was just waiting for him to leave, and would then do whatever he wanted anyway. Paul planned the meeting so that they would have to decide the disposition before he had his last session with the boy this afternoon. Damn the man.

Jack continued to pack his belongings and swear under his breath.

The meeting was scheduled for just before lunch so that everyone would be hungry and restless. Jack hurried to get there but managed to be a couple of minutes late. His colleagues were already seated, gossiping about some female patient's medications. Jack settled himself in the last chair at the table, nodded to the assembled staff, and opened Don Juan's folder.

Head Nurse Alvira looked over at him kindly. She knew, after all these years, how much he hated these meetings. She tried to encourage him, to send him secret signals of support and affection. He did not receive them, but sat there morosely as Paul nattered on, refusing to get to the point.

Alvira said, "And now the moment we've all been waiting for . . . Don Juan De Marco! The World's Greatest Lover! Take it away, Dr. Jack!"

Jack flinched. He wasn't here as Dr. Jack, Super-Shrink, Bad Boy of Meeting Land. He admired and loved Alvira, but this time she had made a mistake. It was no time for joking around, not this time.

All eyes in the room turned to Jack. He looked around the table. Most of the doctors were half his age. Half of those were women. Some of them were allies but most of them were not. He composed himself, assessed the odds, girded his loins, and spoke with as much authority as he could muster, which was a lot, though he seldom displayed his ability to dominate a room.

He said, "As of this minute, I can't be sure about Mr. De Marco. We'll have our last session together this afternoon.

I think it's going to be the important one. I'll know more when it's finished."

Paul looked closely at Jack, surprised at his serious tone. Jack was aware of Paul's scrutiny, but refused to look back at him or alter his course in any way. He went on.

"I've got a hunch about this next session. I have a feeling I'm making real progress with this kid. He's starting to open up, getting a lot more grounded in reality. His interactions are starting to be more reality-based than they were when he arrived. He's moving quickly, Paul. You know as well as I do that some adolescents respond to treatment very rapidly, especially from an acute situation." Jack was trying to dredge up the kind of language and attitude which would be most plausible to Paul and the unwrinkled young doctors.

Alvira saw what he was trying to do. She also saw that it had the same chance of succeeding as your average snowball in Hell. She was right.

Paul said, "Jack, this isn't a treatment conference. This is a disposition conference. We have to decide what to do with the kid on Monday when his ten-day paper expires. Do we ask the judge to commit him? Do we let him go? What, Jack?"

Jack continued to control his temper, responding with cool, professional, aplomb. Never mind the volcano seething inside him. He had to stay nonconfrontational. Never mind what he really wanted to say, which would have left Paul in psychic tatters, or what he really wanted to do, which would have left Paul in physical shreds. The moment called for poise. Jack cloaked himself with a reasonable manner.

"I said," Jack replied, carefully, "that this afternoon

might be a definitive session and I will not know until after I've assessed his condition afterward."

"He's a suicidal patient, Jack. He attempted to kill himself."

Jack tried not to grit his teeth. He relaxed his jaw with an effort.

"Give me a break, Paul. He's not a suicidal patient. It was a flamboyant gesture. Acting out. He made sure he was in a public place so that he knew somebody would call the police. He didn't ingest anything. He didn't cut himself. He didn't cut me. He didn't jump, and he had an hour to do it before I arrived. What he did, Paul, was get in the bucket and come along quietly. That's what he *did*, Paul."

Paul was not convinced.

"You aren't suggesting, are you, that we ought to release him? That's not what you're saying, is it?"

Jack wrestled with his decision, thinking of his next move, trying to get past his own desire to squash Paul like the irritating little insect he was. The room was very quiet, waiting for Jack to speak.

"No," Jack said, "no, I'm not suggesting that."

Paul was headed for the barn at full gallop.

"Okay, then obviously, first thing on Monday, we have to get a circuit court judge over here to take care of it." He was speaking to his secretary officiously, the way he always spoke to her in these meetings. He didn't look at Jack as he kept on dictating to the woman.

"And, also on Monday, we'll have to transfer the patient over to a new therapist." Paul looked up with a swarmy expression, fawning at Jack in a downright disgusting way. "Since that will be your last day, Jack." It was a pointed remark, meant to hurt, but Paul tried to cover it up with a very unconvincing smile, trying to get away with one last dig at Jack without appearing . . . mean.

Paul turned to his favorite flunky.

"Bill, are you up to it? Do you think you can handle him?"

Bill looked a little dubious, but knew exactly what was expected of him. "If he's on medication, of course I can handle him. No problem, Paul."

Paul almost shivered with the pleasure he felt at grinding his heel into Jack's pride. He was completely unaware, of course, of any pleasure in the proceedings. His shiver was unnoted by any of his conscious gray matter. Only the unconscious, reptilian parts knew what a really good time he was having.

"He'll be on medication." Paul looked over at Jack. He wanted more. He wanted everything. He wanted Jack to assume a submissive posture. He wanted groveling and he wanted it immediately.

Jack did his best imitation of a beaten man. He wondered whether it really was an imitation. Maybe it was the real thing. He didn't think so. He thought of the whole procedure as strategic withdrawal.

"Okay." Jack spoke directly to Alvira. "Start him on Mellzac, a hundred milligrams, Q.I.D."

Alvira, startled, looked up from her notebook, in which she had written the medication order. "That's a pretty large dose, Jack . . . is that right, a hundred milligrams four times a day?" She was giving him a chance to correct himself.

"He's going to need it. It ought to put a big smile on his face. Bill can begin to decrease it once he's stabilized and his terror subsides." Jack paused. Since he was apparently going to lose this argument, he might as well have some fun. "And Bill realizes that he no longer needs to be afraid of being attacked by his patient."

Bill squealed, "Paul, make him stop." Jack smiled benignly. Paul motioned to Bill to be quiet. Alvira looked at Paul for approval. Paul nodded. Alvira spoke to Jack, carefully, not sure whether the medication was a joke. The dosage was huge.

"Okay, Jack, what's the story, here? Is that what you really want to give De Marco? If he refuses, should we restrain him and give it to him by injection?" She sounded disillusioned with Jack, with Paul, with all of them.

Jack replied to Alvira, apology in his tone. "Yes, the dosage should be exactly as you transcribed it. About the restraints, absolutely not. You won't need them. Don't worry about it. I'll get him to take the medication. Now, if that's it, I've got to get back to my office."

The sky outside suddenly seemed gray, leaden. The nice spring day had turned back into winter. Jack's heart felt slightly bruised, though he still had a few tricks up his sleeve. He was suddenly tired, not sure whether he had the strength to prevail or even to go on with the afternoon. He rose to leave.

Dr. Paul Showalter stopped him.

"There's just one more thing, Jack." Showalter called toward the door, "Okay, we're ready!"

The door opened instantly. Gloria and someone Jack did not recognize marched toward him. They were holding a sheet cake. Icing camels and gray icing pyramids and plastic palm trees adorned the top of the cake.

Red plastic-looking icing script spelled out GOOD LUCK, JACK! For some reason, there were lighted candles on the cake. More people Jack didn't know, and some that he knew and liked, and some that he knew and disliked, crowded into the conference room. Someone had brought dip and celery. Someone had brought fondue in a hotpot. Someone had brought sparkling cider in a bottle supposed to look like champagne.

There were suddenly big plastic bottles full of off-brand soda pop, a plastic ice bucket full of ice, and plastic glasses on the credenza. Potato salad. Deviled eggs. Potato chips. Cheese balls. The conference table was covered with food and paper plates. Jack could see that Paul was already pouring a little vodka into his ginger ale. He also realized that Alvira was holding his right hand and Gloria was holding his left arm. They were standing very, very close to him, like mamma elephants trying to hold up a failing baby.

He had been so concentrated on Don Juan's fate and the miserable meeting that now he felt as though he had fallen through a trapdoor into an alternate and bizarre universe. He felt that if he tried to speak, he would stutter. He felt that if he tried to walk, he would stumble. He leaned a little on Alvira, and breathed as deeply as he could. He should have anticipated this. But they usually did retirement parties, big ones, off-site. Catered. A piano player. Tuxedos, even. He had let them all know that he didn't want any party. So this was what they did instead.

Alvira let go of his hand and patted him on the back. Gloria let go of his arm and kissed him on the cheek. Then they both moved off and left him standing alone. Someone handed him a paper napkin with a smily face on it and a plastic cup full of something or other. Someone else handed him a piece of cake on a paper plate. He sat down at the table. People went around him to get to the potato chips. Paul and Bill were huddled in a corner, smirking. A woman that he had once taken to dinner, and who once figured in his admittedly meager fantasy life, was telling a friend of hers about her wedding plans.

Alvira brought him a plate of nibblers—olives and cheese, and crackers. She said, "Bear up, honey, the worst is yet to come." He groaned. The room was hot, stuffy. Gloria came to sit beside him.

She said, "I got a postcard from Rocco yesterday. He's going to Istanbul, he got a job on a cruise ship." Jack rolled his eyes. She went away.

A man arrived with whom he had enjoyed a few chess games, a sort of goofy stringbean with a weird sense of humour. He came over, flashed a toothy, evil grin, and said, "The pallbearers will be along in a minute, Jack."

Just then six more men came into the room with balloons. He did not know them. They began to sing "For he's a jolly good fellow, for he's a jolly good fellow . . . nobody can deny." They lined up and a young woman in a hooded raincoat and a mask came in. *Oh no, oh no,* thought Jack, a smile pasted to his unwilling face, . . . *a stripper. Oh, no.*

The young woman put a tape player on the table and removed her boots. Her toenails were painted gold. She started the tape player. Bouzouki music poured out, plaintive throbbing beats of an Eastern drum, flutes. She cast off her raincoat to reveal a full belly-dancing costume. Her skirt and her veil were made of some gauzy, shimmering material. She tucked the end of the veil into a gold belt low on her hips. An iridescent jewel was glued into her navel. Gold coins were sewn to her bra and her belt, and large gold hoops hung from her ears. She took up her finger cymbals and began to move sinuously in front of Dr. Jack.

The dancer's face, though hidden by her mask, seemed to convey a mysterious, even serious, rapture. As the music quickened, the dance became more explicit and the dancer removed her vail, shimmying across the carpet to drape it over Jack's shoulder. She was not, Jack could see, a teenager, nor was she skinny. Substantial was more like it.

He had expected the woman's performance to be a joke, embarrassing to watch. It was not. She danced with passion, transforming the conference room with her full female dignity and beauty. She knelt before Jack, bent backward almost to the floor with her hands weaving in the air above her breasts, then turned over and lay stretched out on the carpet as the music ended. Everyone in the room applauded, and some of the men cheered and whistled.

She rose gracefully, retrieved her veil, pulled on her boots, put on her raincoat, and left without a word. Jack felt he had been strengthened and warmed by her dance, by the rhythm of her swaying hips, by the music. Whoever had hired her, whoever had thought up the idea in the first place probably meant it to be embarrassing to him. So he surmised until he looked at Alvira. Alvira was obviously pleased with herself, an expression of studious innocence vying with laughter. Alvira! Alvira had suggested the dancer! What a sweetheart! What a woman! Jack bowed to her from across the room and blew her a kiss. She laughed and waved back at him.

Paul, who was cross because the Borough of Queens was unlikely to approve of a *danse du ventre* in its conference room if it ever found out about it, tapped with a spoon on the table.

Everybody stopped talking. Paul said the words somebody had to say on these occasions. Pleasure to have worked with you, valued colleague, will miss you, success in whatever you decide to do, don't be a stranger, Token of our esteem . . . blah, blah, blah. Paul handed over a small package, and with a wholly false smile, said, "Now let's hear from our retiree. . . . Speech! Speech! Speech!" To Paul's surprise, Jack rose without protest or reluctance.

He spoke simply, mainly to Alvira, but also to the others.

"I have shared many moments of happiness and sorrow with you over the years. We have fought each other and comforted each other and gossiped about each other and cared about each other like members of a village. We learned the names of each other's spouses and children. We attended funerals together and danced the polka together and ate lunch together and worried about patients and worried about each other.

"Now that it is time for me to go, I know that I will always remember the people here with love and affection, and I will miss you all very much."

There wasn't a dry eye in the house.

19

Doña Inez

*

Don Octavio learns some of the truth.

Jack went back to his office and closed the door. He felt worn out and old. The meeting had been disastrous and the party . . . well, the belly dancer was nice. He opened the package. It was wrapped in metallic *bon voyage* paper and tied up with curly black ribbons. Some joker did that, probably Paul.

Inside the package was a fancy velvet box. Inside the fancy velvet box was a gold pocket watch with a thin gold chain. Inside the gold pocket watch with the gold chain were engraved the words "Today is the first day of the rest of your life" and the dates of his employment like the dates on a tombstone. *Bang, bang*, you're dead, Jack, rest in peace. Trouble our meetings no more. Haunt somebody else. The watch was, itself, handsome and had cost a lot. Paul had probably taken up a collection, extorting donations from people Jack had never met. He thought maybe he could get a jeweller to erase the engraving. But even so, he seldom wore a vest, and never in his life had he ever carried a pocket watch. He thought of certain pictures of quaint Edwardians and their pocket watches. He read the engraving again, groaned, and put his head down on the desk.

There came a knock on the door. He shouted, "Come in!" without raising his head. He expected Paul or Alvira or Gloria or one of his old friends, ready to do farewell scenes. He was wrong. He heard a strange rustling of long skirts. The door closed gently, and a gentle female voice with a charming foreign accent said, "Good afternoon. I hope I'm not intruding . . . I am Mother Michael Ann. In my former life I was Doña Inez, the mother of Don Juan De Marco and the wife of the famous swordsman, Don Antonio. You are, I presume, Don Octavio? May I sit down?"

Jack looked up at her. His eyes were bleary and tired and he rubbed them, but still he seemed to see a stately nun in an old-fashioned habit. Her garments were classical, severe, but the stuff of which they were made was rich, and the tailoring exquisite. The rosary she wore at her waist appeared to be made of precious dark stones separated by sparkling crystals. The crucifix was made of finely wrought, heavy gold. Jack remembered Don Juan's description of the ornate church in the dusty village. He noticed that her right hand was adorned by a signet ring much like Don Juan's, and her left ring finger carried a wide wedding band.

She looked a lot like Don Juan. In fact the theme of his graceful good looks was fully stated in his mother's oval, fine-boned face. When he grew older, he would surely look very much like his mother. Jack judged that she had to be at least forty if she were Don Juan's mother, but her face was unlined and serene. Her hands were well-shaped and the nails had been shaped and polished to a pearly shine. Her eyes were clear and candid. She stood patiently while Dr. Jack collected his wits.

Though speechless with wonder and shock, Jack finally remembered his manners and motioned her to a chair. She sat down gracefully, her silken habit flowing out around the chair. She said, "You seem to be surprised by my clerical attire. As my son probably told you, I retired to the convent shortly after my husband died. Eventually I went on to take the vows which joined me to my church and my sisterhood forever. My son's friend Doña Julia soon joined me at the convent of Santa Maria, where I now hold the position of mother superior. It is a small charitable order. Together, Doña Julia, now Sister Gabriel, and I deliver food to the poor, tend the graves of our dead, and pray for the peace of all souls."

Jack tried to bring this apparition into focus. There was something almost sensuous about the woman's smooth, placid face surrounded by fluid silken cloth. He found himself rather at a loss, but fascinated. A faint fragrance of smoke and sandalwood, like incense, seemed to waft toward him from her hair. He shook his head, as boxers do when they have taken a ferocious blow to the head.

"Excuse my rudeness, Sister. I was not expecting any visitors and I was resting my eyes when you arrived. Would you like a glass of water? I am very interested to meet you, and I want very much to begin discussing your son's case with you. But I am afraid I will have to begin with very elementary questions. For example, may I ask where your convent is located? Perhaps in Mexico?"

"Thank you, I do not care for any water at this time. And, please, I am an abbess. You may call me 'Mother.' But to answer your question, yes, my order has its home in Mexico. San Luís Coatzacoalcos, near Izucar de Matamoros. Perhaps you have heard of it?"

Jack shook his head, which was spinning with wild conjecture. What if Don Juan's story had been true, not in a mythical sense but in plain and honest fact? Dr. Jack, SuperShrink, had just agreed to pour enormously potent drugs into the boy's system. "No, Sister, I did not know the name of the village, nor its location in Mexico. Forgive me my ignorance."

Doña Inez—Mother Michael Ann—forgave him his ignorance, though she suspected more was going on than a simple deficiency in geographic knowledge. She said, kindly, "Not many have heard of our village. It is very small, very far from any busy city."

Jack couldn't bring himself to call her Mother, but he spoke very politely. "How did you know your son was here?"

Doña Inez noticed the omission of her honorific, but ignored the rudeness of his unadorned question. She was sure he didn't mean to be rude. She was a very forgiving woman. She smiled at him, a mother's smile at one of her wayward, confused children.

Jack felt sharply and suddenly the absence of his own mother. That was why he couldn't bring himself to call the nun by her proper title. He had not addressed anyone as "Mother" since the day his mother had died, without even speaking, of a broken heart. At least that is what Jack thought, though the doctors spoke of congestive heart failure and pulmonary distress and other things.

He had not been able to think about his mother, he had been so engulfed in grief about his father, and then the shock had turned him away from the thought of her. He thought, *I still feel like an orphan.* The old songs were right, there was nothing like a mother's love. But when it is gone, there is nothing that can replace it. Half the people in his hospital were there because they had never been mothered, or had been severed from that love too early, or were too hurt to be able to nourish themselves with whatever mothering came their way. *I am one of the lucky ones*, he thought. *I have had so much love. I will be all right.* It was the first time he had admitted to himself that he had been so seriously wounded by the death of his mother. He had lost the thread of the nun's story in his moment of revery.

"Excuse me, Sister, I missed what you were saying. . . . Tell me again how you knew to come here?"

"My son had one of your nurses, Alvira Alvarez, I

believe, call the archdiocese in Mexico City and they contacted me. Of course, I came here as soon as I could."

Jack nodded. Her answer was plausible enough. He found he did not quite believe her yet.

Doña Inez gently prodded the man with a question. "What seems to be my son's problem?"

Jack waved his hands in the air. His mouth opened and closed like a goldfish's. No words issued from him. The thought of describing Don Juan's problem to this nun was more than Jack could handle at the moment. Not a prudish man as far as language was concerned, he nevertheless felt a sudden rush of very inconvenient shyness and modesty. He could think of no suitable words to describe her son's problems. Speechlessness was not a condition to which he was accustomed. It alarmed him.

His wild gestures and evident inability to talk alarmed the mother superior in turn.

She said sharply, "Is it serious? Please tell me!"

Jack pulled himself together. "No, no, Sister, it is not. Don't worry. All will be well. But we do need to talk."

He drew a deep breath and plunged into the topic of Don Juan's troubles. The mother superior concluded that he seemed incapable of addressing her correctly and decided not to instruct him any further. She waited while he framed another question. The man seemed to have some sort of stammer or other speech difficulty. His face was quite red, she noticed. She hoped he was not on the brink of apoplexy. She attempted to reassure him with an angelic smile, but he only grew redder. Finally, he seemed to catch his breath and spoke almost coherently.

"Sister Inez. Did you notice as your son grew up, anything unusual about him?"

The abbess smiled knowingly and affectionately. "I most certainly did notice."

Jack was encouraged by her reply. "How would you describe it?"

The abbess looked at him kindly. The man understood very little, but he had a good heart, she could see that.

"You may not realize this, as you are not, evidently, conversant with Roman Catholic decorum. I have taken vows similar to the marriage vow. I am now a Bride of Christ, pledged to chastity for the rest of my days. My devotion to that chastity commands that I maintain a certain modesty of speech and thought, Don Octavio. It would be best, I am sure, if my son describes what is special about him. I am certain that he will give you every detail you could possibly desire."

Jack almost whimpered out loud at her graceful rejection of his question, but he did not give up.

"Well, Sister, perhaps you would tell me this, if I am not being too personal: Why did you enter the convent?"

She bowed her head and replied piously: "The decision was not mine. I was called by God."

Dr. Jack's knowledge of the convent, vocations, and such matters had mostly been acquired from an old Audrey Hepburn movie. He wished he had paid more attention to it. He fidgeted in his chair, trying to come up with an acceptable way to proceed, while the nun sat as still as cool marble, her hands folded out of sight in the apron of her gown.

Jack was game, if nothing else. He fought to find a way around her obstinacy. He said, "What about this? To protect your modesty, you need do nothing but nod your head yes or no. I will recount the information your son gave me, and you can just indicate whether you can confirm it."

The nun said nothing and did not look at him. Even though she did not respond, Jack began to summarize Don Juan's story. "Your son, who is named Don Juan De Marco grew up in Mexico. Since he was an infant, or at least since he was two years old, women have been strongly attracted to him. In fact they could be described as throwing themselves at him with reckless abandon. At the age of sixteen, he had an affair with a young married woman, the woman you mentioned, his friend, Doña Julia."

Jack stopped for a moment.

"I know these matters must be painful for you to contemplate. But in order to help your son I need to have some precise information. I am relating to you what your son has told me, and I need to verify what he has said." The nun was still silent and unmoving. Her eyes were hidden by the shadow of her wimple. Jack kept talking.

"Doña Julia's husband, Don Alfonzo, a much older man, according to your son, killed your husband, Don Antonio, in a duel. Then your son killed Don Alfonzo immediately afterward in a second duel. Your son was driven to kill by a murderous rage, which he soon regretted. He held himself at least partly responsible for the death of his father.

"You recognized that your son needed to get away from the village, and therefore, arranged to have him travel to Cadiz on a tramp steamer. What happened after that, we do not need to discuss at this time. For now, I need only to know about your husband, Don Juan's father, Don Antonio, and about the man your son killed. I am sorry, but I need to know about your relationships with both men, and with your son."

The nun was not angry, but she was adamant. "As I said before, Don Octavio, I think it would be far better if you would discuss these matters directly with my son. As I have told you, my vows to God do not allow me to discuss certain aspects of my past with any but my confessor."

Jack regarded her scruples with impatience. He had never had much use for religion of any kind, having seen, in the course of his professional life, some of its more harmful effects on the weakened and vulnerable mind. And in spite of his recent attack of shyness, he regarded modesty as, in general, only a shield for deception. He understood that this was not the case with the woman before him. Still, his voice was sharper and harsher than he realized when he spoke again.

"Madam, with all due respect to the vows you have undertaken and the sanctity of those vows, you must realize that your son is currently locked up inside a ward of this state hospital. It is not, in my opinion, an environment which is likely to do him much good unless we can understand his history and what has brought him here into my care.

"This coming Monday, only two days away, he will have a hearing before a judge to determine whether he should be committed to this institution for the next twelve months. If he is dangerous to himself or others, then the place for him is certainly here. In order, Madam, for me to tell whether he needs such close supervision, you must give me some clear, unequivocal, precise pieces of information about his past." Jack had actually, in his perplexity and distress, found a perfectly acceptable form of address. He waited for her reply.

The mother superior sat up, if anything, straighter in her chair and fingered her beads. Her voice was remote and invited no argument. "You will find the answers you need within my son, Don Octavio."

Jack lost his temper and all sense of decorum. He leaned over his desk and almost shouted at the nun. "Madam, what I will find within your son is several hundred milligrams of Mellzac, a potent antipsychotic drug. I have looked within his mind since he was brought to this hospital, and what I have found is that he is in a great deal of emotional pain which he is attempting to hide by a pose of heroic grandeur. I have seen within him pain of such an intensity that he tried to take his own life, which is why he is in this hospital. He threatened my life, too. His attempt was serious enough to involve several fire companies and a squad of policemen. He could have been killed by the policemen at any time if he had carried a gun instead of a sword. Next time he might. So I have to know the source of his pain and I have to try to help him, but I absolutely, Madam, must have your help." Jack felt suddenly that he was guilty of exaggerating, even lying, but he wanted, with a reckless intensity, to get through her calm façade. *I would shake her*, he thought. *I would kiss her violently, I would weep on her shoulder, I would throw myself at her feet here and now if I thought it would do any good*. His train of thought shocked him. He felt that he was blushing and fell silent, waiting for her reply.

She said, hesitantly, "I love my son and would do anything to help him. But what you wish me to remember and to tell you, a stranger, these are matters of this world, a world I have renounced, Don Octavio, not of the spiritual world I have chosen. It is not that I will not speak, but that I cannot."

Jack moved to the chair next to her. He spoke urgently to the spot where her whimple hid her ear.

"I don't think I've made myself clear. I have been to see your son's grandmother, Catherine De Marco. She told me that neither you nor your son ever lived in Mexico. She says that you met Tony, your husband, in Queens, where he worked in a dry-cleaning establishment. And that, until very recently, she saw her grandson only once in her life, in Phoenix, Arizona. She also says that five years ago, in Phoenix, your husband died in a car crash. In addition to that . . ."

He was carried away by the sound of his own voice, until suddenly he realized that she was weeping. Tears streamed from her downcast eyes and fell onto the cloth of her robe. She did not even move to hide her face or wipe the tears from her cheeks. They simply fell, as if she scarcely felt them. Jack's heart lurched as he remembered his own mother crying in just that unprotected way when his father lay dying. Jack looked away, to hide the tears which sprang to his own eyes. He offered her a tissue which she took but did not use. She held it, unaware of it, unaware of the tears, only aware of her own sorrow.

Jack's voice was full of genuine regret for having caused her pain. He said, 'I'm sorry. I don't mean to hurt you. But I must ask you to try to understand, Sister. I need to know the truth."

She turned toward him and looked into his eyes, seeing the unshed tears and the desire of this baffled but goodhearted man to help her son.

She spoke gently, as if to a child. He felt waves of affection radiating from her, as if she had taken him to her bosom to comfort him.

She said, "Do you know the Bible, Don Octavio?"

Jack's religious education was sketchy. "A little. I know only a little."

"Corinthians?"

Jack said, "Not really . . ."

" 'The things which are seen are temporal; but the things which are not seen are eternal. . . . We walk by faith, not by sight.' "

The woman looked at Jack with pity and tenderness. She was a very beautiful and wise woman, with great knowledge of love and loss. Though chaste and celibate, she knew and loved the struggles of men to find happiness. Though she knew such struggles were doomed to failure on this earth, she believed that the effort was noble and admirable, and would find a reward in Paradise, where all struggles would cease and human failure would be impossible. She considered how to help the man who had asked for her help.

She spoke to him with regret and affection, like a good mother to a cherished man who is struggling with the realities of life and love.

"The truth, Don Octavio, is what is inside us. I cannot help you find that."

Jack reached toward the nun and began to thank her, to ask her forgiveness, but before he could speak, Doña Inez, Mother Michael Ann, rose from her chair and left

Jack's office. Jack went to his office window to regain his composure and stare at the daffodils.

The sun had broken through the earlier clouds. He saw Don Juan's mother skimming over the grass, her fine silk habit streaming out behind her like a cloak as she danced. She had taken off her black shoes and stockings. Her bare feet seemed hardly to touch the ground as she stepped lightly on the lawn of the mental hospital. Jack felt as though he had been daydreaming. Surely the mother superior would keep her shoes on. He wondered if he was mistaken, but when he looked again, there was no nun on the grass. Dr. Jack went back to packing books. He mulled over his regrets about the encounter with Don Juan's mother. He knew now that he had pushed too hard and might never get another opportunity to speak with her. He felt that he had botched a chance to learn what was real about Don Juan, and yet he felt curiously refreshed and joyous to have reclaimed the memory of his own mother. He absentmindedly threw books in boxes and began to plan his final session with Don Juan.

20

Donna Ana

*

In which Don Juan and his doctor share mysteries and masks.

D r. Jack's mood was oddly reflective and peaceful. He thought without bitterness about his parents' deaths, and contemplated his own without fear. "I will do the best I can," he reassured himself. "A man can do no more." It was the sort of platitude he had used on his strife-torn patients almost every day for thirty years. But now he thought that it might be true, even for himself. *Retirement is a kind of death,* he thought. *I am saying good-bye to all these familiar things and people. I have only one task left, and that is to take care of Don Juan. Then I must learn to live for myself, without any structure. As if I were a child in the summertime and Marilyn, my darling wife, were my playmate. But with no one to tell us what to do or call us in to supper at night. I have spent so much time tangled up in schedules, so many hours driving back and forth, so much energy in evading and complying and calculating. All of that is over.* He shivered, as if a cold wind had touched the back of his neck.

He didn't want to think any more about his own immediate future. He turned his attention instead to the problem of his last session with Don Juan. In some sense, the boy's story was true. Exaggeration and confusion entered into it, no doubt about that. But it also contained the profound truth of a man's discovery of the miraculous powers of women. Dr. Jack sorted through what he had learned or guessed, and decided the best place to start was with Don Juan's family configuration.

Don Juan's attachment to his mother, and the terms with which he described her implied to the doctor that the boy still thought she was perfect, immaculate, almost a virginal figure. Whether the emphasis on chastity were cultural, personal, or the result of incomplete maturation, it might be the key to the whole situation. Dr. Jack decided to explore that aspect of Don Juan's belief system.

When his patient arrived only a short time later, Jack noticed that the young man's days in the hospital had been rough on his grooming. For the first time, Don Juan's beard looked scruffy. He was in need of a shampoo. His cape was wrinkled, too. He moved at once to the window of Jack's office and stared out at the lawn. Jack went to stand beside him. Doña Inez was cavorting, once again, on the grass, unshod. Jack knew himself to be unqualified to comment on the rules of holy orders, but he was pretty sure that a barefoot romp in public was not completely orthodox for the leader of a convent. On the other hand, it was certainly a charming sight.

Her son, too, was enchanted by the sight of Mother Superior Michael Ann tripping lightly over the lawn. He glowed with filial delight, as he turned to Jack for confirmation. He wanted the doctor to share the delightful vision of his mother tripping lightly over the fresh spring lawn.

"See, Don Octavio, isn't she exactly as I described her to you?"

Jack did not want to join Don Juan in praise of his mother, not in this session. He had to move quickly.

He said, "Yes, she is, Don Juan. An extraordinary woman in every way. I had a long conversation with her earlier today. She told me, among other things, that your first love, Doña Julia, has become a nun at the same convent where your mother is the abbess. I wonder how you feel about Doña Julia's taking the veil?"

Don Juan shrugged. He said, "I heard that she had turned religious. I have nothing against that, for her or for my mother. If it makes them happy, so be it." The young man's voice was indifferent, bored. He turned reluctantly from the window and headed for the couch, where he sat down rather gracelessly, not with his usual athletic and remarkable ease, but as if his back hurt. He examined his slightly unkempt hands while he spoke, avoiding Jack's eyes.

"I told my mother she could go back home today, but I'll miss her. She has a way of putting me in touch with what's real."

Jack recognized the tone of a patient trying to please a doctor by using the jargon. He was surprised to hear it employed by Don Juan, who had never before indulged in such prosaic language. Jack sat down and looked at the boy, trying to decide on the best way to approach the next topic. He reluctantly decided to administer a brutal verbal shock, hoping that Don Juan might defend himself in a way that would allow the doctor to understand him better. If sufficiently surprised, he might even be reattached to reality.

Jack said, in his most neutral tone, "There is something, Don Juan, that I must ask you. It is regarding matters both painful and delicate, and touches on your deepest feelings of respect and love, and you may think of it as offensive, but still I feel it is my duty to ask." Jack concentrated on keeping his voice absolutely clear of any emotional shading as he probed the most sensitive of boyish secrets, a youth's intense, idealistic love for his mother.

Jack asked, "Why are you so certain that your mother was not having an affair with Don Alfonzo?"

Rage boiled up in the young man, as Jack suspected it might. Don Juan jumped from the sofa and began to pace, growing more angry every second. His fingers felt for his missing sword. His face grew red. An ugly scowl disfigured his normally pleasing appearance.

Jack felt sorry that he had trampled on the boy's feelings to such an extent but he persevered. "Married women do, for one reason or another, sometimes love men other than their husbands. Look at your own experience with married women, for example with Doña Julia and the Sultana. It is not unthinkable, to me, at least, that such a thing could have happened in the case of your mother's private life." Jack waited for the boy to speak.

Don Juan snarled at Jack. "My mother was *not* having an affair!"

Jack, still maintaining his neutral tone, said, "You can understand how the thought occurred to me when you told me how your father died. You said that he looked into your mother's eyes, suffered a moment of distraction, and then was killed. I keep wondering what he saw in her eyes."

Jack thought of the tears on Doña Inez's cheeks, as she cried so bitterly in his office. He was sorry he had to speak so bluntly about such a kind and loving woman. But her son had rejected reality for some reason. Unacceptable disillusionment about his mother could drive a man to hide from reality. Jack went on, allowing his voice to become more gentle, more fatherly, though what he had to say was harsh. "I've never been clear about what your mother was really saying when she cried out. 'I will lose both of them,' that's what she said. But did she mean 'both my husband and my son', or did she mean 'both my lovers?' "

Don Juan shouted at Jack. "My *mother* was *not* having an *affair!*" The young man prowled around the office, pushing away the thought that his mother could have betrayed both his father and himself.

Jack waited to see how the don would handle the idea. He suggested, "You understand why one might suppose—"

Don Juan lost his cool manner completely. He screamed, "*Shut up! Shut up about my mother!*" The boy grabbed a vase from the shelf and threw it as hard as he could past Jack's head. It was impossible to know whether the boy meant to hurt the doctor or missed him on purpose. Jack was reaching for the panic button under his desk when the boy began to talk to him again. Jack did not press the button, which would have brought security to the office within seconds, but his hand stayed on it.

The young man's voice was full of hatred and scorn. "My mother did not use me to cover up an illicit carnal affair! What vile filth! What coarse, crude lies! My father saw in her eyes only the purest, most spiritual, most divine love any woman has ever given to a man. You filthy liar! You think I don't know what's going on with you, but I do."

Don Juan sneered at the doctor, who remained alert to the possibility of violence. He remembered other times when he had to call for help: the fragile young woman who had demolished his office, the old man who had pushed him over and broken his wrist; the businessman who had tried to jump out the barred window. He knew that provoking a depressed patient to anger could be dangerous, but it could also be the first step to healing. Depression was often only a scar over rage. As he had on the cherry picker, Jack concentrated on making himself a pool of calm emotion, slowing his breathing and even his heartbeat, like a hunger stalking shy game. His face was a monument of peace as his patient spewed forth his contempt. The young man's voice was full of hatred and pain, and he looked into Jack's eyes as if what he saw there was unbearably ugly. He hissed at Jack as if he were delivering a curse, "You need me for a transfusion because your own blood has turned to dust and clogged your heart."

Juan moved toward Jack, who did not flinch, but kept

his eyes on the young man's face and his hand on the panic button which would summon orderlies bearing restraints. Don Juan leaned over the doctor and spoke with deadly, quiet intensity. "Your need for so-called 'reality' will kill you. It will destroy you, this foul desire to see only a rotten, depraved world where love is dead, where mothers betray their sons and husbands, where there are only whores. Your vicious lust to paint God's beautiful world with poisonous falsehood will fill your own veins until all the life in you is gone, replaced by the dry residue of sophists and clerks, the drab colors of prison walls."

Don Juan's voice was no longer that of a wounded boy, but the proud, singing voice of the bard through whom the god speaks.

"My world of sparkling perfection is no less real than your base, polluted earth, Don Octavio, except that in my world, you can breathe! The green, sweet forests of my world contain the pearly innocent young dryads and goddesses who would be glad to love even you if you could only open your eyes. But you have sewn your own eyes shut and can remember only the sight of the vile pit of despair into which you have thrown all that is inspiring your world."

Once before Don Juan had held a knife to the doctor's heart. When they were on the cherry picker together, he had spared the doctor. This time, with no weapon but his own youth, Don Juan showed no mercy. His intent was to inflict pain. His voice was heavy with the scorn of the beautiful young for their scarred and weary elders. "Why do you wish to assassinate all beauty and all true love? What happens to your soul when your hair grows gray and thin? Does your spirit grow gross and infirm along with your wornout body? Why do you want to pervert love and suck it bone dry of all its glories? Do you envy those who feel the pangs and pleasures of passion? Why do you bother to call what you do by the name of love anymore?

Jack pulled his professional skills closely around him,

placating the raging boy by admitting him to the reality of a grown man. He spoke quietly, and from the heart. "Perhaps you are right. My world is not perfect. It contains infirmity and fear and death and old age. But it also contains love. And it wants life to continue, not to end with one loss or a thousand, but to keep on trying, no matter how hard that may be."

Don Juan went back to the window to gaze out to where his mother walked, slowly now, in her clumsy nun's shoes, over the cold earth. He was no longer filled with rage, but with sadness. Jack saw how thin the boy's shoulders were, how very young he looked, how alone.

Jack said, very softly, "I don't know if you realize it, but this will be our last session. I'm retiring on Monday. I have already said good-bye to my life here at the hospital. On Monday you will become the patient of Dr. Dunsmore. I'm sorry."

Don Juan regretted his outburst, but his pride made it difficult to apologize. He went back to the sofa and sat down quietly. Jack could see that the storm was over.

"I, too, am sorry, Don Octavio. I will tell you about Donna Ana, how she took away my heart and gave me reason to die. You can then decide if I should be set free. Our wager will have been completed." He took both chess knights from the desk, leaving only the queen.

Jack walked over and took all the chess pieces, the queen and all the men on the table, and packed them together into their tooled-leather carrying case. Jack did not want to remind the boy in words that the wager did not really exist because he had never agreed to it, but the gesture clearly meant the end of games, and the don's face showed that he understood, though he did not accept, Jack's demonstration.

The doctor felt overwhelming regret, knowing that he had already agreed to medicate the boy and that Don Juan would surely never pass the scrutiny of a judge on Monday in his current state of bedraggled grandeur. Don Juan would more than likely have to remain locked away for a year or more. It seemed monstrous that the boy still believed that he could talk himself out of the hospital by charming the doctor.

Jack, nevertheless, wanted to know what the boy had to say. "Please . . . tell me about Donna Ana."

Don Juan patted his hair, trying to regain his normally suave manner, and lowered his voice to a persuasive, melodic note, as he began to tell the story of his love for Donna Ana.

"On the second day after I sailed from the Sultana and all those wonderful orphan princesses, my ship was caught in a terrible storm. The vessel was buffeted by huge waves, taller than the smokestacks, taller than the flagpole outside your office. The wind howled and the waves lifted the ship out of the water. The ship buried herself deeper in the water after every mountainous surge had passed. Passengers and crew rushed around, screaming and looking for ways to save themselves. It became obvious even to me, no sailor, that the ship was going down. I jumped overboard and eventually secured a small rowboat, in which I drifted in the burning sun for days, or at least hours. I caught a flying fish in my hands and ate it raw. Sharks circled my little boat. A blessed rainstorm came at last and I caught fresh water in my hat and my boots. Morsels of raw fish and sips of dirty water sustained me as I drifted on the briny deep, carried I knew not where."

Don Juan's beguiling and soothing voice washed over Jack. Don Juan looked at Jack to see how this was going over. Jack appeared to be happy with it.

Jack's alarm at Don Juan's earlier agitation subsided, as Jack pictured to himself the blue sea and the boots full of water. It occurred to him that he was going to miss these tales of splendid, extravagant adventure. A longing washed over the doctor, a yearning for strong experience, for the colors of rare flowers and music and spicy food and perfumed tea, for foreign ports and the sound of unknown languages spoken in old, cobbled streets.

Don Juan's seductive voice filled the room with sunlight and blue skies. "Finally I landed, half drowned and castaway, on the island of Eros. We will call it Eros; it matters not which ocean on which I drifted, whether the Aegean, the South Seas or the Caribbean."

Jack drifted, too, considering the freedom which would go with his loss of a job, considering the currents of fate and losing track of what Don Juan was saying. Then he picked up the thread of the story. A woman had appeared.

". . . She was seventeen, with hair like golden wheat rippling in the wind, glossy as a raven's wing. Her eyes were golden, too, touched with fire like opals, like a cat's eyes in the dark. Her brow was white, untouched by the cruel hand of time or worry. Her cheeks were like the rising sun, blushing and delicate. And her lips, oh, her sweet lips, sweeter than wine or ripe cherries, her lips were divine portals to bliss, Don Octavio! And when she found me like a piece of salt-soaked driftwood on her beach, she raised me up like a fallen god, as if I had washed into her arms on streams of divine grace, not by the accidents of wind, water, and weather.

"That was how I found my Donna Ana."

The boy was like a weaver, making patterns for the doctor to admire. Jack's own concerns receded as he was carried into the intricacies of Don Juan's story.

He sighed. "There are on this fair earth some dull, misguided men who cannot believe that a single soul, born in Heaven, may split into twin spirits and fall like shooting stars to earth, where over oceans and continents, great cities and desolate wastelands, their magnetic forces will finally bring them together again, merging the lorn, lost pairs again into a perfect unity. Some do not believe this. But I know it is true. How else to explain love at first sight, which lasts through all eternity, except that it began in eternity and only corrects a regrettable error by Fate?

Such a love enveloped my Donna Ana and me from that first moment on the shore."

Jack felt he had entered a strange mental state of lightness and balance, as if he were a fencer or an archer, poised in the moment. He also felt as if Marilyn's hand was on his shoulder, her kiss on his brow. The two of them were surely like twin fires, grown together until neither existed alone. He thought, with no regret, that even if he began immediately he would never be able to build with anyone else the love he shared with Marilyn. There simply wasn't time. It took a long time to love a woman. He smiled at the thought of the two of them as shooting stars, racing each other through the atmosphere to some unknown harbor.

Don Juan was not unaware of the effect he was having on the doctor and he approved, relaxing as he spoke melodically of true love.

"We were convinced that there was no other life beneath the sky but ours. We believed that we would never die and that the gods would always smile upon us. We kissed and embraced each other as if each moment were our last and as if there could be no end to the time we would share."

Jack could almost hear the surf and the rustle of the wind in the palms, smell the spice winds and feel the girl's hair as it brushed his cheek. Sunlight streamed in his open window and warmed his face. He could hear, in the distance, a bird singing its heart out.

Don Juan's eyes seemed to be focused very far away. "Our kisses were delicious but, to my surprise, they were exceedingly pure. Though we spent every moment together, we were not united in technically complete bliss. The situation was novel and piquant but also frustrating, and I did all I could to persuade her. Morning and night, over our dainty meals of island vegetables, in our shady bower, on the picnic table, I never ceased to plead. Finally, one night, as we lay naked in our hammock,

Donna Ana spoke into my ear. 'Yes, my darling,' she said, 'I will be yours completely. But you must promise me that we will be together for all time, that we will live here on this beach forever and that, should cruel circumstance ever part us, it will be to this very bower on this very shore that we will return, each of us alone to wait, if necessary, through all eternity for the other to return.' What reply could I make, enflamed with love and so near to my goal? I said 'I love you.' She said 'Promise me.' I said, 'I promise,' and so we swore a solemn oath that bound us to each other and to a certain course of action in case of barbaric accidents of fate. Then we made love again and again, renewing our vows with every kiss, every caress. It was a honeymoon made in Heaven."

Jack considered that most honeymoons were overrated. Usually the participants were tired and nervous and much too self-conscious for the bliss they expected. But he granted the possibility of an unflawed vacation in Paradise, with love as the main attraction. He began to form a plan that would take him to just such a condition. His plan became firmer as the don continued to paint a portrait of uninterrupted joy.

"I was as happy as it is given to any man to be on this earth, Don Octavio. We spent the next morning sitting on the beach, watching the sharks grazing in the lagoon, counting the waves, our arms around each other. Day after day we spent fishing and lounging on the beach, making love without a care in the world. We fixed ourselves delicate snacks and built exquisite sandcastles. The weather was cloudless and cooling breezes refreshed us every afternoon. She wore only the barest minimum of clothing, and I wore only my mask and a loin cloth. I never removed my mask, but I was tanned all over, kissed by the sun and Donna Ana as thoroughly as a man has ever been kissed.

"I was as blissful, dare I say it, as an infant at the breast. As far as I was concerned, God could have re-opened the Garden of Eden right there and sold the snake to a traveling circus. Not a rotten apple in sight, not a worry in the world, my friend. All my apples were silver and gold.

"It was, of course, at that precise moment that her questions began."

Jack smiled to himself. There were certain parallels with his own experience.

"She asked me why I wore the mask. Would I be wearing it throughout our life together? What was the vow I had sworn regarding the mask? Would it not represent an inconvenience and embarrassment to our children should we ever have any? Why couldn't I just tell her, and then we would talk it over? What a good time she was having!"

Jack and his patient exchanged knowing looks, males unable to figure out the perverse wish of women to know awkward facts to insist upon having all the data, to the destruction of happiness. *Just like psychiatrists*, thought Jack, *just like me*.

Don Juan made a gesture of comic hopelessness. "I had no choice but to relate the sad tale of my affair with Doña Julia and its result, and my vow to cover my shame with my mask. Donna Ana quickly deduced that she was not, as she had supposed, my first love."

Don Juan sighed an exaggerated sigh of wronged innocence. "My beloved Donna Ana told me that she would make a valiant effort to accept that she was not the absolute first woman ever to enjoy my favor. Then she begged me to tell her, with the same honesty, how many others there had been. I tried to evade her questions, but she persisted, promising that no matter what the answer, she would not blame me, if only I told the truth.

"That would have been a very good time for me to lie."

Don Juan and Jack both regarded the virtues of the prudent lie.

The young man explained his failure to assess the situation correctly. He said, sadly, "Truth, Don Octavio, is a terrible habit, more difficult to break than the chains of the worst addiction and so, sadly, I told her the truth.

"I said, 'Including you, Donna Ana, there have been, exactly, one thousand five hundred and two.'"

Don Juan put his hand to his head, as if he had a sudden headache.

He spoke with dry humor. "I could see that this was a sum substantially greater than the one she had in mind. It was not possible for her to overlook such a large number of women. Though she had promised to hold me harmless if I would only be frank with her, she immediately blamed me for my past. She could not forgive my retroactive infidelities, even though all of my sinful lapses took place before I ever met her. There was no logic in the woman."

Jack was alert again, though still relaxed, as if he rested on a beach full of sunlight, where young lovers had troubles of the sort that could be cured with a kiss. Jack was in a romantic haze, and he was enjoying it. He considered that even under the worst circumstances, lovers need not end up like Romeo and Juliet. He thought of the terrible fights he had had with Marilyn after that trip to Rhodes, when she was grieving for her mother. He had said too much, then, without doubt. There were many times in a man's life when he ought to temper the truth with prudence.

In the meantime, Don Juan was describing a classical scene, depicted on ten thousand Greek vases. "She ran from me, like a gazelle from the panther. I ran after her, calling her name. I caught her and held her to me. I told her that the heavens and the earth were made for us. I called her my sweetheart, my darling. I said, 'My life sparkles in your eye like a gemstone, like the vital spark of my inmost being! I am only a pale reflection, only a wraith, only a shadow on the sand without your love.' I fell to my knees and prayed to her as if she were a goddess.

"But my words were of no use. For the pain I had caused her, I removed my mask, my face naked and covered with tears. I offered to make the mask and my sorrow hers forever, along with my body and my soul. I told her that with the mask I gave her my shame, my history, my undying love."

Don Juan began to pace around the office again, maddened by the memory of his grovelling attempts to appease Donna Ana.

He said, "I renounced even the memory of my first love, Doña Julia, swearing never to entertain even so much as a nostalgic passing thought of that woman. Still my darling was unmoved. My true love's heart had become like flint, a field of sharp stones on which at every moment I suffered additional wounds. It was awful, Don Octavio. If you have never suffered at the hands of a woman you love, you will have no idea of the heartache I endured."

Jack thought that Don Juan might be embellishing the truth just a small amount, but he was in no mood to point this out to the boy. Dr. Jack was, on the contrary, feeling extraordinarily fine, refreshed, as if he had been meditating. Or praying.

Don Juan resumed pacing, his arms folded over his heart, as though to protect it from further harm.

"The next part, Don Octavio, is hard for me to relate, even to you, even though I have revealed to you many secrets I would not have spoken to a lesser man. Donna Ana turned on me, Don Octavio, like a harpy, like a fury, like a witch. She shrieked with laughter. She pointed her finger at me as if it were a razor-sharp knife.

"She said to me, her devoted lover, 'Have you enjoyed my performance, my sweet naive little fool? Did you really think that I had fallen for you? Did you believe that I loved you madly, passionately, eternally? Really? Did you actually think you were the only sailor ever to wash up here on my shore, or who was pushed into this port by a deceptive wind, or was left behind when his ship sailed off without him? Did you really think you could satisfy me with your weak, pale imitation of love? You poor booby!

You probably even thought I was a virgin, didn't you? Well, for your own information, there have been so many damp sailors washed up on my beach that I stopped counting a long time ago.' She strutted about, hissing wrathfully, an enraged and dangerous swan, but when I looked into her eyes, I seemed to see a bird with a broken wing, deceiving the hunter by a ruse. Of course, I did not believe her for a moment. She was making it all up."

Jack thought that, for a young man claiming such vast experience of women, Don Juan had an almost fantastic devotion to a notion of their purity where all other men were concerned. It was a subject Jack did not care to raise, considering the don's earlier reaction when his mother's chastity came under question. He decided to grant Don Juan an undisturbed faith in Donna Ana's virginity, even though he himself had private doubts.

Don Juan suddenly sounded tired, as if a real sorrow had stepped in to obliterate his dreams of perfect love and heroic quarrels. "It didn't matter, Don Octavio, that I knew she was only trying to hurt me, and was as innocent as a snowflake. In those few brief moments of conversation, I had lost the only woman I can ever really love. She walked off wearing my mask on her face and my heart on her sleeve. I later learned that she had sailed off on the yacht of an American photographer. I myself hopped a freighter a few days later, hoping to track her down. I returned to the neighborhood of my grandmother, and pursued the serious work of trying to locate my lost sweetheart. I had no luck at all until, quite by chance, I ran across a centerfold with her picture. I had no doubt it was her. She was still wearing my mask."

Don Juan shook himself as if to remove the cobwebs of the real world. "My lips still feel her kiss—a long, long kiss of youth and love and beauty—all concentrated like the rays of a burning sun into one focus, kindled from above—the blood's lava flowing, the pulse ablaze, an eruption of heart and soul and sense into one, tremendous, flaming cataclysm!

"She fills my head night and day, Don Octavio, until there is no way to separate us." Don Juan walked to the window and gazed out at the sky, which had grown dark while he talked. Evening was upon them.

Tears flooded Don Juan's unhappy young face. He moved closer to Jack, as if to find shelter from the night. He said, "Who am I?"

Jack looked at the weary face of the boy and felt his own eyes sting with tears—whether for himself or for the Don, he could not tell. He stood up and put his arm around Don Juan's thin, narrow shoulders.

"Sit down and rest yourself, my young friend. I will tell you what I believe. Yes, I do believe. You are the gallant Don Juan, the greatest lover the world has ever known. No woman has ever left your arms unsatisfied, and you are on a quest to find the perfect love of the adorable Donna Ana."

Don Juan looked slightly surprised.

"And who are you?" he asked Jack.

"I am Don Octavio del Flores, wed to the beautiful Doña Lucita, the light of my life. You have seen through all my masks." Jack laughed happily, kindly. "But I will tell you something else, straight from the heart and man to man. You don't know everything there is to know about women and you don't know everything there is to know about love! There's a lot more! A lot more! You are the great Don Juan, but you are only a boy. Wait, just wait, until you have held your woman in your arms after she has given birth to your child! Wait, until you have passed many quarrels, many heartbreaks, and are still alive, still together, and she is still a mystery waiting to enfold you! Wait until you face death together like two warrior comrades! Then come back and tell me that nonsense about only the young can love! You ain't seen nothin' yet, kiddo!"

He patted Don Juan on the shoulder and told him they had to leave. Jack felt just fine, and even Don Juan had stopped crying. The two of them went on down the hallway, a new lilt in Jack's step, a new firmness in Don Juan's.

They stopped at the medication station. The nurse on duty, not Gloria, not Alvira, but one of the very young ones, helped him with his request while Don Juan waited for him. Jack returned with a cup of water and some pills. He held them out to his patient.

Don Juan said, "But I thought you believed me, Don Octavio!"

"I do," said Jack, "I believe that you are Don Juan. But there are a lot of people around here who don't. And I don't run the place. You need to take the pills that will be brought to you four times a day, without fail and without argument."

Don Juan began to understand. He examined Jack for signs of lying or cheating. He found none. He said, "Then, my dear friend, I will do as you ask."

Don Juan held out his hand and Jack poured four capsules into his palm. Don Juan swallowed the pills without even resorting to the glass of water. Then he smiled.

Jack said, choosing his words with care, "A man may have many truths within himself. The truths he cherishes may burn with the light of a huge bonfire, so that he feels they must shine forth from his eyes for all to see. A man may feel a great desire to speak those great truths in a voice like a great golden trumpet. But it becomes a man well to keep his deepest truths to himself, hidden in his heart for only God and his true love to share. I tell you this, not so that you may abandon the wisdom of your own soul, but so that you may ponder on it, and someday use it in a moment of great need. Guidance will come to you if your love is strong. There is no need to speak further. I must bid you good night and wish you godspeed."

They shook hands warmly. Don Juan went back to his room and Don Octavio went home to Doña Lucita.

21

Earth

*

Don Octavio contemplates his future.

The next morning was a chilly but glorious Saturday, marred only by Jack's perplexity about his last case. Jack did not care to dwell on it. He intended, instead, to dwell completely in the present moment, a morning in which he had tangerines to eat and delicious, illicit, caffeinated strong black coffee to drink. He sat at the kitchen table while he sipped the coffee and peeled the tangerine. He was wearing a bathrobe Marilyn had given him several years ago, which he had never before worn. It was silk paisley on the outside, warm terry cloth on the inside. Too fancy, he used to think. He was aware of his own naked body under the robe, its weaknesses and its surprisingly strong desires. His gray chest hair curled against the terry cloth. He pulled the robe closer around himself.

The kitchen was full of sunlight. Their ginger cat lay on a patch of sunlight on the table, where she knew she didn't belong. Instead of shooing her off the table, he scratched her under the chin, petting her until she purred loudly.

He looked out the kitchen window.

He could see Marilyn digging in the garden, pulling out dead weeds, turning over the dirt with a trowel. He noticed even from the window that all the paint was worn off the wooden handle of the trowel. Marilyn had worked on this garden for as long as he had worked at the hospital. It was spectacular, and in the summer had the controlled wildness of an English garden. She grew roses and lavender, tomatoes and moonflowers, azaleas and lemon balm, marigolds and clematis. Moss, the first green velvet moss of early spring, grew between the bricks of the garden walk. Silver grasses grew beside a small fish pond. It was a magical garden and Marilyn worked on it nearly every day from the time the last snow melted to the end of autumn.

A little packet of nasturtium seeds lay on the ground beside her. The seeds wouldn't sprout unless the ground was still cold when they were planted. Marilyn had told him that. She had told him a lot that he hadn't listened to, but now he found that many things she said were echoing in his mind, not just the content but the sad tone.

She looked fragile and intent out there on the chilly ground, trying to encourage life. Might be too late. The moment for the nasturtiums might have passed already. You had to nick the seeds with a knife to get them started, the coverings were so tough. The peonies were already coming up. The winter had been hard on the azaleas. She was worried about the forsythia. It was growing into the neighbor's yard. The winter had also been hard on the rabbits. She hadn't seen a single baby rabbit yet. There was no end to the number of things Marilyn had told him. Or maybe she had said those things in some other spring. He had understood very little about the garden, especially in the last few years. But he could still try.

Jack got dressed in his good blue jeans, never worn before, bought by Marilyn, and a new white shirt. He put on the straw hat he used to wear back when he used to mow the lawn himself, before he had asked Marilyn to hire some kid to do the yard work. There had been so many things he'd given up without thinking. He was suddenly aware of how patient Marilyn had been with him, how persistently she had tried to reach him, while he was off in his own world. He'd been an oaf. He shook off the uncomfortable thought of his cloddishness and went back to the kitchen. The cat rolled up to him, looking for more attention. When she didn't get it, the cat jumped down from the table to go look for a better spot.

He fixed a cup of coffee for Marilyn. He picked out a pretty mug decorated with apples and pears. He even remembered to put cream and sugar in it. He put the mug on a saucer with a small cookie and took it out to her. He sat down on a garden chair near her. She got up slowly, stiffly, with a little pain from her knees. She came and sat near him on a low garden wall. She took off her gardening gloves, which were caked with mud, and took up the cup of coffee, warming her hands as she looked into his face.

It was, in a way, more familiar to her than her own face, yet there was, today, something surprising, different. She was about to comment on it, when Jack began to talk.

His voice was different, still, calm. "It's strange," he said, "but suddenly I have this need to know all about you."

Marilyn laughed. "Oh, Jack, I'm the broad who's served you coffee every morning for thirty-two years."

"I know that. I know all the facts, Marilyn. I know about the coffee cups, and coffee spoons and the children and the years that we have measured together. I just can't seem to connect them properly, I can't seem to realize that they happened to you and me. It's as if time were pleated, and all those facts are in the folded part. All I can see is you and me, sitting here after a lifetime of love, and I don't know anything about you."

Marilyn looked down as Jack reached for her hand. She said, "What do you want to know?"

Jack covered her fragile hand with his large, clumsy fist

in the tenderest of gestures. When he spoke, it was in a low and gentle tone. "I need to know all about you. I want to know what you hope for, what you fear. Dreams that you have lost along the way, while you were taking care of the children, taking care of me. I want to know all that you can tell me, that I should already know, but that I never noticed because I was too busy thinking about myself."

Marilyn began to laugh, not a spiteful laugh but a big hearty belly laugh, startling in such a small woman. She took back her hand and held her middle, convulsed with mirth.

Jack felt confused and a little hurt. "What's so funny?"

And then, suddenly, she started to cry, the locks were opened and the water poured forth. "I thought you'd never ask," she said, "you've acted like a zombie for a year, Jack. I've been so scared. I thought, I really did, that our life together was over. I didn't know how to get your attention. You seemed to be a million miles away. . . ."

She cried some more. He gathered her up into his arms and patted her back, holding her close as she sobbed against his chest. They sat entwined like that for a long time in the garden. He smoothed her hair and dried her eyes with his shirttail. They both grew calmer, and after a while they went back into the house and shared a tangerine.

Jack went off to the hospital to pack up more books and trophies and statuettes and papers. Marilyn went back to work in the garden. She put a fresh cassette of her favorite songs into the portable player. Violas and harpsichords and grand baroque trumpets accompanied her work. The sun was warmer on her back than it had been earlier. She hummed to herself as she folded the big nasturtium seeds into the earth.

A slender, young, emerald-green grass snake, alarmed by the disturbance she was making in the garden, sped away from her hand toward the daffodils. After an instant of surprise, Marilyn smiled benevolently at her fellow creature and went on digging.

22

Marilyn

*

*In which Don Octavio and Doña Lucita
decide what to do next.*

As Jack drove home through the darkened streets, the
car stuffed with books and things he used to love,
he thought about his long career of bringing people to the
point of understanding what they needed to do. He
thought of the patience, the long hours of attentive silence
it had taken, every time, while he listened and reflected
emotions and steered. He had been, at his best, an unseen
ocean current for those frail human ships, taking them
home.

He realized that he had never once applied the same
methods to his family. That was perfectly proper, but now
there was something he wanted Marilyn to do, and it
wasn't going to be easy to ask her. He would have to
prepare the groundwork very carefully. What he wanted
was to abandon the material life they shared so that they
could explore the other lives that they might be neglecting.
He wanted to sell or rent the house, pack up the furniture,
go away to strange shores and explore alluring new worlds.
He wanted to drop out of all the habits that had been fine
for them while he was Mr. Doctor and she was Earth
Mother to the Brood. But now they were just two people

who needed to find a new way home, a new home in each other's hearts. But it was hard for a woman to give up her domain for the utterly unknown. He would have to approach the topic very gently indeed.

Jack was hungry when he got home. Marilyn fixed him a chicken salad sandwich and sat down with him at the kitchen table. She was dressed in a deep pink velvety exercise suit. The velour seemed to glow and so did her clean scrubbed face. Her hair was tied back with a cherry-red ribbon and she wore a light perfume with hints of citrus and cinnamon. He noticed none of the details but recognized with awe that, at fifty-eight, she still looked to him like the most desirable and lovely woman he had ever seen.

When Jack had finished eating the sandwich, he reached over to take her hand. His voice was serious, the same sonorous tone he would use to convince his colleagues of the importance of a theory.

"I think we should talk, Marilyn. I think it is time for a major change in our lives together. Please hear me out. I know it is going to be a big shock to you, but I want you to listen to me."

Marilyn's spine stiffened. She stood up. She said, "Stop! Stop right there, Jonathan L. Mickler! We have determined that what is eating you isn't a terminal disease, unless you count middle-aged angst as fatal. It isn't a dimwitted blonde that's addling your wits, according to your account. It isn't anything except the prospect of retirement, and you're getting panicky! You said yesterday you wanted to know all about me, and there you are, my darling fool, about to tell me *again* what you want. Well, come into my parlor, sweetheart, and I will tell you all about it! March!"

She stood there like an angel with a flaming sword and pointed to the living room.

He marched. He sat down. She paced, he thought, like a lioness. A lioness in a cage. A terrible chill came over him, and he had all he could do to keep quiet, and not jump up and beg her to be merciful. Fat lot of good that would do. *I'm dinner. I can tell. Might as well lay down now and get it over with.* Jack hoped it wouldn't hurt too much.

When Marilyn started to speak, her voice was low, so that he had to lean forward to catch her words, but she gained power quickly. Soon her words were all too clear to him.

"We have been together thirty-two years. We have been in this house almost as long as that. We have buried and mourned our fathers and our mothers. We have waved good-bye to our children and held our grandchildren in our arms. You bet your sweet ass it is time for a change, my darling." Her voice was dry, devoid of sentiment or any romance as far as he could tell.

Jack's heart felt as if it were breaking. He had left everything alone too long. It was all too late, she was going to sail off without him. He stifled a moan of pain, and put his hand over his eyes.

She said, "Jack, listen to me. Stop whimpering. This is going to hurt me more than it does you." She did not smile, but there was a hint of mirth in her voice. Jack clung to that hint as though it were a raft.

She prowled around the room. "You have told me that you wanted to go out like Halley's comet. Well, yes, maybe we will.

"But maybe, just maybe, you aren't going to be the pilot on this asteroid. Maybe you get to be the first interstellar passenger. Look at me while I talk to you. This is important. I want to be absolutely sure you understand me."

Jack raised his agonized eyes to her face. She nodded, like a master chef approving the main course. *I'm dinner,* Jack thought again. *Really barbecue this time.*

"Now this is a great house, Jack, don't get me wrong. It is historic and beautiful and quaint and all of that. It also has six bedrooms and two acres of backyard. You told me that you knew the facts. I don't think you do. I think you haven't faced one single fact since you decided to retire.

"The furnace, for example, is twenty years old. The house needs painting, inside and out. The front steps are crumbling. The chair you are sitting on is, in a word, shot. The carpet is worn almost through in spots. All of the appliances are the exact same age, and they are all going to go at the same time."

He said, "Marilyn—"

She said, "Hush! The six bedrooms are full of wornout furniture. The bookcases are overflowing. I have five complete sets of formal dinnerware and, at last count, four dozen wineglasses, though neither of us can drink much anymore. We have not only hundreds of long-playing phonograph records, but original one-sided seventy-eights with Enrico Caruso and Harry Lauder singing their little hearts out."

She took a deep breath. She didn't want to hurt him, but she needed to tell the truth. Her voice became much gentler. "We have all the photographs from, by my count, six different households, thousands of photographs. Some of them, we don't even know who those people are! Your mother and my mother, your aunts, my grandmother, you and me, even our children, we have all kept newspaper clippings and *Life* magazines and love letters and foreign coins and souvenirs and postcards and *New Yorker* magazines and Civil War medals and baby shoes and now they are all here, and I don't know what to do with them. They are important. I love them. But I don't know what to do with them. There are the school papers and report cards and death certificates and our own medical records and all the rest of the filing in this house, and out in that car you have no doubt brought home another ton of stuff from your office."

Jack bowed his head. He knew what she was talking about. He just didn't care to think about it.

He said, "Your garden—"

She said, "Right. My garden. I love it. But it is a lot of work. It is done, Jack. It's my Sistine Chapel, maybe, but it is done now! I am tired of fighting the Japanese beetles and the bindweed and the blight! I am tired of it, Jack! Enough is enough! It is time to leave the garden! Time to leave the house! Let's sell it, Jack. It is too big for us, and it is just weighing us down, weighing me down. We need to sort out the stuff, give the photos and the archives to the kids, dispose of the furniture, and travel light for a change."

Jack looked at her as if she had just unexpectedly grown wings and a halo. His eyes were as round as dinner plates.

She hoped he was following thus far because the rest of it was going to be harder for him.

"Now, I don't want you to misunderstand. I have been grateful, really grateful, that I got to stay home with the kids. But there were things I wanted to do. I wanted to be an archaeologist. I learned Greek so that I could read Homer. I have forgotten all the Greek, and I am too old to dig, but I want to go and see Athens. I want to go to Samos, and to Crete.

"I want to walk on the Sacred Way and contemplate the mysteries. I want to visit the Oracle and the lions of Delos. I want to see Hadrian's Arch and the Parthenon and the Warrior Vase. I want to go to Mycenae and stand in the Lion Gate. Excuse me, but I want to go to the British Museum. And, darling, I want to go back to Paris and Aspen and London and Barbados, where you saw hotel rooms and delivered lectures and I saw the sights with the other wives. This time I want us to see things together."

He made a strangled sound.

"I want to go to Mexico and climb the Mayan pyramids and admire the treasures of the archeological museum and the murals of Diego Rivera. I want to go to Spain and see the Alhambra, to the South of France and drink a lot of golden wine while having picnics at scenic Roman ruins. And then I want to go to Hawaii and look into the heart of a volcano. I want to watch the lava slide into the sea with a hissing noise. I want to lie on the beach and wear flowers in my hair and learn to do the hula with all the other tourists. I want to go where the palm trees rustle in the breeze. I want to see the dawn come up like thunder, and I want you to be there, too. Then we can come back to a nice little condo and rest up while we plan our next moves. What do you say?"

Jack said, "Oh, yes, my darling, my dear, yes, indeed." He was astounded. He would never cease to be amazed at the surprises life dished up. And Marilyn. Who sat down on the wornout sofa next to the ginger cat. They both looked extremely smug.

She said, "Of course it will take a little while to sell the house and get everything taken care of. The kids have offered to take care of the house and the cat and the stuff if we want to start right away. I know you've been emotionally invested on this Don Juan saga, so, maybe, we should start with the volcano and the beach and the hula and work up to the Parthenon, instead of the other way around."

Jack said, "Yes, maybe the volcano first. And there's an island called Eros—"

"Oh, yes," she said, "You mean Paros. Mediterranean. Off the beaten track. There's an art school and a temple to Aphrodite in a pretty good state of preservation. Okay. We'll make sure we hit Paros. Nice place for a rest."

He looked at his wife with stunned admiration. She had known, without his telling her, what they needed and had granted his fondest wish without his asking. He was slightly out of breath from the speed with which she had moved, and he felt a strong urge, which he resisted, to suggest that maybe he needed a little more time to think it over, get used to the idea. Her daring thrilled him and he decided to follow her to the ends of the earth without hesitation, at once, if possible.

"Doña Lucita."

She said, "What did you say?"

He said, "I'm Don Octavio del Flores, that's who I am. And you are Doña Lucita, the queen of my heaven, the light of my life, who was almost lost to me. I am yours to command, my darling. I adore you. Now come to me and let me show you how I love you, let me count the ways, let me cover your faces with a thousand, then a hundred kisses, then another thousand kisses."

She laughed, said, "You silly thing!" and led him upstairs to bed.

23

Judgment

*

In which Don Juan removes one mask and assumes another.

On Monday morning, Jack left for work very early. Marilyn was already on the phone to real estate agents. She put her hand over the phone as she kissed him good-bye.

She said, "Don't worry. Everything is going to be all right. Go get 'em, Tiger! And come home just as soon as you can."

He thought, *Even if I grow afraid of abandoning my home and my chair and my career and my life, I won't be able to chicken out. Marilyn has got the wheels turning and before I know it I will be gazing into the molten heart of a volcano. Wonders will never cease.*

He would have been perfectly happy if he hadn't had doubts about the fate of Don Juan. He had given him an enormous, quite unjustifiable dose of Mellzac, and planted a suggestion for an escape route. Had he drugged the gallant lover into a stupor from which he would never recover no matter what happened at the hearing? Had he been explicit enough in his suggestion? Had he killed the very spirit he had tried to help?

Jack knew from experience and observation that pas-

sionate romantic daring was certain to land a man in hot
water. And it would likely ensure the further incarceration of Don Juan and justify the continuing application of
severe chemicals to his brain until the verve that sparkled
in him was utterly extinguished. Sometimes the rules and
goals of Jack's profession seemed to him to resemble
fundamental sins, crimes of the calloused heart rather
than guides to the healing arts.

Jack thought that in previous centuries executioners
used to take the job as a family obligation. The position
was passed down as a duty from father to son. But Jack
had chosen his calling of his own free will.

It was his obligation to participate in what he believed
to be very wrong, a procedure akin to condemning the Lord
Krishna to a jail term without probation. And probably just
as effective. Jack had seen it happen before with bright
but strange teenagers. They were chained into conformity
without the least hope of mercy.

Whatever talents they might have had were wasted in
the effort to twist themselves into a desperate imitation of
what was presented to them as normal behavior. Real
grief, passionate love, intense devotion to an art, all were
thrown away in the heat of the psychiatric melting pot.
Good little citizens were supposed to pop out like ginger-
bread men at the end of the process. It sickened Jack to
think of how many times he had failed to fight for some
lost but valuable soul. And this morning, it was too late to
fight anymore for Don Juan. Jack had no option but to be
present as a witness to whatever happened.

By the time he got to the hospital, his soul was as cold
and heavy as steel, chilled by remorse and regret. He
walked to his office as if to the end of the world. He had a
few favorite books left to pack. He set the rest out in the
hallway—GET THEM WHILE THEY'RE HOT! FREE BOOKS! FREE
STUFF!—and dumped pills and paper clips from his desk
into a plastic trash bag, saving only the gold pens he had
gotten on his fifth, tenth, fifteenth, twentieth and twenty-

fifth employment anniversaries. Each pen had a borough crest with a different little artificial jewel. The jewels were supposed to indicate the year. Another physician who lasted forty years had gotten an artificial diamond. *I will never reach that rhinestone*, he thought. *I will be spared that at least*. The pens were handsome trophies of endurance, and he decided he might as well keep them.

He was dressed in his Official Three-Piece Suit. The dumb gold watch was in the watch pocket of his vest, and he could feel it ticking as he carted the last of his belongings out to the car. Marilyn had helped him determine how he was supposed to display the chain and gave him her grandfather's Masonic watch fob to dress it up. He would never understand how she kept all these bits of instructive information straight. She found that old watch fob without even having to paw through the dozens of jewelry boxes and envelopes in every closet. She found it at once, right in a shoebox under the stairs, in an envelope together with medals from the Great War.

The chain and fob looked very fine on his vest. People would be pleased to see that he was wearing the watch. Some of the people who donated money for his gift probably could not afford it. He rather liked his magisterial, even presidential air in this outfit.

Also, he believed in dressing up for the hearings. It never hurt to demonstrate your respect for the circuit judge by wearing a tie. He felt as though he were dressed for a funeral, which was the other kind of occasion calling for a three-piece suit. There had been a lot of them in recent years. One more, and only a symbolic one at that, shouldn't hurt.

Jack sat at the empty desk which was no longer his, in the office which was no longer his, waiting for a patient who would not be his after today. It would have been more satisfactory to go out in a blaze of glory, but he was glad enough to be leaving in any way at all. Just get through the day, he told himself. Just get through the hearing, and then try to forget it.

He had his session and case notes for Don Juan in front of him, but he did not read them. Nothing Jack could do or say at this late moment could help rescue Don Juan from the gray, featureless world of the institution. Jack mused that once, when he had just started in his profession, the hospital had seemed the most vivid place in the world, full of sharp insights and raging drama. Something had happened to the hospital or to the doctor and now he felt that it was a place where hopes were killed. His young patient would never survive a long stay in this joyless place. But Jack could do nothing to change the outcome of the hearing. Don Juan's valiant belief in love and beauty would or would not be saved. His fate was now in the hands of the gods. Jack found himself curiously peaceful, resigned to accept whatever fate decreed. He waited for Don Juan to arrive.

Which he did, right on time, accompanied by Gloria. But Jack hardly recognized him. His hair was limp, slicked back, with an unattractive hint of oiliness about it. He wore a faded, ordinary, wrinkled T-shirt and blue jeans without any style. Instead of boots, he had on a pair of wornout cheap sneakers. No cape, no mask, no ruffled shirt, no brocaded vest, and no hint of the swashbuckling incarnation of romance in which Jack had started to believe over the course of the last ten days. It was as if that other young man had vanished, to be submerged in this travesty. Yet the aquiline nose, the long, tilted eyes, the soft mouth were all the same as ever.

Jack said a cheery good morning but he was unable to hide completely his disappointment at having lost the caped romantic who had transformed his recent life. Don Juan was in too much of a stupor to notice the tone in Jack's voice and stumbled over to the chair. He spoke in an indistinct, blurred mumble. "Good morning. . . ."

Jack said, "How are you feeling?"

Don Juan said, "Kind of . . . stoned. Like I'm walking in a dream, you know? I'm having trouble keeping a grip on anything."

Jack said, "You'll feel better by tomorrow morning. You took *all* the medication?"

Don Juan said, "Yeah. All of it. What do you think of this outfit, Doc? Gloria helped me pick it out." He smiled a blurred, lopsided smile at the thought of Gloria. "They had all this old stuff in a box back there. I wanted to wear one with a picture on it, but it was too small. . . ." Don Juan's voice trailed off and he stared into space for a few moments.

Jack said, gently, "You look just fine. Don't worry about it. We have to go to the hearing now, okay?" He wondered if the boy were too spaced out to realize what was going on or to help himself at all. Perhaps he had miscalculated, after all, and this vague boy was all that remained of the don.

Don Juan nodded. They left the office together. Jack walked slowly to accommodate the shambling boy. When they arrived at the conference room, Jack helped the boy into his seat and they waited for the judge together. Alvira, Paul, Bill, and the young glossy doctors arrayed themselves around the table. Paul appeared to be about to comment on the changed appearance of Don Juan when the judge came in.

Jack knew the judge, Harold Ryland. They had conferred a long time ago on a big case where a young man had done away with his whole family, and over the years, had worked on a finding homes for a long string of sad, confused throwaway children. Ryland was black, about Jack's age and carried the same weary air of having seen too much suffering. He was a very strong, dignified man, and known to be both merciful and fair. Jack felt that it was fortunate they got Ryland and not some hotshot kid. Also Ryland had signed the original paper and was familiar with the case.

The judge stood across the table from Don Juan and spoke directly to him. Ryland seemed to be robed with the full majesty of the law, though he wore an ordinary brown suit. He was an emissary from the courts of justice, and he was standing on a pedestal built of history.

"Do you understand why we're here, young man?"

Don Juan shrugged, his eyes wandering. He looked shifty and uncomfortable.

"Well, I am Judge Ryland of the Eighth Circuit Court of the Borough of Queens in the State of New York. Last Friday I signed a paper saying that since you had tried to kill yourself, the authorities, that's the State of New York and Borough of Queens, could keep you here on a temporary basis. After a certain amount of time, in this case ten days, they had to release you or convene a hearing so that a judge could decide whether or not there was sufficient cause to sign another paper for you to stay here for up to a year. That is what we are doing today, and I am the judge who will decide whether you must stay in the hospital under the care of these doctors. Do you understand me so far?"

Don Juan nodded and looked down at his hands.

Judge Ryland, satisfied enough to go on, continued to explain the situation. "I see that you have waived your right to representation by a lawyer or social worker. If you don't understand what we are doing here, or need me to explain anything, please speak up. Otherwise we will proceed. I want to be absolutely sure you understand the consequences of this hearing before we proceed any further. I can commit you to a longer stay here in the hospital only if I learn that you are still a danger to yourself or others, or if you are so out of touch with reality that you need the kind of close supervision and treatment a facility like this provides. Do you understand?"

Don Juan nodded again, and looked over at Jack, as if for reassurance. Jack nodded at the boy, trying to encourage him, trying to beam wordless messages of hope and rebellion to him from across the table.

Ryland would have been happier if someone were acting as counsel to the boy, even informally, but he was willing to work with the situation. He spoke carefully and clearly, trying to make sure that the boy heard and understood every word. "I have read the opinions of the hospital, but I would like you to tell me, in your own words, something about yourself and your problems. For example, where you grew up, where you went to school, how you got along with your friends, something about your parents, and what made you want to kill yourself. I am very interested in knowing how you feel right now."

Jack could not bear the prospect of hearing his patient repeat his wild story in public. The sinuous limbs of the girls in the seraglio, the wonderful magic island and the pirates just would not play in this barren conference room, before this very real judge. Jack looked at the floor and wished he were someplace else, a thousand miles away.

Don Juan began to speak, mumbling a little, slurring a little, but getting his words out clearly enough so that everyone in the room understood him. "My name is John Arnold De Marco. I was born in Astoria. Me and my parents moved to Phoenix when I was a kid. I hated school. It was awful. I couldn't stand any of the other kids. . . ." He drifted a moment. "They were always making fun of me because my father was Italian and my mother was Mexican. They called me names."

Paul looked thunderstruck. Of all of the outrageous things he had anticipated hearing Don Juan say, this prosaic account of ordinary boyhood trouble was the most unexpected. Paul's mouth hung slightly open. He snapped it shut and began to feel pleased at the way things were going. He couldn't be sure, of course, but it looked as if he had been right all along. Vindication was just around the corner. He began to rearrange his assessment of the situation. A smug, pleased smile played around the corners of his mouth. His brow lost its usual frown. His eyes began to glow with the happiness of a man who does not, after all, have to deal with thorny facts. He knew that within six months they could have this delusional young man off medication and out of the hospital.

Don Juan went on, slowly, working against the drug to get the words out. "I had a crush on a girl. . . . It was bad, she never gave me the time of day. She laughed at me, too. When I was sixteen, my father was killed in a car crash just outside of town. He was alone in the car. Fell asleep at the wheel, that's what they said. My mother, who had always been sort of flaky, well, she, I guess you could say, she flipped out. Anyway, she'd been having these affairs on and off and my father knew about them, and I guess when he died, she felt guilty. She decided to go off and become a nun. Within three weeks of my dad's death, she was in a convent somewhere in Mexico."

Bill Dunsmore thought, *This is my patient, now. With this kind of material, I could publish, and not just in the journals, either. I could be the next Oliver Sacks. Religious fervor, guilt, death, rejection, and delusions of such a flamboyant nature, maybe inheritable suicidal tendencies, conversion phenomena, hell, I could actually do it.* A mildly gleeful expression crept across his face. He and Paul nodded to each other, sharing the anticipation of months, even years of complex treatment and delightful meetings on the topic of the delusional boy and his cure.

Don Juan started to whine a little, his voice slow and nasal. "There I was, my mom had retired to the convent. I was all alone. I didn't know where to go, I didn't know what to do. I stayed with my aunt and uncle in Phoenix for a while, long enough to finish out the school year."

Paul was feeling more comfortable every minute. The story was one that justified all of his insistence on medications. He did not trust Jack and knew that Jack had never really accepted the medication-based treatment plan. Now even Jack would have to admit that he, Paul, had been right all along. It was a prospect he enjoyed contemplating.

Paul carefully studied Jack's face, looking for signs of chagrin, or remorse for his stubborn ways. Jack's face was alarmingly, blandly, and perfectly innocent. It made Paul temporarily uneasy, but he shook off all doubts. The case could not be more satisfactory. Jack could not possibly do or say anything to spoil Paul's enjoyment.

But Jack was no longer staring hopelessly at his hands in the anticipation of catastrophe. A quiet, barely noticeable song of hope had begun in his soul. He almost felt like holding his breath.

Don Juan swung into the main part of his story.

"Then one day I picked up a magazine and there was this centerfold. It was love at first sight. I had to find her. I knew she wouldn't go for me the way I was, the way I am. . . . I had been reading this book about Don Juan so I decided to put on a mask and go for it. I became Don Juan."

Paul, Bill, and Alvira all stared at Jack. He did not stare back.

Paul's vision of his future grew rosier every minute. He saw himself on a stage, accepting the Nobel prize for medicine, the man who cured Don Juan, the discoverer of unknown oceanic depths of the psyche, the explorer of fabulous mythical islands of theory, a star. No one would ever argue with him again.

Don Juan's voice, in the meantime, took on the aggrieved tone of the thwarted teenaged punk trailing an uncooperative female.

"I tried to find her. I looked everywhere for her. I named her Donna Ana after Don Juan's girl. The magazine wouldn't do anything to help. They wouldn't give me any information. I called them a hundred times."

Ryland scribbled in his notebook, nodding to Don Juan.

"Then one day, this woman, I think she was a temp,

she took pity on me and gave me the girl's phone number. I called it over and over again, always getting her answering machine. I never left a message but I didn't give up. Finally, late one night a couple of weeks ago, I called her up and some guy answered. Then she got on the phone. I told her that I loved her and that we were meant to be together. She called me a creep and some other things and threatened to call the cops. Then she hung up on me."

Bill was quietly ecstatic. Every element of the story suggested a brilliant academic approach to his feverish brain. He saw himself signing autographs, giving lectures, impressing women, as he demonstrated his suave and knowing analysis of this complex and difficult case. He saw himself in time supervising the teaching program at the hospital. He would be the grand old man, just a touch of gray at his temples, quoted with reverence by adoring female students, who would visit his office after hours to ask his advice and share glasses of excellent sherry with him. His face shone with the splendor of the career he saw unfolding before him, all based on the robust illness of this lovestruck young patient.

Alvira looked over at Bill. She knew all about his ambitions, which flared up like acne whenever he was allowed into the sun. She felt sorry for the don, who had been so beautiful and so sweet to everyone. He now seemed broken and ordinary. She renewed her promise to herself that she would never get sick, and if she did, she would stay away from all physicians unless they could prove that their organs of ambition had been excised. Which, in her opinion, was an operation performed all too infrequently. She wished that the meeting were over, that the day were over, and she were asleep in her own blessedly lonely bed at home.

Ryland examined the boy's face carefully, and then returned to his note taking. Jack watched the boy fighting to tell them a story they could accept, letting himself become ignoble, giving up in order to survive. He thought,

No! No, Don Juan must never give up! Keep your white plume! Don't let them take you alive! But he said nothing.

Paul seemed to sense something amiss. He felt proud of his own wisdom, but still uneasy. There were currents in the room he did not understand, warm breezes and potentials that disturbed his complacency, his profound satisfaction with the effect of drug treatment on the wayward don.

Things seemed almost too perfect. Paul had no reason to trust the smiles of fate; in his experience, whenever fate smiled, she had just dropped a banana peel in his path. On the rare occasions when he felt happiness, he immediately rushed to conceal it, lest it be snatched away. This was one of the occasions and his face was tired with the effort to fight off a grin of sheer joy. His reputation would rise, his wife would admire him, his staff would adore him. If only it were all true, Don Juan's story as he was telling it to the judge, there would be months of delicate calibration of medication, careful exploration of the effects of various psychotropic combinations on the young man's delusions.

Don Juan seemed to be embarrassed at what he had to say. "I felt as if my life were over at this time. I decided to kill myself, or at least make people believe I wanted to do it, and maybe get some attention or something. Anyway, that's what I did. It was all pretty stupid. I knew that girl would not even be sorry if I died right in front of her. I don't know what I was thinking. I never, really, intended to kill myself. I wanted somebody to notice me. That's all."

The boy seemed to be searching for words. He looked the judge in the eye for a long moment and then said, "And that's all. I never meant to hurt myself or Dr. Jack here, and I'm real sorry I put everybody to all this trouble."

The room was completely silent as the Don, Paul, Bill, Alvira, and Jack waited for the judge to speak. The younger doctors just waited for the meeting to be over.

Judge Ryland looked back at the boy and said, "Thank you. This has been very helpful. Now I want to tell you something, Mr. De Marco. You are going to have to behave yourself. No phoning women you don't know in the middle of the night. No chasing women at all. No mask, no cape, no sword. No climbing around on billboards getting the police and the fire departments all upset. Do you understand? Do you think you can behave, now?"

Don Juan said, "Yes." Within Don Juan's stuporous state, Jack could almost detect a smile.

The judge said, "You can go back to your room now."

Don Juan left the conference room.

Judge Ryland delivered his verdict.

"Doctors, this seems like a perfectly normal kid to me. I've had a few fantasies about centerfolds myself. And there have been times I've been a fool for love. I bet you all have, too. I'm certainly not committing the boy to an institution for having a fantasy that went a little too far. Let him go."

Paul said, "Let him go? Let him go? There are months, literally months, if not years of treatment ahead! What are you saying?"

Judge Ryland said, "You heard me, Paul. Let him out of here, today." He shook his head in disgust, muttering, "Doctors! Not an ounce of common sense in the whole sorry bunch of you. Now, if you will excuse me, I have to get back to the real world."

Alvira could have hugged him, just for the scorn in his voice as he packed his notes into his briefcase and departed. He left a room full of dashed ambitions and stunned physicians, all babbling at once.

Bill said, "That can't be right! He was going to be mine!"

Paul said, "What did you do, Jack? How did this happen?"

Jack said, "I guess he's cured. Thank God for medication."

There was not a trace of irony in his voice, but his heart began to sing a hymn of joyous revolution, and he silently uttered the sweet triumphant cry of a prisoner stepping through the prison doors, finished with his sentence and retiring with his own kind of honor. He sidled out of the room without a wave or a word or a backward glance, the hubbub receding from his hearing. His colleagues were so enmeshed in their own confusion, they did not even see him step out of the conference room and out of their lives. All except Alvira, who watched him walk out, and thought, *Doctor Jack is a fine man and I wish him good luck. God will look after him. Surely goodness and mercy will follow him all the days of his life.* Alvira smiled at her friend, who disappeared into the corridor as if in a puff of smoke through a trapdoor. He was heading for Don Juan's room.

24

The Island

*

In which truth and fantasy, reality and dream, lunatics and lovers, memories and myths are all reconciled with each other beneath the golden sunlight of a tropical beach; at least temporarily.

Jack walked through the quiet hallway, loosening his tie and considering the fate of his patient. He thought, *The medications I gave him dulled Don Juan's glittering surface so that he could fit into the pack. He told that roomful of tedious doctors exactly what they expected to hear. But whether he was confused or cunning, I don't know. The truth is within him and will never die. Unless, of course, it has been killed by the drugs.*

Jack winced at the thought of his own complicity in Don Juan's shabby, colorless appearance. Worry made him walk more quickly toward Don Juan's room. He stopped at the nurses' station to get Don Juan's belongings. Gloria had them ready, neatly packed into a brown paper bag, except the sword, which she had wrapped in multiple layers of butcher's paper and tied up with string. She handed the sword-shaped package to the doctor with a curiously antique gesture, the maiden arming the knight. She murmured, "Say good-bye to him for me, will you?"

Jack patted the girl's cheek. "I will, Gloria. Don't worry." He took off his badge and handed it to her. "Please, give this to Paul with my compliments."

She smiled and nodded, then showed Jack Don Juan's mask, folded into a small, tidy bundle like a handkerchief. "And you give this to him, too. I washed and ironed it for him, and maybe he'll need it." She tucked the mask into Jack's breast pocket and stood on tiptoe to kiss his cheek. "Take care of yourself, Dr. Jack."

He said he would, and started back down the corridor again.

As Jack carried the sword in his left hand, its balanced, flexible weight changed his gait to that of a gallant swordsman. He began, without much awareness, to consider the practical ramifications of carrying a sword. He would need, he thought, a holster for it. Scabbard? Something. He had somewhere at home a tooled-leather belt from Spain. It would be just right for the sword, if he could still get into it. Of course he couldn't wear a sword to work. But he didn't have to go to work anymore. Maybe a pair of boots, too. Not cowboy boots—Paul wore cowboy boots—but swashbuckling boots to go with the sword. Of course the weapon belonged, strictly speaking, to Don Juan, but that could be solved. He could buy a sword just like Don Juan's. And he could take fencing lessons, too. His step became lighter, his stride longer and his back straighter as he walked toward his rendezvous with the boy. He was conscious of none of these changes in his posture. He was only aware of an unusual sense of cheerful masculinity and general well-being.

Jack met Don Juan outside his room, and handed over the paper bag. He took the woozy boy's elbow and gently guided him down the corridor toward the front door. He said, "The drugs will wear off soon. By the end of this day you will feel once again the passionate beauty of life, I promise, Don Juan."

Don Juan said, "Thank you. You are a good man and a

true friend. I will never forget what you have done for me, Doctor. . . . Don Octavio . . . ?" The boy stopped and looked at Jack. Still muddled by the drugs, Don Juan's voice was blurred as he asked, "Who are you again?"

"Let us leave this place before we talk more, my friend," Jack said quietly. As he steered the wobbly young man toward freedom, the bronze doors of the hospital swung open before them, revealing the golden sunlight of a spring day. They stepped lightly into freedom together, the man and the boy, patient and doctor, both liberated from the gray institution which threatened to hold them in its stone grip forever.

Don Juan was still dizzy and confused from the medication and blinded by the sunlight. His hair, however, had begun to curl and twine, no longer so lank and lifeless. His eyes were no longer quite so dull and he stood almost steady, weaving only a little. He said, "And who are you, can you tell me now, please?"

Jack laughed happily. He almost sang as he recited his newly polished and sparkling identity to Don Juan.

"My name is Don Octavio del Flores. I am the son of a great wizard, the wise and heroic Don Bernardino del Flores, and his gentle loving wife, Doña Rosa. I have inherited from them vast estates full of flowers and precious illuminated volumes of rare learning, which it will take my lifetime to comprehend. I am married to the splendid, faithful, wise, and beautiful Doña Lucita, light of my life, who will guide my footsteps to wonders and treasures few men have ever been fortunate enough to see." Jack laughed again.

"And, my young friend, I am the world's greatest psychiatrist. In my time I have cured a thousand and three hopeless patients. No wounded mind has ever left my sanctuary unchanged. I have led each step by step from the darkest corner of night into the sunlight and the strong currents of life itself. Their faces linger in my memory like summer days, full of promise and newfound joy." He gently led the boy out of the shadow of the mental hospital into the sunshine.

Jack pressed the boy's hand and said, "Go with God, Don Juan De Marco. Be comforted and make sons to carry on your name, daughters to teach you humility. Be well, Don Juan, and be happy. Perhaps someday we will meet again."

The boy bowed, regaining some of his courtly manner, and smiled for the first time since the hearing. The sullen, unfocused expression he had worn all day lightened with the smile, and he waved graciously as he turned and began to walk again. He seemed to grow taller and more dignified now that he was free, though he still lurched just a little. Jack stood still in the shadows as he watched Don Juan moving away. The boy seemed to be enveloped in a blaze of sunlight that obscured his shabby clothes, as if he walked on a cloud of glory.

Jack looked into the sunlight surrounding that slender, gallant figure, and had the sensation of looking back into a world without limits, into the Garden before the Fall, when everything was possible and love was everywhere. He remembered his own youth in a haze of beauty. He was filled with happiness as he thought of his own journey, just begun, toward the unknown, toward his mysterious, beloved wife, and maybe even his own magic island in the middle of an uncharted sea.

Jack stood on the shadowy threshold of his past, watching Don Juan walk away and it seemed to him that an opportunity was escaping, an important part of his future was vanishing around a corner. There was something else he ought to do, something which tantalized him almost like a wave of déjà vu. He knew he was not yet finished and would never be content unless he could discover the proper deed for this occasion. He could never be sure that Don Juan would not just vanish into the city, that the drugs hadn't killed the amorous demigod within the boy, and he would never know the end of the story unless he found the key in the next few minutes.

He felt the embrace of a tidal force, urging him toward some unimaginable act. Some vital clue was leading him gently forward; some forgotten song of romance, sentiment, and opulent desire was teasing his mind with unbidden images. His mind conjured up a multicolored balloon outlined against the skyline of the Emerald City. He seemed to hear the guide of souls, with staff and winged feet, suggesting that now was the time to make tracks. He needed to travel, and to a world in which anything could happen. His old life had spit him out, left him a castaway on an unknown shore, just as the pirates had abandoned Don Juan.

When had he begun to want that other world, that vision in which the real and the imaginary danced without hindrance or shyness toward good adventure? He had said an affectionate farewell to Don Juan, but why did he assume that he had to part with this young man who embodied all that he most cherished? Why did he feel it necessary to plod away from that part of his life which insisted that truth and beauty were indeed one? Why must he automatically reject the fragrant and iridescent vision of boundless generosity? Of unerring perfection? Why should he accept the dreary, painful sadness of pedestrian, quotidian, mundane existence? Why couldn't he mount on mighty wings, soar above the plains and the ocean, above the clouds?

He suddenly knew exactly what he had to do next. It was against all sense and wisdom, it threw logic and knowledge and practical considerations and caution overboard. It was not so much a plan as a play, a grand flourish of imaginary trumpets announcing his new life. Jack ran after Don Juan and it may have been his imagination, but he could have sworn that his feet barely touched the ground as he flew over the lawn. Don Juan turned around and smiled. They were in perfect agreement as they walked quietly together to Jack's car, got in and drove away from the hospital to Jack's home, where Marilyn was surprised but not offended to welcome an unexpected guest for dinner.

Jack, knowing now exactly what he wanted, moved like the wind. He solved each difficulty without delay, resolved each conflict, persuaded each obstacle to come along or step aside. He cajoled, he begged, he humbly prayed. He packed, he phoned, he drove, he paid and all logistic snags and all objections melted away, in a delirious, ecstatic harmony of needs and means.

It was only a matter of hours until Jack, Marilyn, and Don Juan were seated on a great blue-and-white transatlantic jetliner, thundering through the night sky. Don Juan and Marilyn chatted away as if they had known each other forever, but Jack held Marilyn's hand and kissed it frequently. He was well aware of the blandishments and alluring sweetness of the boy in the window seat. Marilyn found his desire to hold her hand entirely understandable and rather endearing. She patted him reassuringly at frequent intervals, while Don Juan spoke softly into her ear.

She felt, rather than heard, his warm, silky and soothing voice recounting fabulous, delicately phrased adventures and expounding a thoughtful but delightful naive philosophy of absolute love, spiced with outrageous and completely enjoyable compliments to her fine cheekbones, her sensitive, alluring eyes, and her good taste in clothes. Though her husband had mentioned the strong influence the young man had exerted upon him, it was a different matter entirely to feel that influence on herself.

She was surprised to find her usual reticence with strangers so easily overcome. Between Don Juan's voice on her left and her husband's comforting hand in hers on her right, she felt enveloped in love and piquant male mysteries. Even better, she sensed in herself a renewed certainty of her own beauty and power, and reflected in those admiring masculine eyes, nothing cruel or ugly or unsightly. Her struggles with the mirror over the long dry months, her own revulsion at the unstoppable ruin of her neck and hands and breasts, her shame, all vanished as if they had never happened, as if they had never mattered at all. Don Juan avoided mentioning Donna Ana's name to Marilyn, but spoke to her as if she were the only woman in the world, as if his only reason for existing was to sit eternally beside her on an airplane over the ocean.

Jack, however, was struggling with doubts and half-stunned with the enormity of his folly. He tried to prepare himself against disappointment and disillusionment, which would logically arise from this adventure, and found himself oddly suffused by a warm contentment undermining all doubt and fear. He was on the knees of the gods, for sure, lured to faith by hope and the glamour of his own newborn freedom. He wanted everything beautiful to be true, and he wanted to see it all with his own eyes, though he was old enough to have learned better. He felt profoundly foolish but also deeply thrilled as he secretly imagined the vindication of beliefs he had given up years ago. He stroked Marilyn's hand and gave in to immense impulsive waves of gratitude. Not every woman would be delighted to jump on a jet plane and fly halfway around the world at a moment's notice, in the company of at least one, more likely two, lunatics.

Jack and Marilyn and Don Juan flew through the night sky for many hours, as the stars wheeled around them and fellow passengers smiled at their happiness. The steward asked Jack if they were on their honeymoon or celebrating some anniversary. Jack said, with pride, that they certainly were, and the steward brought them tiny bottles of champagne compliments of the captain. They landed as the sun was coming up, and they caught a bus to the port, thrilled by the sound of soft foreign syllables and the sight of marble ruins and palm trees.

They could not read the street signs, but Marilyn had bought a book of phrases in the airport and found the correct pier, where a small ferryboat was waiting. A wedding party was in progress on the ferry, and musicians played invigorating, probably bawdy, folk songs at which the bride blushed and the relatives cheered. Then the band played sentimental songs and everyone wept. Jack and Marilyn and Don Juan drank a few toasts and danced a few steps. It was all very friendly and romantic and the wedding party waved good-bye to them as they got off at an island harbor.

They engaged a tiny sailboat with eyes painted on the prow and a weathered old fisherman to sail it for them. The sailboat skimmed over the dark blue sea and the fisherman offered them a bottle of wine with some olives and dark bread, as the hospitality of the boat. They all had a snack and several drinks and were happily jetlagged and tipsy when they reached the island.

Marilyn bought them all straw hats and a big bottle of sun-drenched sweet wine and some cheese and more bread, and they set off on an old, old path leading up from the town. They walked slowly in the green shade of the olive trees, enjoying the salt breeze and admiring the banks of scarlet flowers which grew on the hillside above them. From time to time they sat down on the column drums that marked the ruins of ancient temples and tombs. As they rested and shared the wine and bread, Marilyn told them stories of the old gods and heroes, and every time they rose, they all seemed lighter and stronger.

Jack remembered that he still had one of Don Juan's belongings. He took the black silk mask out of his pocket and offered it to the boy. Don Juan shook his head and threw the mask up into the air. They all laughed and watched it tumble away in the wind. Then they linked arms, and set off again, ready for whatever might happen.

As they walked, their legs brushed against lavender and thyme which grew by the side of the road. The air

was filled with sweet, enchanting fragrance. Soon the
path turned downward, and the sound of the sea grew
louder. Don Juan handed his cape to Jack and began to
run ahead. He disappeared behind a grassy sand dune.
They could hear his voice calling, but the words were
carried away by the breeze.

Jack and Marilyn climbed down the final few yards to
the beach. Don Juan was a long way down the curving
shore, alone, still waving and calling, though his voice was
faint with distance and dismay.

The two older lovers hurried toward him, thinking to
comfort him and console him. When they were only a very
short distance away, Jack saw a figure walking toward
them from the far curve of the shore. It was a young
woman, tall and tanned, with long silken hair, a mask,
and few clothes. She was as graceful as an antelope and
absolutely at home on the sugary sand. As she caught sight
of the young man, she plucked off her mask and threw it
into the air with a cry of pure joy. Her feet were bare and
her arms were flung out in welcome as she ran swiftly and
gracefully through the golden sunlight toward Don Juan.

The boy and girl embraced as if all the world were
cheering their love, as if all the brilliance of the sun were
in their arms. And they kissed a long, long kiss of youth
and love and happiness, as if they were two pure spirits of
absolute love newly hatched on the original beach of the
original magical island in a world without sin or limits or
prudence or sadness or death. They were as close as two
feathers on a single soaring wing. Time passed above
them, leaving them suspended in that eternal, impossibly
flawless moment before practical problems and baggage
and babies and fatigue and worries can mar the luminous
surface of passionate romance.

Jack's eyes filled with tears as he watched them. He
was almost blinded by their blazing beauty and the terrible
perfection of their love. He turned toward Marilyn, and
she drew him into an embrace as profound, a kiss as

deeply passionate, and a love far richer than he had ever imagined. Jack hugged his wife and laughed with pure happiness.

"I don't think my last patient will ever be cured! He suffers from a rare and persistent romantic dream. He yearned for perfect love and he has found it. Those two young people and you and I may dance in the fires of Hell and we may grow so old that we cannot dance, but we will, nevertheless, be forever young, forever beautiful, and forever, oh, my sweetheart, madly in love!"

"I believe you, yes, I do, my darling husband, yes, I do, with all my heart and soul, and I plan to prove it to you over and over again until you scream for mercy. But now this minute, now, my reckless passionate hero, my own Don Octavio, now what do we do?"

Jack waved his hand at the sugary white sand, at the ancient olive trees and the wine-dark sea. Then he laughed, and bowed to his woman, doffing an imaginary hat with an imaginary feather.

"Anything we want, anything at all, anything, anything my sweet and gentle, beautiful wife."

JEAN BLAKE WHITE graduated from Rye High School in 1959. She studied painting at the Rhode Island School of Design and psychology at Goucher College, graduating from the latter with a bachelor's degree and a Phi Beta Kappa key. Her paintings are on display in private collections in Louisville, Chicago, Los Angeles, London, Chevy Chase, Seattle, and Boston. Her poems have been published in various literary magazines in the United States and England. A collection of her poems, *Book I*, is about to be published as a Newton illustrated book in association with a Llamagraphics, Inc. software application. Her essays have appeared on the Baltimore Sunpapers Op-Ed Page. She is currently working on a novel, *Life Class*.

There's an epidemic with 27 million victims. And no visible symptoms.

It's an epidemic of people who can't read.

Believe it or not, 27 million Americans are functionally illiterate, about one adult in five.

The solution to this problem is you... when you join the fight against illiteracy. So call the Coalition for Literacy at toll-free **1-800-228-8813** and volunteer.

Volunteer Against Illiteracy. The only degree you need is a degree of caring.